Threadwalkers

Joanna Volavka

Threadwalkers

© 2017 by Joanna Volavka

For permission requests, write to the publisher, addressed "Attention: Permissions Coordinator," at the address below.
50/50 Press, LLC
PO Box 197
1590 Route 146
Rexford, NY 12148

http://www.5050press.com

ISBN-13: 9781947048119
ISBN-10: 1947048112

Edited by: Megan Cassidy-Hall
Cover Design: Megan Cassidy-Hall
This book is a work of fiction. Names, characters, places, and incidents are products of the author's imagination or are used fictitiously. Any resemblance to actual events, locales, or persons, living or dead, is entirely coincidental.
Printed in the U.S.A.   First Edition, October 2017

To my 13-year-old self: Look kid; we did it!

Chapter 1

Miranda Woodward heard voices. Not the normal kind everyone hears when they're thinking, and not the kind that make people question your sanity or send you to therapy. Miranda heard *conversations*. Usually she only noticed fragments. As soon as she concentrated on them, the voices stopped, but sometimes they continued for minutes at a time while she stood as still as possible. Listening.

She noticed them first when she was about five years old, sitting on the beige living room carpet with her toy airplane, piloted by her favorite plastic dinosaur. She heard someone whispering across the room, a voice that didn't belong to her father or mother. She tipped her head to one side, her dark brown hair tumbling around her shoulders, before looking up at her parents, her brown eyes wide.

"Shhh!" Miranda said, the dino-plane hovering in mid-air. "I'm trying to hear!"

Her mother had opened her mouth to scold her for her rudeness, but her father stopped the conversation and instead scooped Miranda up into his arms and carried her to her bedroom.

1

She sat on the bed hugging the little airplane while he asked her what she'd heard, but she hadn't been able to catch the words. He didn't seem worried, but she felt a little scared all the same.

"Is it ghosts?" she whispered to her dad.

"Let's not talk to your mom about them, okay?" he replied. And she hadn't mentioned them to her mother since. For a while, the voices felt like a magical, wonderful secret between Miranda and her father, but after a while, the secret started to get stale. In fact, every time she tried to talk to her dad about the mysterious voices, he'd be interested in what she heard, but then he never wanted to discuss them further. By the time she was eight, Miranda stopped telling him about the voices in frustration, and by the time she was twelve, she'd had stopped hearing them anyway. Or maybe she'd just stopped noticing them. It was like they'd gone away. At least, they had until six months ago, when everything changed.

"Hey, are you coming or what?" Miranda's best friend Jae Rogers was standing about ten paces away, one hand on her hip, tapping her yellow Converse on the gravel lot. Jae was a couple of inches taller than Miranda and had curly dark hair and intense gray eyes. She was wearing her usual jeans and flannel shirt over a tank top, and as usual, she always had the best accessories and managed to make her outfits look cool. Today's necklace was a string of giant, neon plastic gummy bears. Their other friend, Abby McInnis, had driven the three of them to the Henley Corn Maze, but wasn't out of the car yet.

Miranda could see Abby's straight blonde hair swinging as she pulled the rearview mirror over to check her makeup. Abby had skipped her usual skirt for a pair of shorts and a three-quarter length sleeved top that Miranda had once coveted, back when clothes seemed like a bigger deal. Miranda looked down at her own outfit: jeans, t-shirt, ballet flats. Boring, but it worked. She hadn't worn much else lately.

"Well?" Jae said.

Miranda shook herself and tried to grin at Jae. "Sorry, I was just thinking about, um, the maze." The only voices she could hear just then were parents calling for kids and the kids shrieking with delight from the edges of the corn maze she'd talked her two best friends into doing with her for her birthday. Miranda felt a little childish; after all, shouldn't sixteen-year-olds be too old for corn mazes? But she and her dad had always gone every year, and she didn't want to miss it this year, just because things were different. Her friends seemed to understand; they both immediately agreed to go with her as soon as she asked.

"Well then think and walk," Jae said, reaching out for Miranda. Abby climbed out of the driver's seat, where she'd been touching up her lipstick, and marched across the gravel in her brown boots.

"We're walking, we're walking!" she said, waving her arms at Jae, who rolled her eyes.

Abby linked arms with Miranda and hauled her along toward Jae who grabbed Miranda's other arm, and the three of them set off toward the entrance as the sun set behind the trees, leaving a golden pink glow on the clouds. The smell of wood smoke drifted past them, and Miranda pulled on a button-up shirt to have some sleeves against the cool night air.

They cut across the corner of the adjacent field where bales of hay marked the edge of the play area. A handful of young kids with their parents played corn hole on the lawn. The ticket kiosk stood on the opposite side, with a little stand selling hot apple cider and coffee beside the door to the main produce shop. The man at the ticket kiosk handed them a large red flag as they paid along with a small score card listing eight stations.

"Find each station inside, doesn't matter what order, and use the hole puncher to mark it off. The punchers are all different shapes, so don't try to cheat. And if you get lost or stuck, wave the flag and whoever's on the tower in the center of the maze will help you out." He smiled. "You girls have fun."

They started toward the well-lit entrance to the maze, though the path faded into long shadows within about ten feet, the corn blocking most of the quickly fading sunlight. Abby reached into her slouchy, patchwork satchel and pulled out a flashlight. She clicked it on. They all lit their matching glowing necklaces and stepped inside, following the trodden dirt path straight into the tall corn. A cool breeze rustled the corn stalks, sounding like whispers in the deepening darkness. Crickets and frogs sang from the trees lining the edge of the field, and from somewhere else in the maze, children laughed and squealed.

Miranda didn't talk much, but watched her friends checking the little map in the flashlight beam. The light illuminated the bottom halves of their faces, so that their eyes seemed to melt into shadowy pools above their cheeks.

"This is kind of creepy," Abby said after a while, as they stopped at an intersection. "Which way are we supposed to go?"

"Not sure," Miranda said. "It changes every year." The maze turned in on itself several times, and so far, they hadn't found any of the hole punching stations. Miranda peered down both directions of the new path they now faced.

"Y'all are such wimps," Jae laughed. "Little kids are in here. What's the big deal? Let's just start going to the left, keep on making every left turn, and we'll find everything. Right?"

"I guess that makes sense." Abby shrugged. "But if you get us more lost, I'm going to kick your butt, Jae Rogers."

"Yeah, yeah, say it like you mean it," Jae shot back.

"So," Miranda began as they took the nearest left-hand path, "you agreed to come to the corn maze if I'd let you plan the rest of the night. What's after this?"

"We can't tell you. Spoilers!" Jae said, spinning around to walk backwards for a couple of steps, and nearly crashing into a wall of corn. Abby laughed.

"Come on, just a hint." Miranda stopped beside Abby, grinning and leaning against her friend's shoulder. "Are we going where I think we're going? Please, please, please, tell me I get to finally be in on this tradition!" She couldn't help thinking of the rumors that floated through the school about a House, and of the cryptic things both of her friends had said after their sixteenth birthdays. They hadn't exactly tried to keep it a secret from her, but at the same time, she'd never heard the full story from them either. It bothered her a little that her best friends wouldn't fully share something so important. They insisted the secrecy was part of the tradition, and while part of Miranda understood and even appreciated that it would be a surprise, she was tired of being left out.

"No hints, Randi!" Abby said, still laughing. "You'll find out when you find out." Abby leaned in a little closer and whispered, "But yes, we're going where you think we're going. Just try to act a little surprised."

Miranda sighed, but let Abby take her arm and pull her into the lead, handing Jae the map as they began to trace the edge of the pathway, turning left twice before being forced to go to the right. With Abby holding onto her, Miranda felt a little better, and tried to shove anything but the corn maze out of her mind. After several minutes, Miranda was fairly certain they had gone in a circle. She glanced at Abby, hoping her friend wouldn't be frustrated, but Abby was facing the other direction, so she couldn't tell what her friend might be thinking. Miranda took a deep breath to apologize.

"Come this way," someone said behind them.

"Come what way?" asked Miranda, looking behind her.

"What?" Abby asked, turning to look, too. "What are you looking at?"

"Jae said we should go that way," Miranda said, "but I don't see which way she meant."

"I didn't say anything," Jae replied, stepping around the corner with the flashlight and map in her hands. "I'm just trying to figure out where we are."

"But I was sure…" Miranda turned to peer into the corn to their right to see if there was a path parallel to theirs. She could just see another opening through the stalks, but it looked empty. Miranda shivered.

"Why now?" she whispered.

"Why what?" Abby asked. She had stopped walked and was watching Miranda, her pale hair twisting slightly in the light breeze.

"Nothing," Miranda answered. Surely the ghost voices weren't in the corn maze. *Surely*.

"If you're trying to freak us out, it's kind of working," Jae said.

"I'm not trying to freak anyone out!" Miranda snapped. Then, in a softer voice, she asked, "Y'all really didn't hear anything?"

"No?" Abby said, crossing her arms across her chest and taking a step back from Miranda.

"It's got to be that way," the voice whispered.

Miranda spun to her left, staring straight into the corn. She thought for just a moment that she saw something moving behind the stalks, but the breeze made it hard to tell for sure. Turning back to her friends, she took a deep breath and started walking again.

"Let's just go."

Her friends followed behind her in silence, though when she looked behind her to make sure they were coming, it seemed like they were avoiding eye contact. She sighed and slowed down enough to squish herself between them and link arms again.

"I'm sorry," she said, careful not to look directly at either one of them. "I thought this would be fun, but it's...different. Without my dad. I guess things are just a little weird, you know?"

"We know," Abby said, giving her arm a squeeze. "It's okay. Let's just find our way through this maze." Miranda looked up at her friend, who was smiling at her. She turned to Jae who shrugged and smiled, too.

"Sandwich?" Jae asked, and suddenly the two girls leaned hard into Miranda. She burst out laughing and wiped away the dampness in her eyes as the other two tried to smash her in the game they'd invented when they were eight.

The mood lightened, and the girls continued along the path. After several left turns, they walked straight into a dead end with a wooden post inside. A string with a star-shaped hole-puncher dangled from a nail on top of it. Miranda punched their score card while Jae checked to see where the other seven stations might be.

"I think if we keep doing this left-hand-turn thing, it'll work," Abby said, looking over Jae's shoulder. "I mean, we've only been in here something like twenty minutes, right?"

"No way, it's got to be longer than that." Jae pulled out her cell phone and checked the time. The glow from the screen made Miranda squint after so long in the relative darkness. "You're right. It's only been twenty-three minutes!"

"Yeah, well, we've got to go faster than this if we're going to get through this whole maze," Abby said.

"Sorry I made y'all do this," Miranda mumbled. She didn't want her friends to be bored, or worse, to think she was lame for wanting to do a kids' thing.

"No!" Abby reached out and hooked arms with her again. "I didn't mean it like that, Randi. I just mean we have other places to go tonight, too."

"No spoilers!" Jae sang again, trotting back down the path and hanging a left. "Are y'all coming, or what?"

Abby and Miranda took off after her. For the next hour, they ambled through the maze, singing as many Disney songs as they could think of at the top of their lungs. Every so often they stopped to check their phones or the map, but they made good time, and soon they had all but the last station punched. The darkness settled around them, and the clear sky sparkled with stars. The light from the play area and ticket kiosk cast long, sharp shadows when they got close to the edge of the maze, but when they walked along the far side, Miranda saw the thicker part of stars straight across the center of the sky where the Milky Way spun. They reached the last station. As Jae punched their card, Miranda's phone beeped.

"Ugh, it's probably Mom," she said, pulling it out of her pocket. As it came loose, she fumbled, and it bounced across the straw and dirt into the edge of the corn.

"I want to go get some cider before we leave," Abby said, as she and Jae stopped and waited for Miranda to fish her phone out of the dust and corn leaves on the ground. In the soft yellow light from Abby's flashlight, Miranda dug through the pile until her hand closed around the phone. She opened her messages and saw several missed calls from her mother, though her phone never rang the whole time they were inside the maze.

"Why don't y'all go on ahead?" Miranda suggested, dusting off her phone. "I want to make sure Mom's okay."

"We aren't supposed to separate," Abby said.

"It's okay. I'll be right behind you," Miranda said. She didn't want her friends overhearing the conversation in case her mom was upset again. Her mom was doing better, but still. "Just leave me the flag and I'll catch up in a minute."

Jae handed her the flag. "Don't be long, Randi. We've got places to go." Abby and Jae walked off into the darkness, arm in arm. Just then a text message popped up.

9

Heading home now. Let me know when you get this. Hope you're having fun! Love, Mom

She wrote back: *Finishing corn maze now, having a great time. See you tomorrow!*

"That's not the way to go. Come this way. This way. Alone. Come alone."

Miranda jumped. "Who's there? Are you following us? You're freaking me out."

She held the phone up, swiping her flashlight app open to light up the path around her. She didn't see anything but corn, and the wooden post with the hole-punch still swinging from its nail.

A rustling noise to the right made her turn, and she took a step back, but tripped on a rock and tumbled backwards, landing hard, still clinging to her phone and the flag. Her legs trembled as she got to her feet and ran down the path after her friends. The wind picked up and the corn leaned and swayed as she ran, bowing into the path in front of her, brushing her face, the silk and leaves getting caught in her hair. Footsteps and laughing voices ahead made Miranda slow down and try to catch her breath; she didn't need her friends thinking she got scared being alone in the dark. As she rounded the corner, she put on a smile, which vanished again almost instantly. She faced an empty path.

A bird called in the trees to the left. The corn stopped swaying, but the stalks kept rustling as if moved by a wind she could no longer feel. Miranda clutched the flag tighter and started walking again, glancing to the left and right as she went. She thought she saw someone go around the corner ahead of her, and she hurried to catch up to them, but when she reached the turn, no one was there.

"Stop and think, Miranda," she whispered to herself. "The store is lit up. Look for lights and go that way."

Standing on tip-toes, Miranda scanned the cornfield as far to the edge as possible and soon picked out where the lights looked strongest. She began winding through the corn in that direction, careful to stay on the path and not cut through any of the corn barriers, no matter how tempting a straight line might be. Finally, she burst from the exit, sweating in the cold air and breathing hard. Her friends looked up at her from a picnic table by the snack stand, clutching steaming cups. Miranda handed the flag back to an employee at the maze exit and went to join her friends.

"Whoa, what happened to you?" Jae asked. Her breath swirled over her cup to mix with the steam.

"I tripped," Miranda said. She looked down at her sweaty self and dusted off her pants.

"We can't leave you alone for five minutes, can we?" Abby asked. She reached out and plucked a piece of corn silk from Miranda's hair. "Come have some cider. Then we have *plans*."

Miranda sat across from Jae as Abby passed her a steaming Styrofoam cup of cider. She wrapped her hands around the cup, and let the warmth seep into her fingers, her shoulders relaxing. She looked back at the corn maze, where a dad with his small daughter emerged, laughing and holding hands. *I wish I could talk to my Dad*, she thought. *He'd know if this was the voices.* The corn rustled and leaned to the left as the breeze shifted, and Miranda smelled wood smoke again. The children who were playing with their parents earlier got in their minivan to leave, and the dad with his daughter approached the snack bar, the little girl singing about hot chocolate. Across the parking lot, a row of enormous pumpkins appeared briefly in headlights, future giant jack-o'-lanterns for Halloween.

Miranda breathed in, enjoying the cider, and smoke, and the musky smell of early autumn. It reminded her of just a few years ago, where fall meant jumping into leaf piles while her mother yelled at her to stop making a mess. She took a tentative sip of the cider, letting its spicy warmth trickle down into her stomach, and smiled to herself.

"Don't get too comfy there, Cupcake," Jae said, poking Miranda's shoulder. "Finish your cider and then we're heading out. After all, it's your sixteenth birthday. You're the last one, thank God."

"So, are we going where I think we're going?" Miranda asked. She felt an excited swoop in her stomach. The strange encounter from the maze pushed to the back of her mind, drowned by anticipation of finally getting in on the not-so-secret Henley High School birthday tradition.

"Oh yeah," Jae said.

"Of course we are," Abby nodded solemnly. "Everyone goes to the haunted house for their sixteenth birthday."

"So." Jae leaned forward, her curly hair tumbling around her face until it disappeared into a shadow. "Are you ready to be initiated into the Henley High Society of the Haunted?"

Chapter 2

Miranda clambered into the back seat of Abby's little blue Volvo hatchback and kicked her feet up sideways on the seat as they headed further from the edge of town, away from the corn maze and on to an area not as well-lit. She leaned against the cool glass of the back-seat window, watching the stars follow her as the last few houses flew past and then disappeared, swallowed by the night to be replaced by thick trees and near complete darkness. The sky looked like velvet with tiny sparkles shining on it, vivid in the absence of even street lights. She sat up and leaned between the others' seats, peering down the road.

"So, are we really going to the old Henley House?" Miranda asked, as she tried to follow the direction they were taking down familiar roads. *Strange that I haven't been this way before,* she thought.

"You'll see," Jae said from the front passenger seat. Her friends were chatting quietly but she couldn't quite make out what they were saying above the road noise.

Miranda rolled her eyes and settled into the backseat of the car. At least it was nearly over, and they'd all be on a level playing field again. After about thirty minutes, Miranda could tell that Abby was taking them on a long series of random turns down two-lane roads, deserted on a Friday night when most folks were back in town at restaurants or the local movie theater. At long last, a yellow glow in the darkness loomed on their right, and Abby slowed the car, coming to a stop opposite a driveway with a huge, wrought-iron gate, flanked by a thick, tall hedge. An arch over the gate proclaimed this the entrance to Greenlawn Cemetery.

Miranda's stomach opened into a deep chasm of anxiety as she tried to draw her eyes away from the gates. "We're not actually going into the *cemetery*," she said. She hoped her friends didn't hear her voice shaking. Greenlawn was a place she knew all too well, though she hadn't visited it in six months.

"Don't be ridiculous." Abby said. She glanced at the wrought iron gates, then turned off the engine and got out of the car. "Don't even look over there."

"Turn around." Jae said, climbing out, too.

Forcing herself to look away from the dreaded grass hills with their shadowy gravestones, Miranda turned and instead looked up at a massive old farmhouse, looming in the darkness behind her. Two of the house's upper windows had broken, gaping holes in the glass. Finally, she got out of the car.

Even though she knew this had to be the Henley House all the kids talked about in school, Miranda hadn't realized exactly where it was. And of course, she wouldn't have noticed this house in particular the last time she was here. It was daylight then. She'd been with her mother, and it had felt like they were trudging together through a long, dark tunnel with a black hole at the other end, where time slowed to nothing and every happy feeling got sucked out of them, one molecule at a time, for all eternity.

Miranda could picture the headstone they'd gathered around, the carved letters on it like gashes in her own heart: *Samuel Woodward.* Miranda felt herself flush with irritation. Why hadn't Jae and Abby told her this is where they were going? Didn't they know how much she hated this place? How hard it was to be so near?

Jae reached out and touched Miranda's shoulder. She was chewing her lower lip and twirling a piece of her curly hair, like she always did when she was nervous. "Listen, Randi, if you want to leave, we can leave. We'll just tell you what's supposed to happen and then nobody will know the difference. It's just that this is the place, and there's not another abandoned house around here to take you to."

"We were hoping that if it was just the three of us, it would be okay," Abby said, standing beside Jae. "We know how much you've wanted to be in on this, but we should have told you where it was. I'm sorry. Do you want to just head back to my house?"

Miranda considered it. She'd been hearing about the Society of the Haunted, that rite of passage that every sixteen-year-old in their school faced, since Abby's oldest sister went through it nearly ten years earlier. Everyone on campus knew about it. She'd been looking forward to it for years. Her friends had been talking about it for months. But now that she was here, realizing how close it was to the cemetery, she wasn't so sure anymore. On the other hand, her friends were here with her. She thought about how they were both trying so hard to make her sixteenth birthday a good one, and how they'd wandered the entire corn maze with her. She didn't want to disappoint them or let them think she was scared, and most of all she didn't want to miss out on a chance she wouldn't get again.

After a long minute, Miranda reached into the backseat and grabbed her button-up. She turned her back to Greenlawn with a shiver and took in the huge, two-story farmhouse nestled behind a pair of ancient walnut trees, about a hundred feet back from the road. The bits of siding she saw in the moonlight were crooked, and the windows looked like gaping portals into a void. One of the shutters banged against the cracked siding in the breeze, the rusted hinge that barely held it in place groaning in protest.

"Here, I brought extra flashlights," Abby said, pressing one into Miranda's hand. Miranda blinked and realized she was facing the cemetery gates again. Abby spoke in a slightly too bright, sunshine tone, and Miranda knew she was still a little worried. "I know it's weird to be here," Abby continued, "but I'm really glad you decided to do this. We don't want you to miss out."

"She's right," Jae said, with a half-smile. She reached out and took Miranda's free hand, gave it a squeeze, and then gently but firmly pulled her to face the house again, their backs to the cemetery. "Try not to think about that place. Concentrate on this one."

Miranda took a deep breath and focused again on the house in front of her. "What the hell?" she muttered, and led the way to the bottom of the warped front porch steps, hanging on tightly to Jae's hand, Abby right on their heels.

The door to the house stood slightly ajar, but the room beyond remained hidden in shadows. The porch looked solid enough, and the parts they illuminated with their flashlights showed what might have once been white paint, faded to a dingy gray and peeling away from the wood. The steps looked warped, and when Jae put her foot on the first one, it creaked, but held.

"Come on, you two," Jae whispered. "Let's go."

"Wait." Miranda pulled her hand from Jae's grasp. The hair on the back of her neck prickled as she looked up at the open front door. She thought of the voices from the maze, unsure if she was ready for more just yet. The Henley House looked like just the sort of place for ghost voices. "What exactly are we going to do in there?"

"Initiation. Can't tell you more until we're inside," Abby said. As her friends climbed the porch steps, Miranda wavered at the bottom, not wanting to follow, but also not wanting to be alone in the dark, especially across from the cemetery. She looked up at Abby, who now stood at the top. "It's not like we're going to get arrested for trespassing. No one's here. Are you coming or what?"

Leave it to Abby to think of the one thing I wasn't *worried about,* Miranda thought. She willed her heart to stop pounding and took the first step. She creaked her way up to the porch and all three of them leaned into the doorway.

Up close, Miranda saw moonlight coming through the windows cast a little illumination into the foyer. A steep staircase rose about ten feet back from the front door, and wide openings led into rooms on either side of the entryway. She didn't want her friends to think she was scared. Glancing down to avoid holes, she squeezed between them and into the house.

The dark of the entryway enveloped Miranda, and the floorboards groaned as she inched toward the center of the space, away from the yawning mouth of the stairs that vanished into the dark above her. A soft noise to her right made her jump, and she pivoted to face the open door as Jae and Abby stepped into the hall behind her. The three of them stood in silence as the old house shifted and creaked around them.

Miranda reached for her friends and clasped their hands. Her ears strained to pick up any sounds that might not just be the house settling, but she couldn't find anything. Not even a whisper. After a long minute, she took a slow, deep breath and dropped their hands.

"Okay, we're here. Now what?" she whispered.

"We're going to stay until midnight," Jae whispered back. Miranda noticed Jae's usual straight posture hunched toward the middle of the group, as if she leaned away from something beside her.

"Why?" Miranda asked.

"Because it's your birthday," Abby said. Her full volume voice echoed in the darkness.

"It's the First Rule of Initiation into the Society of the Haunted," Jae said, her gummy bears reflecting red and yellow in the glow from the flashlight. Jae always had a flair for the dramatic.

Miranda folded her arms and raised her eyebrows. She had heard stories about the supposedly haunted house for years, but nobody had ever explained exactly what happened when you were actually there. In fact, now that she thought about it, she couldn't remember anything specific at all except how pissed she'd been, not to mention downright hurt, to find out her best friends had gone without her on their sixteenth birthdays. She hadn't spoken to them for a week, until finally Abby cornered her after school one day, her face red from crying, and Miranda had felt so awful that she'd forgiven them. Now that she stood in the house itself, however, she couldn't help but wonder what the point of the whole thing was.

"It's just an old house, Miranda." Abby cut into her thoughts. She turned and led the way into the right-hand room, motioning for the other two to follow. "Come on. Let's find a place to sit."

The room they entered looked like an old parlor. A huge, gilded mirror hung above a blackened fireplace, so dirty it looked gray, its surface buried under years of dust. A lumpy, pale gray shape to their left turned out to be a broken davenport, draped in an old sheet by whoever last lived in the house, its legs warping from the humidity that came into the house in the North Carolina summers.

The girls circled the room, pausing to look out the windows, while Jae shone her flashlight into the empty, cobwebbed corners. They found a few empty bottles piled on the hearth but no other signs of life. Abby pulled a small towel out of her satchel and set it on the floor, then took a seat and looked expectantly at the other two. Jae shrugged at Miranda and the two of them sat on the floor opposite her.

"I don't get it," Miranda whispered as she leaned close to her friends. "So, we just stay here until midnight? And then what?"

"We can't tell you yet because of the Rules," Jae answered. "You only get to find out the secret at *exactly midnight*. That's Rule Two."

"This is ridiculous," Miranda said. The dust made her eyes water and she didn't know what she might be sitting in on the dirty floor in her favorite jeans. She looked around the musty room and back at her two friends, who were Cheshire-cat smiling at each other in the darkness, and tried to ignore the twinge of irritation. She wanted to be there. She wanted to be part of the group. This was how she could stay part of the group. Miranda closed her eyes. When she opened them again, Abby and Jae were watching her.

"Abby's sisters brought Abby for her birthday," Jae said. "My brother brought me."

"I remember," Miranda said, folding her arms again. "And you didn't bring me."

"We couldn't. I told you that. It's part of the tradition." Abby smoothed her shirt and glanced at the fireplace. "Although, I'm not sure how long this has been going on."

"So, who started the rules?" Miranda thought about Abby's two older sisters, though they rarely hung out with the younger girls. One lived away at college and the other was about to graduate from high school in the spring, so they didn't have much time to spend with Abby anymore. If this had been going on at least as long as their sixteenth birthdays, the tradition was at least ten years old.

"I dunno, it's just passed down," Jae said. "My brother taught me. And no one gets to know about it until they turn sixteen. Then, and only then, those of us who have already been *initiated* get to bring a new initiate into the fold and show them the ways of the Society."

"Um, what?"

"Jae, knock it off," Abby said.

"I'm creating atmosphere!"

"You're creating crap," Abby said. She turned to Miranda. "Basically, it's just a thing people have been doing forever. If you're going to survive the next couple of years at this school, you need to have the experience."

"Gotcha." Miranda uncrossed her arms and tried to get comfortable on the floor. They were doing their best to show her around, so she decided to play along. Maybe it would be fun after all. "So, this is the Rite of Passage Tour, huh?"

"Only the best for you." Jae checked her watch. "We've got about fifteen minutes until midnight. Time for Rule Three."

Jae rummaged in her own bag and pulled out three pillar candles, handing one to each of the other two. She pulled a lighter from her pocket and lit her candle. "I hereby begin the Initiation as I light the flame of knowledge." She passed the lighter to Abby.

"I light my flame," Abby said, clicking the lighter and holding the tiny flame to her candle's wick. It quickly caught and the flickering candlelight on her two friends made them look almost otherworldly to Miranda as she took the lighter from Abby.

"I light my flame," she said quietly, lighting the candle in front of her.

Abby and Jae reached out to her and the three of them held hands in a triangle above the trio of little flames, their shadows dancing around them on the walls of the old house, reaching up into the darkness. Miranda wondered if she was unknowingly getting pulled into some weird occult group, and glanced behind her to make sure nothing was sneaking up on them, but the room was empty except for the furniture. When Jae spoke again, it startled Miranda, and she jumped. Abby suppressed a giggle.

"I, Jae Rogers, offer passage into the Society of the Haunted." She leaned forward the whispered to Miranda. "Now you ask me for passage."

"What?" Miranda whispered back. "Um, can I have passage?"

"Honestly, Randi, you suck at this. Give it a little, y'know, drama."

Miranda swallowed to clear her throat and tried to make her voice sound as solemn as Jae's. "I, Miranda Woodward, request passage into the Society of..."

"Of the Haunted," Abby whispered.

"Of the Haunted," Miranda finished.

"Good," Jae said. "Now repeat after me: I, then say your name, do solemnly swear."

"I, Miranda Woodward, do solemnly swear," Miranda said. She looked up at her two friends. Jae was concentrating on her candle, but Abby was watching her, biting her bottom lip to keep from giggling again. It made Miranda feel a little better to know Abby wasn't taking this thing so seriously. It couldn't be anything scary if Abby was laughing. Her friend was kind and intelligent, but awful about scary stuff.

"That I will uphold the Rules of the Society," Jae continued.

"That I will uphold the Rules of the Society," Miranda repeated.

"And will not speak of anything that happens tonight," Jae said.

"And will not speak of anything that happens tonight."

"Or I will eat wax."

"Or I will eat...wax?"

"Don't ask," Abby whispered. "I don't get that part either."

"Welcome, Miranda Jane Woodward, into the Society of the Haunted," Jae said. She threw her hands up in the air and wiggled her fingers. "Now Rule Four!"

"The last one," Abby said, giving Miranda an encouraging smile, who shifted on the dusty floor. "You've got to go to the top of the stairs and wait until midnight."

"You're joking," Miranda said. She glanced at Jae, but both of her friends now looked completely serious. "Come on, you're not going to make me go up there alone."

"That's how it works," Abby said. "You've got to climb the stairs and stand at the top landing until at least midnight."

"How will I know it's time to come down?"

"You'll know," Jae said. "Besides, your story has to be right if people ask you about it later. Come on, Randi. Just do it."

Miranda scrambled to her feet and brushed off her jeans. Her friends didn't move, so she took her flashlight and picked her way back to the hall alone, careful to watch where she stepped. The floor seemed solid enough inside the house, but the creaking boards unsettled her. She stopped at the foot of the staircase and glanced back at her friends. They smiled at her in the flickering candlelight.

The banister on the wall curled down to the floor in a single, long piece of dark wood, worn smooth by countless people's hands running along it over the decades. The stairs looked slick but darker in the center, as if the old varnish had worn away at some point under the weight of so many teenagers running up and down. The narrow beam of the flashlight illuminated the corners of the steps where a few cobwebs shivered in the air, clumps of dust dangling from them. A cold draft came through a crack in the front door and tickled the back of Miranda's neck, making her skin prickle again. She closed her eyes for just a moment, then took the first step.

A loud crack made her nearly fall off the stair and she swung her flashlight around as the sounds of her friends roaring with laughter filled the old house. She turned the light's beam to them and they pointed to the bottle Jae held by the neck, ready to knock it into the fireplace again.

"Not funny!" Miranda called.

"Just get up there," Jae called back. "You're wasting time!"

Miranda turned back to the stairs. This time she didn't hesitate, but hustled to the top of the landing, not wanting to linger on any one step longer than necessary. Her hand trembled as she shone the flashlight down the long hallway, flanked by closed doors, to the end where another narrow door opened onto what looked like a bathroom with tile on the floor and walls. Miranda glanced back down the stairs and called into the darkness.

"Okay, I'm upstairs now."

"Good!" Abby called back. "Now we just wait until midnight. Good luck!"

Miranda inched away from the top step, pressing her back against the wall to better see in every direction. Snatches of her friends' voices drifted up to her as they whispered to each other, and she found it comforting to hear them and know she wasn't really alone. Even with what they said about everyone coming there, the house made her uneasy, and her stomach twisted. She glanced at her phone: eight minutes to go. Miranda pulled her button-up shirt around herself, willing the minutes to pass so they could leave. Something about the house nagged at her. It seemed somehow familiar though she was sure she'd never been there before in her life.

"Almost time!" Jae called.

Miranda looked at her phone again: 11:59pm. She chewed her pinkie fingernail and waited for the little numbers to tick over to twelve, closer and closer to midnight. As the time changed, she froze, listening: above the whispers of the girls on the first floor, someone else spoke.

"...ought to take better care, it's not like—" a quiet voice said from the far end of the hall.

"It's the way things have to be, I'm afraid," murmured another voice.

"But she's bound to find out..." replied the first, getting louder.

A shadowy figure stepped from one of the rooms on the left-hand side of the hallway, paused, and then vanished through the wall opposite it. Miranda screamed.

Threadwalkers

Chapter 3

Miranda thundered down the stairs, slipping on the wood worn so smooth by years of feet so that she had to yank on the banister to keep from falling. Her friends came tearing out of the side parlor, each clutching a pair of glass bottles as if they were about to throw them.

"What's wrong?" Abby asked, her eyes wide. "We haven't done anything yet."

"This isn't funny!" Miranda shouted, pushing past them, and running out the front door. She didn't stop until she reached Abby's car, where she tried hauling on the handle even though Abby locked up when they went inside.

"What's not funny?" Jae demanded, marching out of the house, still holding the bottles. She looked from Miranda, to Abby walking up behind them, and back again. Abby held the three candles, now snuffed. "We didn't do anything! Well, I didn't anyway."

"I didn't either," Abby said. "What happened?"

"You didn't send me there to see that, that *thing*?" Miranda shouted, wheeling on them. It was all too much—being left out and then sent up by herself, only to have someone or some*thing* come out of nowhere. She balled her fists and felt her entire body tense with anger and fear.

"What *thing*?" Jae tossed the glass bottles toward the porch and crossed her arms. "Miranda, we don't know what you're talking about. It's just, y'know, like a dare. There isn't anything up there."

"We were getting ready to scream and smash the bottles into the fireplace when you came barreling down the stairs at us," Abby said, tucking the candles into her backpack. Miranda looked frightened as she pointed back at the house, though it didn't help her calm down any to know her friend was scared, too. "That's all that really happens. The house is totally abandoned, has been for years. It's just a prank everyone does." Abby pulled out her keys and let them all into the car.

Miranda climbed into the back seat and curled into the corner, shaking. She saw her friends exchange glances as they got into their seats. Abby backed out of the long driveway and pulled onto the road back to town. Miranda didn't want to look at them, so she stared out the window.

Twenty minutes later they turned into Jae's driveway and climbed out of the car. They hadn't spoken for the entire ride, and Miranda felt herself getting more and more tired as she came down from the terror of the house. All she wanted to do was sleep and not talk to her friends any more. She walked around to the back of the Volvo to get her overnight bag. Jae went to unlock the front door, but Abby hung back with Miranda to help her gather their things from the trunk.

"I'm really sorry you got freaked out, Randi" Abby said. "It's not supposed to actually be scary. It's just the people downstairs shouting to scare the person, and then everyone leaves."

"So, you didn't see the guy in the upstairs hallway?"

"The *guy*?" Abby's jaw dropped. "No! There's never been anyone there."

"And you didn't hear them talking?" Miranda watched her friend closely, but Abby genuinely didn't seem to know what she was talking about.

"No! I didn't hear anything! Now *I'm* kind of freaking out," Abby said. "I hope there isn't some random person living in there!" She hugged her overnight bag close to her chest and shut the trunk.

Miranda leaned heavily against the car. Abby wasn't the type to lie. Maybe they hadn't put her up to that on purpose. Maybe it was just another weird Miranda thing. She wished again that she could call her dad and talk it through with him.

"Randi?" Abby's quiet voice interrupted her thoughts. "Should we go inside now?"

Miranda nodded and went inside, her stomach twisting again. Maybe it *was* just someone squatting in the upstairs part of the house. She'd probably scared the crap out of whoever it was by being there in the middle of the night. Maybe that guy was even more freaked out than she was. Miranda's insides began to relax as she thought about some poor person she'd probably terrorized when she screamed and went careening out of the house.

She stepped into Jae's living room with her overnight bag, and any lingering frustration and fear dropped from her. The girls had the entire living room decorated with purple streamers and balloons. A big hand-painted poster that said "Happy Sixteenth, Miranda!" hung above the TV. Jae handed her a sparkly purple headband they'd passed back and forth since Abby got it on her ninth birthday. It had once said "Happy Birthday," but now read more like "H pp irthd y."

"Listen," Miranda said, stepping into the middle of the room. She suddenly felt guilty about yelling at them. "Y'all are the best. "I'm sorry I got so freaked out."

"It's okay," Jae said quickly, her easy smile radiating across her face. "We don't have to ever go back there again anyway, not now that you're in. Because whatever happened, that totally counted."

"That's right," Abby added. "And you don't have any younger siblings so we don't have to do it for anybody else."

"So that's the whole thing?" Miranda asked, plunking herself onto the couch. "You just go, light candles, wait until midnight, and scream?"

"Pretty much," Jae said. She tossed one of her mother's throw pillows onto the floor and leaned back against it. "So, what movie are we going to watch?"

"*Lord of the Rings*?" Abby asked, her voice hopeful.

"Not again," Jae groaned and looked at Miranda, a pained expression on her face. "Please, Randi, pick something besides those long-ass hobbit movies."

"What about *North by Northwest*?" Miranda asked.

"Ooh, that's a classic," Abby said. She flopped forward onto her sleeping bag and hooked her feet up on the couch.

Jae sighed, but she tossed Miranda the remote anyway. "All right. Since it's your birthday, and it's not a hobbit movie. But if I can't sleep tonight, it's your fault."

They spent the rest of the night chatting and watching Hitchcock movies until they slowly drifted off in the living room, curled in their sleeping bags. Miranda was awake last. Her thoughts drifted back to the Henley House and the weird thing she saw upstairs. It *must* have been a person that she startled, and the more she thought about it, the more ridiculous she felt for getting so angry and scared. She was thankful that her friends weren't the type to go to school on Monday and tell everyone about it. She and Abby and Jae had been friends for so long that, despite a couple of rough patches in middle school, they'd always had each other's backs. She snuggled into her sleeping bag between the other two girls and finally fell asleep around 4 o'clock in the morning.

After a few short hours of sleep and too many pancakes made by Jae's mom, Abby drove them both home. They went to Miranda's house first, where they both got out of the car to wish her happy birthday again and say goodbye until Monday. She hugged each of her friends, then rummaged in her purse for her house key as they pulled away. As she fit the key into the front door lock, she paused.

The hair on the back of Miranda's neck prickled, and she held her breath. The shadowy figure from last night loomed in her mind as she listened for the voice she halfway expected behind her. She didn't want to look but knew she needed to move. Something on the sidewalk stood just out of Miranda's peripheral vision. Her stomach twinged. As she worked up the courage to turn, the door flew open. She screamed, and her keys jangled onto the cement stoop where she dropped them.

"Ahhh!" Miranda's mother screamed, too, holding the door open. She leaned around her daughter to look into the front yard. "Miranda, are you okay? What's going on?"

Miranda spun and looked at the sidewalk and front yard, too, but didn't see anything. "I could've sworn there was...nothing, I guess," she finished. "I'm fine, Mom. Sorry about that. You just startled me when you opened the door." Miranda ducked around her mother into the bright hallway, daylight pouring through the open door behind her.

"All right..." Her mother glanced outside, then closed the front door, and pulled Miranda into a bear hug. "Happy birthday, sweetie! I can't believe you're already sixteen!"

"Yeah, me either," Miranda said. She usually pushed her mom away, but today she let her mother keep squeezing her as she tried to shake the feeling that someone or something outside had been watching her.

"How was the corn maze?" her mom asked, letting go. Her mother was still wearing purple nursing scrubs from an overnight shift at the hospital. She smelled like the orange scented cleaner that they used in the children's wing.

"It was good," Miranda said, dropping her overnight bag at the foot of the stairs in the living room.

"Just good?"

"Well, I guess it was fun, but it wasn't the same." Miranda shrugged. She didn't have to explain what she meant to her mother. Nothing was the same for either of them anymore, no matter how much they had both tried to find some kind of normal in their lives.

"I know, sweetie." Her mother put a hand on her shoulder. "I'm glad you got to go. Your dad would be glad you went, too."

"Yeah. I know." Miranda looked at her mom's face. Her mother looked tired, but that could just be from working overnight. Then again, she always looked a little tired these days. Miranda was often tired, too, with the nightmares. She understood not being able to sleep.

While her mom made coffee, Miranda sat at the kitchen table, which was buried under at least a week's worth of junk mail. The sunlight stretched across the ceiling, coming in from slits in the mini-blinds, and she imagined them as fingers, creeping toward the light fixture. As she watched her mom wash a couple of mugs, she felt something press against her legs. She reached down to pet her fluffy black and white cat, Perkins, but when she reached the point where his head should be, there was just air. She grinned, thinking he had rolled over to ask for a belly rub, and looked down.

At her feet sat a petite orange tabby cat. It mewed at her and hopped right up to curl into her lap. Miranda pulled back, startled, but also pleased that it was so friendly. She slowly reached down to stroke the little cat, and glanced around the room, looking for her own fluffy black and white fur-ball, but he wasn't in sight.

"Where did you come from, cutie?" she whispered. The cat just closed its eyes and purred. Was the little cat a surprise birthday gift? "Mom, where did the cat come from?"

Her mother glanced over her shoulder from the sink, where she was drying the last few dishes. "That's a strange question, Miranda. Probably the living room. Why?"

Miranda was puzzled. Her mom hadn't mentioned getting another cat, and she felt certain that they would've picked one out together anyway. But Perkins didn't like other cats, so it was especially weird to think of her mom going and getting another one, and even weirder to not acknowledge it. In any case, she wondered where Perkins might be, since he usually sat on her feet under the table. After a while, the orange tabby jumped down again and trotted across the kitchen floor toward the water dish in front of the pantry.

Miranda leaned down to look under the table, but her cat wasn't there. "Mom, have you seen Perkins this morning?"

"Who?" Her mother poured a cup of coffee and glanced over her shoulder at Miranda. "Perkins? That sounds like a butler's name."

"Yes, Perkins, he—Oh. Yeah, well, the butler name... that was the point, right? He's black and white. Like he's wearing a little tuxedo?" Her mother didn't answer, so she continued. "I figured he'd be following that other cat around. I didn't know we were getting a new cat. You should've told me."

"New cat?" Her mother looked confused, and Miranda resisted the urge to roll her eyes. She wasn't in the mood for games.

"The orange cat." Miranda pointed to the little cat, who was now working on cleaning the food bowl of every last crumb. "It's right there."

"You mean Polly?" Her mother put down her coffee cup and walked toward the cat, glancing at Miranda, a worried expression on her face. "She looks the same as always, Miranda. What are you talking about?"

"Looks the same as always for what?" Miranda held out her hands. What was her mother playing at? "I seriously don't know what's going on here. Where is my cat?"

"Miranda, you're worrying me. Did you sleep all right?" her mother asked, reaching out to put the back of her hand on Miranda's forehead. "I know you girls stayed up late last night. Are you feeling okay?"

"Where is Perkins?" Miranda demanded as she jerked her head away from her mother's touch. "Is this some kind of prank? Did Jae put you up to this?"

"What are you talking about? Who is Perkins?"

"PERKINS. MY CAT."

"Do not raise your voice at me, Miranda Jane," her mother snapped. "I don't know who Perkins is, and this isn't funny." Her mother plunked another large cup of coffee in front of Miranda, along with a bottle of cinnamon syrup. Miranda knew her mother had probably picked the syrup up as a special treat, but she didn't want coffee when her mother was pretending not to know about the cat they'd had since Miranda was five years old.

"Fine. I'm going to look for him."

Miranda pushed back from the table and stomped into the living room, where she knelt down and started looking under the sofa and end tables for her black and white cat. What was going on with her mom? Was she losing her mind? Why was she acting like Perkins wasn't around? It wasn't funny. Miranda fought back tears of frustration as she reached into the back corners beneath the sofa. It was like she and her mother were having two different conversations. Her head started to hurt a little, and she sniffed hard.

Where was Perkins? Miranda flung open the coat closet and checked behind the shoe rack inside, thinking about her fluffy cat being lost, or even stuck somewhere. She rubbed her temples with her fingers, willing her thoughts to slow down so she could figure out what was happening. Maybe she just hadn't seen him. Maybe he was mad about the new cat and hiding under her bed. He always hid under the bed when something upset him, like a storm, or an unexpected knock on the door. Maybe he was hiding and refusing to come out.

She rushed upstairs, looking under her bed and in her own closet. She even dug through the pile of laundry on the closet floor in just case he'd made a nest, but Perkins wasn't there. He wasn't anywhere in her room. She crossed the hall and went into her mother's room, lifting the bed skirt to look for the telltale reflection of Perkins's bright golden eyes, but the only things under the bed were some storage bins with her mother's winter clothes. Miranda leaned back on her heels and tried to steady her breathing and not panic. Perkins was probably hiding somewhere and she just hadn't seen him. He'd come out for dinner. He couldn't really be gone. She couldn't lose her cat on top of everything else. Taking another shaky breath, Miranda got to her feet and walked back downstairs, flopping onto the couch.

After a while, Miranda's mother came and took the seat at the other end of the couch, still clutching her coffee cup. "Sweet Pea, are you sure there isn't anything you want to talk about?" Her voice sounded softer than usual.

"No," Miranda snapped, and immediately regretted it. She glanced up under her eyelashes, now wet with tears, to find her mother watching her, brows furrowed. Miranda didn't want to hurt her mother. She just wanted to know where her cat was, and what this other cat was doing in their house. Why was her mother still not telling her? Miranda felt frustration bubbling up again but with her mother sitting there, she tried her best to hold it inside.

She'd spent the better part of the last six months trying to protect her mother, to keep her from having anything extra on her plate. Miranda had helped set up the bills on auto-pay, and she'd started packing both of their lunches at night before bed just to give her mom a little bit of breathing room. It was hard enough that they skated around the topic of her dad all the time, and Miranda knew that the therapist had just recommended that her mother increase her dosage of anti-depressants. She was glad her mom was sleeping again, but she'd never realized how fragile her mother was, before. Maybe this thing with the new cat was just bad timing on her mom's part, and she needed to let it go. She set aside her worry for Perkins, hoping he'd turn up before too long, sat up straighter, and sighed, "Really, Mom, I'm fine."

"I know you are," her mother said, running her finger along the top of her cup absently. "I just know you're getting older, and it can be hard to talk to your mom about things. But I'll always be here if you need me. Okay?"

"Okay, Mom." Miranda looked down at her black ballet flats, still a little muddy from the yard around the Henley House.

Should she tell her mother about the house? The voices? Her mom looked much older than a year ago, maybe evidence of the extra shifts at the hospital to help cover the bills. The prominent creases around her eyes showed and a thin strip of gray in her dark hair betrayed the slack in her usual hair routine. She wanted so badly to talk to someone about the strange things happening, and her mother sat there, just within reach. Miranda took a deep breath, but just then her mother smiled at her.

"I'm sorry I've been pushing you, Pea," she said before Miranda could say anything. "This isn't easy for either of us."

"Yeah, I know," Miranda said.

The oven timer beeped. Miranda's mother jumped up, leaving her coffee cup behind, and walked back to the kitchen. Miranda slowly got up and followed her. The smell of cinnamon and butter wafted across the room, and Miranda took a deep breath. Cinnamon rolls were her favorite, and her mother hadn't baked them since before. She hadn't really baked anything in the last six months. Miranda liked watching her mom carefully working the buns out of the pan with a knife.

Since the end of March that year, her mother had insisted they both see a therapist, and to Miranda's horror, they saw the same one. She knew Dr. Trestle wasn't allowed to repeat anything to her mother, but she still never quite trusted the woman, fearing some so-called revelation might get back to her mom. She didn't know why it mattered to her. The voices were getting louder, but Miranda didn't want her mother to be even more upset than she already was, and she was pretty sure having a daughter who heard disembodied voices would rank as "upsetting." Her mom had enough to deal with in her own grief, working through the fog until they found the right medication to help her sleep, to help her cope. It wasn't as if knowing about the hollow inside Miranda's chest would make her mom feel any better.

And then there were the nightmares. When the nightmares got bad, she did break down and tell Dr. Trestle about them, who gave her a temporary prescription for a sleep aid. She used it once, and slept right through her alarm the next day, missed the bus, and vowed never to use it again. At least the nightmares got her up on time. What good was a doctor whose only solution was pills? She didn't want to talk to anyone except her dad, and he was the one person not available.

Miranda's mother tried to talk to her about her dad a few times those first weeks. She kept sitting beside Miranda, asking how she felt, asking through watery eyes how she was doing. Miranda always shook her head and forced a smile, trying to be brave or strong or whatever it was she thought her mother needed her to be. Her mother would nod, as if she somehow knew about the emptiness, or as if she had her own floodgate keeping things inside, and they wound up sitting in silence more and more. The silence between them stretched, even as the spring turned into summer which went racing into the fall.

Eventually, her mother stopped asking, and they fell into a routine of small talk. *How was your day, mine was fine, would you grab me a soda from the fridge?* That sort of thing. And eventually, the gnawing grew less, or at least became such a normal part of her existence that Miranda learned to function despite it. She started spending more time with her friends than at home, and began laughing at their jokes again. Her mother let her stay out past midnight more often, too; if Miranda was participating in life at all, that seemed to be enough for her mom. Just a month ago, her mother stopped taking her to Dr. Trestle. They never mentioned it, but Miranda felt a huge relief all the same when Tuesday came and went without a trip to the therapist's cold office.

Now the evenings were quiet but peaceful. Her mother never cried, at least not in front of Miranda. They ate dinner, watched cooking competitions and bridal shows on TV, and just kept one another company. Their relationship might not be the closest, but Miranda never missed a weeknight dinner if she could help it. On the weekends, though, Miranda went to her friends' houses for dinner, and often stayed over. On weekends, she could pretend to be normal. Miranda glanced up as her mother turned back to her with a plate.

"Make a wish," her mother said, placing a huge, freshly frosted cinnamon roll in front of her. It even had a candle. "Happy sixteenth birthday!"

Miranda blew out the candle. She tried to smile at her mom, who smiled back and kissed the top of her head. She pushed away the thought of the voices, deciding that today wasn't the day to tell her mom, even if she wanted to. Not on her birthday. There would be another time. And besides, first she needed to find Perkins.

As Miranda took her first bite of cinnamon roll, her mother opened the pantry and rummaged in the back. She returned a moment later with two small boxes, one wrapped in bright yellow paper with a large blue bow perched on top of it and one a small shipping box, which she handed to Miranda first. Miranda gave her mother a puzzled look and started to lift the lid from the cardboard box. Her mother reached out and touched her hand.

"This came yesterday. It's from the Coast Guard."

Miranda looked up at her mom, eyes wide. She felt her hands shaking. She didn't know what to say. Her mother's eyes were fixed on the box, and she was talking very fast now.

"I wanted us to do this together. I hate that it's your birthday, but I'm here for you."

"Mom, what is this?"

"I guess the investigation is over, so they released his things earlier this week." Her mother sat down beside her and rested her hand on Miranda's arm. "I'm not even sure what the box is, but this is all they found."

"They didn't find anything else? Six months of searching? A whole investigation?"

"No, Sweet Pea. They said the rest of the plane was swept into the ocean. These washed up on the beach of that island." Her mother sniffed and bit her bottom lip. "And I'm sorry I didn't tell you last night, but I didn't want to ruin your night out with your friends."

Miranda reached over and hugged her mom tightly for a long minute. "No, Mom, it's all right. Let's open it."

She lifted the lid of the box. Inside was a smaller package wrapped in brown paper. Her heart skipped a beat when she saw her name scrawled across the top of the brown package in familiar neat, square handwriting. Her dad's handwriting. It looked like it had been soaked in water, but it was still legible. Under the little package she found her dad's wallet, crusted in sea salt. There was nothing else.

Her mother reached out and touched the cracked leather with one finger. "The wallet's empty except for his driver's license," she said quietly. "I checked. I guess that's how they knew it was his."

Miranda set down the wallet and picked up the little package. She ran her finger along the edge until the found the corner of the packing tape, pulling it so the paper tore away in her hands, revealing a warped cardboard gift box. Her mother leaned in to see as Miranda lifted the flap.

41

Inside, beneath a layer of what used to be white packing paper but was now crispy and yellowed from being waterlogged, she found a small, carved wooden box. Miranda pulled it out and set it on her palm, turning it so they both had a good view. Intricate patterns covered each side, including a large flower inset on the lid. The box seemed undamaged by its exposure to salt water; unlike the wallet, not even a slight salt crust coated its surface.

Miranda peered at the beautiful carvings, and examined the area right around the seam of the lid until she found a tiny button. Using the tip of her fingernail, she pressed it. With a soft *click*, the lid popped open. A rush of spice and salts and something more elusive filled the room, and Miranda and her mother both breathed in the smell of her father, back from a long trip. She reached inside and found a carefully folded piece of paper, and a spool of pale gold thread. She carefully set the spool on the table and, hands trembling, unfolded the paper. The same familiar, boxy handwriting scrawled across the page.

"Read," her mother whispered. So, Miranda read.

My sweet Miranda,

I'm so proud of the young woman you've grown into, and know you're ready to have this now. Keep it with you at all times. This is VITAL.

Miranda glanced at the box and the spool, so she kept on reading.

I'm truly sorry I haven't been able to explain where I've been, or anything else up until now. We have so much to talk about.

Know that your mother and I love you and know that we're always proud of you, and we always will be, no matter what. Keep this safe and work hard in your lessons. The past is present and future.

Love,

Dad

Miranda handed her mother the letter. She could feel herself crying but the numbness inside her chest had reached out to swallow her so that she wasn't sure what else to do. Why was *this* the only thing left? Why had her father chosen such a strange thing for her, and why was he carrying it with him in California six months ago? She leaned into the comforting warmth of her mother's arm and shoulder. Her mother squeezed her and they sat silently for a long time. Eventually, Miranda sat up and scrubbed the back of her hand against her eyes. Her mother gave her a watery smile. Miranda reached for the spool.

"What's this?"

"It's an empty wooden spool," her mother said. "I believe your grandmother used to use some like that."

"Empty?" Curiosity began to overcome the initial shock, and Miranda held the spool up to the light, where the fine golden thread shimmered. She looked from it to her mom, her heart hammering in her chest. "The spool looks empty to you?"

"Miranda, I'm not sure what you're getting at, but yes. I see the same wooden spool you do," her mother replied, an eyebrow arched. "It looks hand-carved, like this box. It's beautiful."

"Weird," Miranda said. She ran her finger over the pale gold thread, feeling the subtle texture of it and wondering why her mother couldn't see it. Then again, her mother also didn't hear the voices, so maybe the voices and the thread were related. Or maybe she was so tired she was starting to see things. Between this and the cat and her weird experience in the old house the night before, she felt unsteady, her thoughts swirling too fast for her to latch onto any single one of them. She shook her head, trying to rid herself of the frightening thoughts and focus on something a little more concrete. She turned to her mom, who was looking at her a little strangely. Miranda put down the spool. "Did dad sew?"

"No... We sent everything to the tailor," her mom said. "Who knows where he picked this up. He was in California for a while right before..." Her mom's voice trailed off.

Miranda picked up the note and read it again. She turned the box upside-down and shook it, but nothing else fell out. She placed the spool back inside the little box and closed the lid with a snap, running her fingertip around the carved flower. Her mother watched her for a while but then nudged the yellow-wrapped gift toward her.

"Open this one, too."

Miranda untied the ribbon and pulled away the paper to reveal a white box. She lifted the lid and stopped. Inside was her mom's gold watch. She didn't know what she'd expected, but it certainly wasn't a watch.

"Oh!" she said. "Didn't dad give you this for your anniversary?"

"Yes," her mom said, smiling. "I want you to have it. See, I even had it engraved for you. You should have a nice watch to wear."

Miranda turned the watch over in her palm. She rubbed her thumb over the shallow lettering on the back of the face: *Miranda Jane Woodward*. It even had her birthday, September 9, in tiny numbers below her middle name.

"Wow." She wasn't sure how else to react. Obviously, this was important to her mother, but it wasn't exactly her style. Still, she put the watch on and looked up at her mother with a hesitant smile. "Thank you, Mom," Miranda said.

"It's not for school," her mom said in a thick voice, her eyes shining with tears. "Just for special occasions. But you ought to have a piece of grownup jewelry. A keepsake."

Her mom reached out, and Miranda again accepted the hug. If she was honest with herself, it felt good to be hugged so tightly. They finished their coffee and cinnamon rolls, reminiscing about all of Miranda's other birthdays, talking more easily than they had in months. Miranda remembered a lot of her birthdays, but not the earliest, and her mother was happy to recount. She talked a long time about Miranda's first birthday, and how her father brought home the wrong cake, and how in front of all the grandparents, she shoved her little one-year-old fists into a cake that said, "Happy Birthday Ashley!"

Miranda's best birthday by far was her thirteenth, when her dad had taken her on a flying lesson. Miranda dearly wanted to be a pilot like her hero, Amelia Earhart. She began retelling the story to her mother, who cringed as Miranda described the swooping feeling of the plane hitting a little pocket of air, like a personal roller coaster in the sky. A love of planes and flying was something she had shared only with her dad, but now as Miranda talked, it didn't feel like such a fun memory anymore. She quickly changed the subject, and they both relaxed a little again.

After breakfast, they went for pedicures and then to Miranda's favorite restaurant for lunch, a seafood place called Dan's, and for the first time in a while, they laughed together, the old memories still carrying them together like boats caught by a breeze that sent them along, side by side.

Miranda sat bolt upright in bed on Sunday morning, her heart pounding. She felt certain she heard a voice in her room, and it said her name. She did a quick mental check of the place. Door: closed. Closet: closed. Hamper: overly full. Backpack: on the ground where she'd dropped it Friday. Posters: Amelia Earhart and Nancy Harkness Love, her two favorite female pilots, on the wall above her desk. Computer: screensaver of photos, mostly of herself with Jae and Abby with a few stills from Hitchcock films thrown in. Nothing looked out of place, but she sat as still as possible all the same, keeping her breathing shallow and straining to hear any other noise.

The house was quiet. Slowly, Miranda forced herself to lean forward and gently touch Polly, who lay curled just within reach. Perkins was still nowhere to be seen. The little cat opened one eye, yawned and stretched out across the entire foot of the bed. Miranda stroked the cat's side for a moment, still debating the sound. As she ran her fingers through the soft, orange fur, Miranda watched the screensaver scroll on her laptop: photos from middle school, photos from when she and Jae and Abby went to Freshman Camp, photos of camping with her parents... And then she noticed something strange: the camping photos had changed.

Sliding off the bed, Miranda walked to the desk and leaned in close to the screen. She had updated the screensaver album earlier in the summer, and Jae and Abby featured prominently, though she included the old family photos all the same to look at her dad from time to time. As she watched the images scroll past, one appeared from her childhood: a photo of herself in a canoe with her mom and dad sitting on either side of her as they paddled past whoever took the photo. At least, that was how she remembered it. Now, however, only her mother sat in the canoe with her. She tapped the keyboard and quickly opened the screensaver album's folder. Her father seemed to have simply vanished from all but the oldest of her photos—the ones from her preschool and kindergarten years.

"Dad!" she whispered. She touched one of the pictures where he used to be. Her breath started coming faster, and she had trouble holding the mouse steady as she scrolled through column after column of photos. Her chest felt hollow again, like it had the night her mother got the call. Miranda flung herself onto the floor, holding her knees up to her chin like she did when she was little, and letting the tears run down her face as she picked at the gold watch still on her wrist. What had happened to the photos? What was happening to *her*? The tears curved along her chin and pooled together, dripping onto her chest. Polly mewed from the bed and jumped down, pressing the top of her head against Miranda's arm.

"I don't want you. I want my Perkins. WHERE IS PERKINS?" she shouted. The tiny cat hissed and ran under the desk. Feeling guilty, Miranda reached in after her, pulling Polly into her lap and holding the cat tightly, even as the feline struggled to get free of the unwanted hug. "I'm sorry, Kitty; I just don't understand what's happening. I'm starting to think I'm going crazy. Maybe I do need to go back to Dr. Trestle..."

She let go of the cat, who leaped back onto the bed and started licking herself all over, ears laid flat against her striped head. Miranda stopped crying and rubbed her face dry with the back of her sleeve, sniffing hard. Then, she noticed a shoe box under her desk where she'd put it months earlier. She pulled it toward her and removed the lid. Inside lay several small items, each belonging to her father, each hidden away after his funeral so they wouldn't end up in the donation bin. She knew her mother kept some of his things, too, but certain memories she wanted all for herself. Somehow it comforted her to have a little piece of her father squirreled away in her room.

Miranda grabbed the box the Coast Guard sent and reached inside to add her dad's empty wallet to her collection. She hadn't looked at it too closely yet because it, more than anything, showed that her dad was really gone. It belonged in the memory stash, for another time when she was ready. From the bottom of the shoebox, she pulled out a battered wallet insert, filled with her school photos.

She'd found the little packet in his dresser months ago. The photos from kindergarten and first grade on the first page looked especially worn. She poked her round, kindergarten face, then turned the little insert page. The other photos she remembered weren't there. Miranda thumbed through the whole insert, but didn't see any of them. She dug through the rest of the box to see if any of them had fallen out, with no success. The photos simply disappeared, like her father had from the screensaver pictures. She set the insert aside and pulled out the tiny hand towel he'd brought her from what he said was the fanciest hotel he ever stayed in for work. It was thick and white, and she rubbed her fingers over the threads for the hundredth time.

She pulled out the last item in the box, a snow globe. Miranda remembered when her father came back from his business trip to Alaska with this trinket, and how much she loved the tiny sled with six dogs pulling it through the swirling, sparkling fake snow. Miranda picked it up and put it flat on her palm, but it didn't have sled dogs any more. Instead, the little glass dome enclosed palm trees and a tiny figure, painted gray, pointing straight ahead. It read "Cabrillo" across the bottom. Miranda stared at the snow globe, trying to remember where she got it, and why she mistook it for the one from Alaska.

"But I didn't mistake it! I know this was the one from Dad when I put it in here," she said aloud.

She shook her head, as if trying to knock a thought loose from her mind, but couldn't settle on why her memory bothered her so much. She placed the snow globe carefully back into its place in the shoebox and picked up the wallet, opening it for the first time. Her mother was right: it looked empty. Her mother must have removed the driver's license already. But when she tried to slide the photo insert into one of the card slots, it seemed to get caught on something. Miranda pulled the little slot as wide as possible. There, in the back and folded in half, was a small piece of thick paper. She used her pinky to pull it far enough forward to pinch the edge, and pulled a business card from the wallet. The front of the card had one line on it, in tiny block type:

Stitch in Time Tailoring

The back had just three letters, "ICE," in her dad's boxy handwriting. She stared at the letters; ICE was the code her dad had insisted she put into her first cell phone, and every phone since, with his and her mother's numbers listed. "ICE" was short for "In case of emergency" and, as he told her, was an easy way for someone else to call for help if anything happened. But there was no phone number on the card.

"What does this mean, Dad?" she whispered, running her fingertip over the little letters. She glanced back at her computer, where the screensaver was scrolling past again, and decided it was time to do some looking. She moved to her desk, opened a browser window, and typed in her dad's name.

The name "Samuel M. Woodward" turned up only a few results for her to sift through, and she quickly found his obituary in the local paper's online archives.

Samuel M. Woodward, aged 47, died Tuesday in a plane crash off the coast of California. He is survived by his wife, Colette Woodward, and his only daughter, Miranda Woodward. Funeral services will be held this Friday at White Memorial Church. The family has requested donations to the local VFW instead of flowers.

Miranda skimmed over it for a few minutes, even though she had long ago memorized it. After a while, she shook her head and did a search for details about the plane crash. Several articles appeared, though with a small plane and not one of the huge, commercial flights the public wasn't as interested so stories were scarce. Private pilots messing up their own lives just didn't hold the attention of the sensation-loving news audience. Before long, Miranda found a website with the description she wanted.

A small plane crashed off the southern California coast on Tuesday, killing five including the pilot. Authorities believe the plane went down due to poor weather conditions. Wreckage has been found along the southern California coast and off Anacapa Island, part of Channel Islands National Park. Local authorities have ruled the crash an accident, and have expressed concern for the native wildlife found on the small island.

Miranda frowned. Was this really all there was? She kept scrolling, but didn't see any other information, except one piece saying that a salvage team recovered all the debris and returned the tiny island to its usual pristine state. As she scrolled back up to the top of the article, she noticed that the date seemed wrong. This article was dated March 21, two days after the date of the crash, but it was from ten years ago, not six months. Maybe there was another crash on March 19 on the same island, a decade earlier? That seemed odd. Maybe the website was glitched. She clicked back over to the tab with the obituary, but the page gave her a 404 error. She re-searched, and found it again, but this time in an archive from years earlier. Miranda rubbed her eyes, unsure she was reading things correctly. No matter where she clicked, there on the screen was the wrong date.

Miranda sat back in her chair, wondering what to do next. She wondered if her computer was screwed up. But her photos were wrong, too. Maybe she should reboot it overnight or something. As she leaned back in the chair, she saw the business card by her elbow. *Stitch in Time Tailoring.* She searched online for "Stitch in Time Tailoring," but nothing came up. Next, she typed "tailor shop." Dozens of entries showed this time, but they all had names like "Thompson's Tailoring" and "Hems and Things." Nothing helpful.

She decided to broaden her search, and typed "Stitch in Time" into the search engine. In moments, she got back dozens of sites talking about the origin of the expression "a stitch in time saves nine" and how it meant to do a little maintenance now to prevent a large problem later, or it meant that solving a problem quickly keeps it from turning into a much bigger one. No surprise there; she'd heard the expression for years. She typed "Sam Woodward + Stitch in Time" and once more got a list of articles about the expression itself. The thing she didn't expect was the eighth entry down the page. It was a link to a page called simply "Stitch in Time," but had an interesting tag line in the preview.

We are there when you need us most. Stitch in Time.

She clicked the link and found, instead of a story or a full website, a plain text ad that had nothing at all to do with her father, at least as far as she could tell. Still, the first line made her heart race.

Are you in need of a good Tailor? When things don't fit, finding someone with the right expertise can make all the difference. The proper fit can change your life! Contact us today, and remember: A Stitch in Time Saves Lives.

Miranda read the ad twice. She flipped the business card over and carefully copied it, unsure why she felt the need to do so. The last line she checked a few times to get it exactly correct, wondering if "Lives" was a typo. As the search engine kept insisting, the original expression was "a stitch in time saves nine;" this one didn't even half rhyme with that. She set the card aside and went to click the link for directions to the advertised Tailor, but couldn't find one. In fact, when she tried to click on the main ad again, the page refused to load.

Miranda's stomach growled; she'd lost track of time and it was early afternoon. Reluctantly, she left her desk and ventured downstairs to find food. When she got to the living room, her mother looked up at her from the couch.

"I ordered a pizza. It'll be here soon," her mother said. "Why don't we watch some TV?"

"I need to finish my homework," Miranda said. She wanted to grab a snack and go back upstairs to keep crawling through links to see if she could find out anything else about this tailor shop.

"Just until lunch gets here." Her mother patted the cushion beside her.

Miranda walked around the couch and sank into the spot beside her mom. Sunday afternoon Bride-a-thon had always ranked as her favorite of their TV shows, and as much as she wanted to know about the strange card in her dad's wallet, she knew that her mom needed her to be there, too. She relaxed as the minutes ticked by and her mother didn't ask anything about the rest of the morning or comment on Miranda's still unfinished homework, leaving her to puzzle over the strange ad.

"You should always know the person you're with really well before you get married," her mother said at the end of one of the shows.

Miranda glanced at her mom, whose face was washed in the blue light of the TV screen, her neck a dark void beneath the shadow of her chin. Though her expression was calm, Miranda could sense that she'd been crying again. Her mom cried a lot. Miranda did, too, up in her room, alone. She wondered whether these bridal shows made her mother feel lonely seeing all those people getting married. It suddenly occurred to Miranda that her mother might start dating again and might even get remarried someday, and her stomach twisted uncomfortably.

"How well did you know Dad when you got married?" she asked. Her mother shifted to look directly at her. Thanks to the birthday gift, this had been the most mention of Samuel Woodward either had made since the funeral, and Miranda hoped the silent barrier that had separated them for months would stay down a while longer.

"I knew him pretty well," her mother answered. "I mean, we dated for over a year before he proposed. He traveled a lot, though, even then." She shook her head, but her gaze drifted to the family photos on the mantle to the right of the TV, including their wedding portrait.

"What do you remember most about him?"

Her mother considered this for a while, tapping her fingers on her knee and still looking at the portrait. "His laugh, I think," she said. "And how hard it was when he traveled. And... just little things. He always left his socks on the bathroom floor, and it drove me nuts."

"I remember his smell," Miranda said. "And his books. What happened to those?"

Her mother tilted her head to the side, her expression unreadable and suddenly strange. "Which books do you mean?"

"The ones he brought back from his trips. You know, the really old ones about the places he'd been. There was one— "

"Don't you have homework to do?" her mother interrupted, turning back to the TV show. It was like a spell was suddenly broken.

Miranda's mouth hung open for a moment in shock. She didn't understand what had just happened. One minute they were actually talking, the thing her mother had wanted to do all summer, and the next her mother was almost *dismissing* her. What the hell? Well if her mother didn't want to talk after all, fine. She stood and stomped back upstairs, slamming the door, and sinking onto the bed.

Maybe it was something she'd said, though she didn't know why books, of all things, would upset her mom. She didn't understand why the trips bothered her mother so much, either. And why couldn't Miranda know what happened to the books? Her mother acted like she didn't know what Miranda was talking about. Miranda heaved a sigh and pulled her backpack onto the desk. She dumped out her textbooks to start her homework and knocked over the carved wooden box in the process. She peeked inside at the spool, then slipped the business card into the box and opened her Spanish book.

Monday afternoon after school, Miranda waved goodbye to Jae and Abby at the front of the building, and she and her mother drove to the DMV. Other than almost rolling past a stop sign when her stomach twisted uncomfortably (which made her regret the extra fries she'd had at lunch) and parking a little too close to another car, she passed the test easily. New driver's license in hand, she borrowed her mother's Honda and drove straight to Jae's house.

She didn't have a parking tag for school, so she still needed to ride the bus, but she felt like the little plastic license in her wallet was a pass for freedom. She couldn't wait to take her friends for a ride around town. Miranda pulled into Jae's driveway and honked the horn, hoping to get Jae and her older brother to come outside to see her. After several minutes, no one opened the door and the curtains didn't twitch, so she turned off the engine and pulled out her phone.

Knock knock! she texted as she walked to the front door, keys still in hand.

Who is this? came the reply.

Don't be silly! Miranda wrote back as she rang the doorbell. After a couple of minutes, the front door opened, and Jae stood there, her curly hair held back in a thick headband and her expression blank.

"Hey! I got my license. Let's go!"

"Go where?" Jae asked, closing the door halfway and leaning on the frame so that her body blocked the view into the house. "We don't buy things from people who— "

"Go anywhere! Go get Abby and go to the mall, or a movie, or something."

"Do I know you?"

Chapter 4

"Very funny," Miranda said, grinning at Jae as she held up the new license. "This makes me like a new person, I get it. Now let's go!"

"Seriously, who are you?" Jae asked. The usual half-grin and bright eyes that usually betrayed Jae's jokes were missing from her face, and Miranda felt herself chest tighten. Jae turned and called over her shoulder. "Mom! Someone's here!"

Jae's mother appeared behind her in the door, a look of mild curiosity on her face. "What's going on?" she asked.

"Hi, Mrs. Rogers. I wanted to see if Jae could come with me to…" Miranda didn't finish her sentence. The blank looks on both of their faces made her even more uneasy, and she shifted her weight onto one foot, rubbing the back of her calf with the other one. She didn't understand what was happening, but it seemed like a weird prank to play. In fact, it didn't seem like a prank at all. Both of them looked completely serious.

"Do you know Jae from school, dear?" Jae's mom asked.

"Mrs. Rogers, you know we've been friends since third grade."

"What was your name again?" the woman asked, as Jae ducked back into the house.

"Miranda. You know, Miranda Woodward." Miranda held out her hands, silently imploring Mrs. Rogers to recognize her. "This isn't funny, y'all."

"I'm sorry, dear, but I don't think Jae knows you," the woman said.

"Okay..." Miranda tried again, but Mrs. Rogers slowly closed the front door in her face. Miranda went back to her car and plopped into the driver's seat, steaming and scared. What had she done? Jae hadn't seemed mad at her that day at school. Surely, this was just a joke... though she'd never known Jae's mother to joke like this. Miranda looked down at the cell phone still in her hand, and hit the call button. Jae answered on the third ring.

"Hello?"

"Good prank. Now do you want to come or not?"

"Who is this?"

"What do you mean, who is this? It's Miranda. Why are you doing this to me? Did I do something wrong?"

"Don't call me anymore, or I'll have my mom call the cops," Jae snapped. She usually had a hard time keeping a straight face when she told a knock-knock joke, but Miranda could tell she wasn't joking. "Don't come here again, either." She hung up.

Miranda sat in their driveway for a full minute before cranking the engine and heading home, tears streaming down her face. Her thoughts raced through every conversation she'd had with Jae that day at school, and from the weekend at her party, trying to remember anything she might have said that would have upset her friend enough to act this way. Had she offended Jae when she got freaked out at the old house? Had she said something stupid and not even realized it? Her hands shaking, she dialed Abby's number, but it went straight to voicemail.

"Hey, it's me. Listen, I was just at Jae's house and she was acting really weird. I need to know what's going on. Did I say something stupid? Please just tell me. Call when you get this. Bye."

When she got home, her mother sat on the couch in her scrubs with a plate of soft cheese and crackers, her feet propped on the coffee table, Polly perched on the couch behind her. It looked like she was headed to another last-minute shift at the hospital soon. She smiled as Miranda closed the front door.

"Hey there, Licensed Driver! How was your first solo cruise?"

"It was weird," Miranda said, plopping onto the couch beside her. "I went over to Jae's house, to see if she wanted to go walk around the mall or something, and she acted like she didn't know me."

"Who, Pea?" her mother asked absently.

"Jae." Miranda looked at her mom, who was spreading cheese onto a fresh cracker.

"Who is Jay? Is he a friend from school? Do I know his parents?" Her mother ate the cracker and started making another.

"No, my friend Jae. She's a girl. You know, Jae Rogers? You used to hang out with her mom that awful year you made me play soccer?" Miranda sighed. "Why is everyone doing this? It's not funny."

"What's not funny?"

"THIS! Why is everyone acting like I don't know my own BEST FRIEND? What is WRONG with you people?" Miranda got up and ran up the stairs.

"Pea, what's the matter?" her mother called, but Miranda slammed her bedroom door and didn't answer.

Miranda collapsed onto the bed, watching the fan whirl overhead, trying to sort out the hollow in her chest. The pain inside her grew, gnawing her insides while she fought back tears.

What had she done wrong? Surely, they'd been friends long enough that if she did or said something, Jae would tell her. She looked up at Amelia Earhart who stood in front of her plane in her flight suit. Did Amelia's friends ever stop speaking to her? She always looked so brave and smart, and Miranda had devoured every book she could find about the aviator, but none of them ever mentioned friends not speaking.

After a while, she heard a soft knock at the door.

"What?" she barked.

"I just came to see if you're all right." Her mother's voice, muffled by the door, sounded strained. "You're upset, and I'm not sure why, but I thought maybe if you wanted to talk about it..."

"There's nothing to talk about, unless you're a freaking mind reader because apparently that's what I need."

"Please don't take that tone with me," her mother snapped back. "I'm trying to help, but I don't know what the problem is. You're the one who came home upset."

Just then Miranda's phone buzzed. She picked it up to read the text message; Abby's number blinked on the screen.

Who is this?

"It's FREAKING ME!" she screamed at the phone. She flung it across the room where it crashed against the opposite wall and fell behind the desk.

"I know it's you!" her mother shouted back. "When you're ready to act your age, let me know!" Her mother's footsteps stomped back down the stairs.

"No, Mom, it's not—AARRRRGGGH!"

Miranda slammed her face into the pillow and screamed. She pounded the bed with her fists like she hadn't since she was about ten, then got up and started pacing around the room. After a while, she sank onto the floor with her back against the bed, exhausted.

"This is ridiculous," she muttered. "I can't think of anything I've done. Why are they acting like this?"

She got up and fished her phone from behind the desk. She leaned over the side of it, stomach across her keyboard, until she reached the phone. The back had popped out and the battery slid under a bunch of cords, so she shoved the desk to one side and used the tips of her fingers to grab it, coughing as dust flew at her. As she pushed the desk back into place, the business card slid from under the keyboard and fell facedown to the floor. She picked it up.

Are you in need of a good Tailor? When things don't fit, finding someone with the right expertise can make all the difference. The proper fit can change your life! Contact us today, and remember: A Stitch in Time Saves Lives.

She read it twice, and then stuck it in her back pocket and put her phone back together. Once her phone rebooted, she opened the maps app and searched for Stitch in Time Tailoring. To her surprise, it showed up immediately, and was only about eight miles away on the other side of town from the high school. Miranda tapped the card on her chin and bit her bottom lip. Maybe this thing with her friends wasn't her fault. Maybe it was. Either way, her life was feeling more and more out of sorts, and she got nothing else out of the visit, she might find some of her dad's clothes that he hadn't picked up. Making a sudden decision, she put the wooden box with the spool inside in her backpack and ran downstairs. Her mother was sitting on the couch again, watching television.

"Are you ready to—" she started to ask, but Miranda interrupted.

"I need to go get something for school, I'll be back later."

"Okay..." Her mother looked at her. "You sure you're all right?"

"I'm fine, Mom. Sorry about earlier. I'm really okay."

"Be safe," her mother said, turning back to the show.

It didn't take Miranda's GPS long to populate directions to a part of town she rarely saw. Henley High, the mall, and her hangouts all stretched to the west, but now she turned east, with the setting sun behind her. She didn't know what she expected to find at the tailor shop, but the need to satisfy her own curiosity, and maybe even find an answer, propelled her. She drove through the nicer part of town, past boutiques and doggie daycare centers, and people with yoga mats going into little fitness centers. As she reached the older part of town, the scenery changed. Most of the store fronts advertised check cashing, liquor, and discount appliances. After a couple of miles, the GPS pinged. She had arrived.

Miranda pulled into a little strip mall and parked her car in front of the shop marked "TAILOR." The "IL" flickered in the middle of the faded, red sign, its neon lights buzzing like cicadas in the distance on a summer afternoon. The other shops looked closed with plywood nailed over their windows and muddled graffiti across their doors. The only other place with lights on was a convenience store on the right-hand side of the strip. The whole place felt melancholic, as if it was holding onto the last vestiges of life that sputtered and blinked in the old signs.

Miranda got out of her car and walked to the tailor shop door. A yellowed *Open* sign dangled on a nail behind the dusty glass window. The shop looked dark, and grime obscured most of the view inside, so she opened the door. A bell tinkled as she stepped into the dimly lit space.

Miranda found herself standing in a narrow lobby. It smelled like old books, with a hint of cinnamon and some other spice that made her think irresistibly of her father, though a rack of clothing took up most of the left-hand wall, and she could see more rows of clothes in clear plastic coverings extending into the back of the shop. A desk blocked her path, occupied by a young woman not much older than herself. Miranda took in the woman's short brown hair and a well-tailored gray jacket, while the woman similarly surveyed Miranda over folded arms. Her hair was curled into a style Miranda could only describe as "vintage," curling under at the bottom to frame her face. She wore bright red lipstick and her nails matched perfectly. Six phones surrounded her, crowding the old desk. Miranda decided they must be decorative, because they were all from different eras: one rotary phone, one olive green with a heavy receiver, and even one with no way to dial, just an earpiece on a cord. A modern computer sat in the exact center.

Behind the woman she saw that besides the racks of clothes, there was a folding screen in the corner like in old movies for women to change in semi-private spaces. The painted screen looked like it would fit in a western set in the 1850s. Miranda debated walking back out the door, but before she could move one way or the other, a reedy voice called from the rear of the shop.

"I'll be there in a moment, no need to worry."

"Can I help you?" the woman asked before the other voice finished. The only sound in the shop was the ticking from a tall grandfather clock in the corner opposite the folding screen.

Miranda fiddled with the strap of her backpack and glanced behind her. "I'm looking for, um, a tailor."

"Obviously," the woman said. "Are you picking up or dropping off?"

"No, I mean, I found one of your business cards, and I came to..."

"Ahh." The young woman's face relaxed into a smile, and she stood up, holding out her hand. "I'm Bridget. I answer the phones and pass along messages for the Tailor. What's your name?"

"Miranda. Uh, Woodward. Miranda Woodward." She shook the woman's hand, and felt her own body relax a little. Glancing to the rear of the shop again, she saw a door open; behind the door, she caught a glimpse of a rack of every color thread imaginable.

"Fantastic," Bridget said. "Please take a seat. The Tailor will see you shortly." She motioned to a spindly, high-backed wooden chair squeezed into the opposite corner by the clock. Miranda sat on the very edge of the seat and waited, while Bridget turned her attention back to the computer and began typing.

After several minutes, marked by the loud ticking of the grandfather clock and the clicking of the computer keys, a tall, thin man emerged from the door with all the thread. He wore a brown jacket with leather patches on the elbows, like an old school professor from a movie. Round, wire-frame glasses perched low on his nose. His thinning hair was combed back, and he wore a carefully-buttoned vest with plaid trousers. She'd never seen anyone not on TV look proper. And stuffy. The tailor stood ram-rod straight and moved with ease that didn't match his apparent age as he walked up to face her behind the counter. Miranda scrambled to her feet, almost dropping her backpack.

"How can I help you, my dear?" He lowered his chin to watch her over the top of his glasses.

"I... um... Is this your ad?" She fished the folded business card out of her bag and pushed it across the counter to him with the ad facing up. Bridget leaned forward to peer at the card with some interest.

"It looks like a handwritten ad," he said. "I assure you that I typically hand out professional business cards."

"It's one of yours. At least I think it is. I saw this online and copied it out," Miranda said, flipping the card over to show them the front. She glanced once more behind her toward the door. As she reached to take the card back, the old man scooped it up.

"Yes, that is me," he said as he ran his thumb across the card. Miranda took a step backward as he snapped his gaze to her. "How did you find it?"

"Well, it was, um, it was in my dad's stuff." Miranda felt her cheeks flush. Now that it came to it, she didn't know what possessed her to even come, but she stood her ground all the same. This old guy wasn't going to intimidate her, not with the disastrous last few days she'd had.

"It is an ad, yes," he said. "But you have to be truly looking for this place in order to find it."

Miranda froze. She looked hard at the man, wondering if he was serious, but he peered back at her, a calm expression on his face.

"So, you found a business card of mine," he continued. "Many people begin the search, but few complete it. And they all come through here at some point or another. I suppose you've been wondering about the disappearances? Usually it's college students looking for a government conspiracy."

"No, it's...um...no," she stammered. What in the world was he talking about? Government conspiracy? She just wanted to know why her dad had this random card, marked "ICE," in his wallet and nothing else.

"Miss Woodward?" the man asked. "How did you find my shop, exactly?"

"Wait. What disappearances?"

"Never mind about those. All in good time." He held up his hands, pressing his fingertips together and gazing at her over the top of them without blinking. "I ask again. How did you find my shop?"

"I was trying to find out what happened to my dad," she whispered. She cleared her throat and said more clearly. "He had one of your cards in his wallet. That's where I got it. But he's gone now. Do you have any of his things that I can pick up?"

"Just as I thought. A disappearance." The man shook his head and turned to walk away, calling back over his shoulder, "I can't help you with that. I'm sure the government is responsible somehow. Why don't you find someone to sue over it?"

"He's dead!" she shouted, startling herself. The man stopped walking, but he didn't turn. Bridget stopped typing. "His name was Samuel Woodward and he's dead and has been for six months but now—" She stopped and bit her tongue.

The old man pivoted, a strange gleam in his eyes. "But now, you're not sure about the time anymore?"

Miranda opened and closed her mouth again. Did this man know about the obituary dates being wrong?

"Samuel Woodward, you say?" the man said, without really asking. He turned to the young woman still sitting at the desk. "Bridget?" The woman reached under the counter, and Miranda braced herself, expecting her to pull out a gun or knife or something. Instead Bridget pulled out a rolodex, a big rotating file with cards filed inside, through which she began to flip.

"Woodward, Woodward. Ah, here it is!" She pulled out a card with spidery writing on it, spotted with age. "Oh, yes. He is long overdue for his pickup."

"Wait, you knew my dad?"

"Did we?" Bridget asked, handing the card to the old man.

"But you have him on your file thing." Miranda's head was spinning with the conversation in which she had a feeling that she was only a partial participant. Her thoughts were flipping so quickly through her brain she felt like her head might have turned into a rolodex, too.

"Then I suppose we must know him," the old man said. "Or not."

"This isn't helping!" Miranda glared at them both. The old man returned her gaze.

"You are very impatient."

"You are very confusing," she shot back at him. She realized that it might have been a bad idea to come here looking for answers without having any clear questions.

"Who are you?" he asked, his voice quiet.

"I told you. I'm Miranda. Who are you?" She was starting to feel impatient. What was the point of this whole thing? She had bigger things to worry about than picking up some old clothes of her dad's, like the weird stuff with her friends and what the hell had happened to her cat.

"I am the Tailor."

"Not helping." Miranda crossed her arms and re-settled her backpack on her shoulders. "You know what? If you don't have anything for me, I'm going to just head out. I'm sorry I wasted your time."

"Miranda Jane Woodward, age sixteen" Bridget said suddenly. She went back to the rolodex and pulled out another card, just as old and spotted as the other. "All right, Miranda, I need to verify who you are."

"You can't be serious." Her agitation increased and she fought the urge to either throw something at them both or to walk out the door, but she also felt a small twinge of curiosity. How did this woman know her middle name, and how old she was? She stepped closer to the desk.

"I'm perfectly serious. We can't give information to the wrong Miranda." She set the card down behind the computer screen, hidden from Miranda's view.

Miranda heaved a sigh. "Fine."

"Thank you. Now, please answer the following questions. Your birthday is...?"

"Two days ago. September ninth."

Bridget took a pen and wrote something. "Siblings?"

"None."

The woman wrote something else. "Mother's full name?"

"Colette Desrosiers Woodward. Nurse. Great baker, bad cook."

"Mm hmm. Pet?"

"A cat. Perkins. At least, it used to be. I think. I'm not sure anymore." Miranda scrunched her face. She could assume that she'd accidentally offended her friends, or that her mom was tired from being overworked and on edge, but she just couldn't explain the cat disappearing.

"Ah. And there we have it." Bridget smiled and leaned back in her chair.

"What?" Miranda looked from Bridget to the old man.

"You have a cat named Perkins, yes?" Bridget pressed.

"Yes. Well, I thought I did."

"And he's not there anymore?" the old man asked, stepping up behind the desk.

"Well, no. When I got home the other day, there was this other cat and my mom acted like she'd never heard of Perkins, and all we have is this orange one named Polly that I've never seen before in my life. I've looked everywhere, but I can't find Perkins."

"Lovely!" Bridget beamed at her.

"How is that lovely? My cat's missing." She looked from one to the other of them. What was up with these crazy people? Had she stepped into the Twilight Zone?

"Only the real Miranda would know her cat's name," the old man said. He was watching her closely and she felt the hair on the back of her neck raise.

"What do you mean, 'real' Miranda? Do you know what happened to Perkins?" Miranda unfolded her arms. Her heart pounded in her ears again, but she hoped she might finally be getting answers and she stepped closer to them.

"You've been having strange experiences," the man said. "Things changing and you don't know why. Objects appearing and disappearing. People's ideas changing mid-sentence." These weren't questions, just simple statements.

"Well, I— " She couldn't deny this, but it was shocking all the same to hear someone actually say it out loud. She thought of her mother's strange behavior when they were talking about her dad's books, and for that matter, the cats. She thought of Jae's sudden switch, and of the photos and the dates for the news articles. She put her hands on the desk and leaned a little closer.

"You have been getting frustrated." The man walked around the desk and stood facing her, his gaze steady behind his glasses.

"Yes, but I—" Miranda took a step back and looked up at him, not daring to believe that this stranger might actually understand what she was going through.

"So, you came to the Tailor!" The man beamed.

"Because things don't fit," she said slowly.

"And you want them to do so again," he finished.

Miranda closed her eyes and shook her head, not because she disagreed, but because of the speed of the conversation. When she opened her eyes again, the old man reached out and took one of her hands in both of his. She tensed, but didn't pull away. Something about him radiated trust, and not just the fact that he seemed to know why she was there without her having to explain.

"It is all right not to understand yet," he said. "You are at the beginning."

"The beginning of what?" Miranda whispered. "Why is everyone doing this to me? I thought this was just a birthday prank, or that I'd said something wrong to my friends, or..."

"You haven't said or done anything wrong," the man said quietly. "Tell me what you want. And be specific." Miranda didn't know how to respond at first, opening and closing her mouth a few times as she searched for the words.

"I want to understand," she said at last. She tipped her head to the side and looked at him again. His silver eyebrows were a little wild and bristly but his blue eyes were clear. "*Who* are you?"

"I told you, I am the Tailor." The man let go of her hand and walked back to the desk, leaning over Bridget's shoulder to peer at the rolodex.

"You said already that you're a tailor."

71

"Not a tailor, *The Tailor*. It is who I am, and it is what I do. I help people when they need answers. You need answers and you are here. I will help you." He smiled. "Come with me."

She followed him to the back of the shop, weaving around racks of clothes to the narrow door marked "Office" with a rack of colorful thread mounted on the back of it. He held the door for her, and as she stepped inside, she looked up at an unexpected vaulted ceiling, set with old-fashioned dark tiles with stars painted across them. Tapestries lined the walls, hanging floor to ceiling, many of them faded, but some bright and colorful, depicting scenes of forests and towns. Each had the same image somewhere on it: a person standing inside of a rectangle. One wide tapestry on the back wall illustrated several rows of people watching something in the distance.

Dominating the left side of the room was a large, carved wooden desk with clawed feet and dozens of drawers, each with a tiny keyhole in the center. Beside the desk, a tall, thin cabinet stood on spindly legs. High above hung an old chandelier with teardrop crystals dangling from the lights, the filaments visible in its pear-shaped bulbs. A white cat was nested on a heap of fabric in the opposite corner. It raised its head and blinked at Miranda, then lay down again went back to sleep. The Tailor settled into a wingchair with green cushions in front of the desk.

"You have questions," he said, "and while I cannot answer all of them, we can at least begin with finding out where you are and maybe where you should go next. Now please take a seat."

He motioned to a small ornate wooden chair against the right-hand wall, nearly invisible against the tapestry behind it. Carved leaves and flowers sprawled across its back and she perched on the edge of it, hesitant to lean against them. Miranda dropped her backpack on the floor at her feet, onto the deep blue carpet.

"When did things start to feel different?"

Miranda thought about all the strange things that had happened that weekend, but also about the more frequent voices she heard and the general ache in her life. But there was one thing that stood out beyond anything else. It had upended her entire life with a single phone call. "Six months ago," she said. "My dad." She kept her eyes the carpet, following the twisting pattern in it to the center of the room.

"How did he die?" the Tailor asked quietly. She sensed him lean forward but didn't look up, afraid that if she looked directly at this man she might break down and cry and she did *not* want to cry in front of a stranger.

"A plane accident." She swallowed and turned her attention to the corner where the cat slept. "I mean, that's what they said, but they never... they never..."

"Never what, Miranda?" the Tailor prompted. As if drawn by an invisible thread, she turned to face him.

"They never found him," she whispered.

"Meaning?"

"We had a funeral and everything, but he just kind of disappeared, along with all the stuff he had with him. Well, almost all of it."

"But you're certain he was on the plane?" the Tailor pressed. Miranda nodded, twisting her hands in her lap.

"They did an investigation. He got on the plane. It was small and had some kind of mechanical problem. Everyone died, and they said it was an accident, but they only sent home his wallet, and like one other thing."

She stopped talking, unsure she was ready to share about the wooden box. This Tailor might know a thing or two about thread, but she didn't want to share that secret just yet. Instead she sat, watching the white cat.

"And now, what doesn't fit for you?" he asked.

"My cat's gone, for one thing. I haven't seen him in a few days, and there's another cat that Mom acts like has been there the whole time. My friends are acting weird. I was afraid I'd said something, but now I'm not so sure. It's like they don't even know me, and their parents are acting the same way. And my mom won't tell me what happened to Dad's books." Miranda hesitated. "I'm not sure I should tell you all of this."

"You are wise," the Tailor said. "But as I am the first person to take you at your word, I am likely also the first person you have trusted since things stopped...fitting."

"Everything is disappearing. It's changing. I don't understand! And my photos are different, and my snow globe is different. It's just...wrong." Miranda finally looked up at the Tailor, wishing she had words for what she was feeling. She was so unsure how else to explain or describe the chaos of her life or how it made her feel like she kept losing her footing in a constant earthquake.

"Is there anything else?" he asked.

Miranda studied his face, but his expression was unreadable. The Tailor seemed trustworthy, but so had the therapist who recommended taking her out of her own school, and so had the doctor who told her mother that she shouldn't be left on her own when she tried to confide her roller coaster of emotions to him after her father's death. None of the adults she'd tried to explain the swirling mess of emotions inside of her had really understood. Even her own friends didn't understand. Not really. She felt alone most of the time when she stopped moving long enough to be aware of her own thoughts.

Miranda glanced at the door and then up at the tapestry hanging behind the huge desk while she weighed what to say next. This one depicted a herd of deer with long, skinny legs, leaping through a forest with hunters on horseback not far behind them. A sudden weight on her lap startled her and she nearly jumped out of the chair, but relaxed as soon as she saw the white cat curled onto her knees.

"That's Penelope," the Tailor said, smiling. "She likes you."

Miranda stroked the cat and took a deep breath.

"Well..." Miranda glanced at her backpack on the floor. "I did get this weird... thing... from my dad."

"Did you, now?" the Tailor asked, raising his eyebrows. "Do you mind telling me about it?"

"It's a box. A wooden one. It's got... Wait," she said, an idea striking her. "Is it yours?"

"Is what mine?" the Tailor asked.

"The box?" Miranda asked, scratching the fluffy cat behind the ears. "I don't know, I just thought it might belong to you."

"That's an interesting idea. I might be able to help you more if you tell me what this box contained." The Tailor stood and walked to the cabinet beside the desk, opening one of the narrow doors. Inside, she glimpsed several large jars and a few cardboard boxes, though none like hers.

"It had a spool of thread," she said.

"Is that so?" the Tailor asked, pivoting to face her, his expression still unreadable. "How curious."

"So, you don't know anything about it?" She reached into her bag and pulled out the box, pressing the little button to make the lid pop open. The held up the spool, and the gossamer gold of the thread nearly sparkled in the office light. Penelope purred louder and began kneading her knees. "I thought you might, since you're a tailor and all."

The Tailor examined the spool and thread without touching either. "It is beautiful thread."

Her pulse quickened and she sat up straighter. "You can see it? The thread?"

"Yes, and I am sure it is very valuable, or it would not have been given. But no, I cannot unlock its mystery for you."

"My mom couldn't see it. Or, she said she couldn't." Miranda sighed. "None of this makes any sense."

"And yet here you are, still asking."

"Well, I thought this would help." She shook her head. "But all I am is more confused."

"Well then, we must find out what you know and what you don't."

"About what? I don't even know what I'm supposed to know."

"Good. You should ask questions." He nodded.

"Okay then. What happened to my dad? Why can I hear voices?"

The Tailor blinked slowly at her and, though she wasn't sure if she imagined it, his eyes might have narrowed slightly at her mention of the voices. "Not those questions yet."

"But you said— "

"We shall get there soon enough." The Tailor reached for the pile of cloth, pulled out small piece of black fabric, and began folding it. "For the time being, we must begin at the beginning. Or at least your own beginning. What do you know of your father's job?"

"Oh." Miranda shifted in the chair, and the cat held onto her knees. "He was a rare book collector, but I guess I don't know much about that."

"Not so," the Tailor countered. "Think. You know more than you realize."

Miranda concentrated on snatches of memories from childhood: her father coming and going, her mother taking her to soccer practice after school, the books that drifted around the house and always smelled like him even when he left for weeks at a time. "I know he traveled a lot, but he was always home for my birthdays. He never missed a single one. Until this year."

"Yes, birthdays are important. What else?"

"He brought back hundreds, maybe thousands of books, including some for me. He had a whole collection of them. When I was little, he read stories to me out of them, even biographies and things. He liked history. I did, too. My favorite stories were all about Amelia Earhart and Nancy Harkness Love and all the WASP pilots from World War Two and he found as many books about them for me as he could. Mom won't tell me what happened to his books." She looked up at the Tailor. "But I don't know what this has to do with this spool of thread."

"We shall see. Continue."

Miranda sighed and thought for another minute. "Well, when I was a kid, I told my friends he was an adventurer, traveling the world in search of lost treasure, like a pirate or like Indiana Jones." She looked at the cat on her lap and curled her fingers into the thick white fur. "When I got older, they quit asking. I think everyone knew I made it up by then, and they didn't understand the rare books thing."

"It is true that your father did not have a traditional job," the Tailor said. "Your pirate story isn't far from the truth."

Miranda looked up at him. "That's ridiculous. No one's actually Indiana Jones. That's not what archaeologist are like for real."

"We all need income. I tailor clothing; your father collected rare books. It is a very fine dance we do, sometimes."

"But what does that have to do with all of this?"

"That is a bit more complicated," the Tailor said. He sighed and leaned back in his chair. He took off his glasses and began polishing them with a handkerchief from his pocket.

"So, explain," Miranda said. She felt irritated, like the conversation was floating around without stopping at a solid answer, like a fly that can't make up its mind where to land, continuing to touch on things and move past them again before she could quite swat it.

The bell on the shop's front door tinkled, and Miranda saw the Tailor stiffen. She heard Bridget speaking to someone whose voice was so low, she couldn't make out what the person was saying, though she could clearly hear Bridget's replies.

"He's in an appointment, you'll have to—"

"I'm afraid we will have to cut this short for today," the Tailor said. "Quickly! Put the spool away! We will continue when you are ready. For now, you must go home and rest and spend time with your mother. She needs you."

"But I—"

"It's time for you to go," the Tailor said.

Threadwalkers

Chapter 5

Miranda stood up suddenly, and Penelope the cat scrambled back to her cloth pile. Miranda's fists curled as she tried to hold in her frustration, and she felt herself quivering. Her face flushed, and her whole body tingled with a heat that started in her toes and raced up her spine and into her face, until it burst out of her. "But you haven't told me anything!" she snapped. "I thought this was supposed to help!"

The Tailor stood and moved to the office door, though he kept glancing toward the front of the shop. "I need to do some research, Miranda. Then there will be more to tell."

Miranda carefully placed the spool back into its box and dropped it in her backpack. The Tailor led her past the little office door and to the back of the shop. One of the tall clothing racks blocked Miranda's view of the front desk, so she couldn't see the newcomer. The Tailor unlocked a heavy security door that opened into the alley behind the shop. Miranda stood, incredulous, looking at it.

"You want me to go out the back? But my car's around front!"

"Which is good, because I don't think you've been seen. Just go down to the end and turn right. As long as there is no one by your vehicle, you should be safe. Go straight home. Make sure you are not seen!"

"I don't understand what's happening!" Miranda threw her hands in the air.

"No more. It is time to go."

"When should I come back?" she asked.

"You'll know when it's time."

Dismissed, Miranda stepped outside and the security door closed behind her with a thud. She stood there for a while, a little overwhelmed and a lot more confused than when she entered. Anger bubbled inside of her, and she wanted to march back inside to demand answers, though she still wasn't sure what questions to ask. She checked her mom's watch and saw she'd only been inside about ten minutes, but the sky was now dark. She followed the alley down to the side of the building and walked back to the front of the shop.

As Miranda unlocked her car, she saw the sign now read Closed. Mini-blinds covered the windows except for a narrow gap, and the whole shop looked even darker than before. Curious, she stepped back to the door and peeked through the little gap in the mini-blinds. A tall man with a bald head stood with his back to the door while Bridget gestured toward the back of the shop. Miranda watched, but couldn't hear anything they were saying. A thick, woolen scarf obscured the man's neck and his clothes were all dark. With a final sigh, she got in her car and drove home, where she found her mother sitting in the den, drinking a cup of coffee while watching an old Reese Witherspoon movie.

"Did you get what you needed?" her mother asked.

"What? Oh. Yeah, I think so."

Miranda went to school the next day with the wooden box still in the bottom of her backpack. Her stomach clenched. She dreaded seeing her friends. She kept thinking about going back to the Tailor shop after school, but knew that the Tailor had explicitly said to wait until she "knew it was time," whatever that meant. As she sat in first period algebra, she kept checking her watch. The minutes dragging by even slower than usual for a 7:30am class. Even though she didn't really expect them to, neither of her friends showed up at their usual corner between classes, and Miranda walked into second period English an hour later, feeling worse than ever. She took a desk in the back of the classroom and bent low over its scratched veneer top. Then Jae walked through the door.

Jae eyed Miranda, giving her a wide berth as she made her way to the front of the classroom and sat down with some girls they never spoke to unless they had a school project together. They were nice enough, but those girls weren't Jae's friends. Miranda felt tears well up behind her eyelids as she watched the back of Jae's head, her tight curls moving back and forth as she chatted and laughed with those other girls. Miranda stood up to leave the room, but the teacher walked in the door, so she decided to wait and see how the class went.

As her English teacher, Mr. James, stood in front of the class to take attendance, Miranda pulled out her homework and set it on her desk. She felt completely alone in a room full of people and wished the ground would open and swallow her up.

Mr. James called each student in turn, glancing up to see a hand raised in response. Miranda waited for her name at the end of the list. Mr. James called, "Shuman," and Alex Shuman raised his hand. Then "Williams," and another raised hand. "Wyatt." Another hand raised, and Mr. James put down his roster. Miranda glanced around the room, then raised her hand.

"Yes?" Mr. James asked, leaning against his desk.

"I'm here, too, but you skipped my name," Miranda said.

"I see you're here, but who are you?" Mr. James picked up his roster and checked it. "I didn't get a memo about a new student."

"I'm not new, Mr. James," she said. She heard the tremor in her own voice. "I'm Miranda Woodward. I've been here all year. I did all the reading!" She held up the book to show him.

"Why don't you head down to the main office and double check that you're in the right class, Miss Woodward," he said, smiling.

"Fine," Miranda said. "Just, fine!" She stood. All the other students, including Jae, stared at her. If she wasn't on the role, then there was no reason to stay in class anymore. Slinging her backpack over one shoulder, she sprinted out the door of the classroom, which closed behind her with a thud. In the hallway, she leaned against the painted cinder-block walls and took several slow, deep breaths the way Dr. Trestle taught her. "In through the nose, breathe in. Out through the mouth, breathe out."

What Mr. James said terrified Miranda. And for him to be so nice about it! Miranda's whole life was disappearing out from under her feet. Did Miranda Woodward even *exist* anymore? She must, or else they wouldn't still see her. She focused on relaxing her clenched fists, her back pressed against the cool, smooth wall. After several minutes, she felt calmer, but still didn't have a clear idea what to do.

The first lunch bell rang. As students spilled into the hallways and toward the cafeteria or their cars, Miranda joined them. She let the crowd carry her until she reached the side door and walked onto the warm asphalt of the student parking lot, squinting in the sudden brightness of mid-morning. No one stopped or questioned her, and she crossed the street to Burger Palace to get something to eat and figure out what to do next. Walking into the restaurant without Jae and Abby felt strange, and she glanced around for anyone she knew, but didn't see anyone. She went to the counter and ordered a basket of fries and a soda. As she chewed the scalding-hot fries, Miranda scrolled through her phone, debating who to call. Her friends were all at school, but they weren't her friends anymore, so her options were rapidly dwindling. She swiped across her mother's number and held it to her ear.

"Miranda?"

"Hi, Mom." She felt her whole body uncoil and her shoulders relax at the sound of her mother's voice. "Can you come get me?"

"What's wrong? Are you all right?"

"I'm just not feeling well," she said. "I'm at lunch. Can you come get me?"

"Let me make sure someone is on call to cover me, and I'll be right there."

Miranda hung up and felt relief for the first time all morning. Her mother still knew her. She smiled and shoved a fry into her mouth. It burned the roof of her mouth, but she didn't care. Her mother knew her. That was all that mattered.

A group of students walked into the restaurant then, and she sank low in the booth, realizing Abby was with them. Abby laughed as she walked up to the counter with the group, a bunch of kids from the advanced placement classes. They got their food and sat at a pair of tables across from Miranda. None of them looked at her. She felt invisible. Then Abby turned to her and waved. Miranda's heart soared. Her face broke into a wide smile as her friend approached her.

"Hey, I saw you earlier this morning. You must be a new transfer. My name's Abby." Her friend beamed at her in a friendly, typical Abby way, but the hollow place in Miranda's chest, the spot that usually ached when she thought of her dad, continued to twinge unpleasantly.

"It's me. Miranda," she whispered. "You know me."

"Well, yeah, I saw you in class this morning, but I'm pretty sure we haven't met before..."

"*I'm your friend,*" Miranda hissed. "We've been friends since *third grade*, Abby."

"Um, okay," Abby said.

"Your name is Abbigail Rachel McInnis and your favorite color is aqua. You used to have a golden retriever named Maggie, who got out of the yard one time and had puppies, and your mom didn't want to keep them, so we took them up into the tree house to try and raise them ourselves. Don't you *remember me?*"

"I'm sorry," Abby said nervously, glancing at the other girls at her table as she took a step back. "I don't know you, and I don't know how you know so much about me, but I need to get back to my friends." She turned and carried her tray to the other table, looking back over her shoulder, but wasn't far enough away for Miranda to miss the last word. "Stalker..."

Miranda got up and threw out the rest of her fries. She took her drink out the door to wait for her mother on the curb. Miranda grimaced and hugged her stomach as she rocked back and forth on the cement ledge, imagining what Abby must be saying about her to the others, talking about the strange girl no one knew, who must have looked up a bunch of personal information about them online.

Ten minutes later, Miranda's mom pulled up and unlocked the passenger door. Miranda climbed in and slumped against the seat, the half empty soda cup still in her hand.

"Don't we need to check you out from the front office?" her mother asked.

"I took care of it." When her mother didn't respond, she sat up a little straighter and looked at her. "Once you're old enough to drive, they let you check yourself out." While not strictly true, students left after lunch all the time. Her mother didn't press it.

As they pulled onto the main road toward home, her mom chatted about work and the nurses' opinions on the latest celebrity gossip. Miranda leaned on the window, watching the trees go by in a blur of yellow and orange, and even some traces of deeper red that hinted at autumn's passing. She caught glimpses of pumpkins and even some early Halloween decorations on a few houses. As her thoughts wandered, she pictured Jae standing at the door of her own house, the cold expression on her face, and Abby walking through Burger Palace without recognizing her. Her vision swirled with black and she felt her stomach twist. She gripped the door handle.

"Stop!" she gasped.

"What?" Her mother looked at her.

"Stop the car! NOW!"

Her mother pulled hard to the right and stopped the car, turning on the hazard lights. Miranda flung herself out of the car and made it no more than five feet away before she vomited. All the fries came back up in a streak across the pavement, and she stumbled a little further away, her stomach lurching and her vision out of focus. She felt her mother's arm around her shoulder, guiding her into the grass off the street, holding her hair back as she vomited again. She couldn't get her footing, and stumbled, but her mother wrapped an arm under her shoulders and held her upright.

"Breathe through your nose," her mother said in her nurse voice.

Miranda took a shallow breath through her nose and felt her stomach turn, but she stopped heaving. Her legs trembled and she leaned on her mother, who led her back to the car and helped her into the front seat.

"Did you eat something funny?" her mother asked, pressing the back of her hand against Miranda's forehead. Her mother's skin felt cool and Miranda kept her eyes closed, trying to ignore the slight lurch in her stomach.

"Just fries," Miranda managed. Her throat burned as she tried to swallow. "I told you I wasn't feeling well."

"Well, you did say you were sick. You didn't tell me you felt nauseated."

"I didn't," Miranda said. "I mean; I didn't feel like it before. Can we go home now?"

"If you're ready," her mother said. Miranda nodded, and her mom got back in the car. She drove slowly, avoiding some of the sharper turns on the way.

At home, Miranda went straight upstairs to her room. Her mother brought her a cool cloth for her forehead, but she didn't feel sick anymore. The feeling passed as quickly as it came, without explanation. She lay on the bed a long time with the cloth over her forehead anyway, running over the last conversation with her friends, trying to think of any reason why they might stop speaking to her, but she couldn't come up with one no matter how hard she picked it apart.

She woke with a start from an unintended nap some time later. Brushing away the still-vaguely-damp cloth, she blinked toward her feet and found herself looking at Polly.

"Miao?" the little cat mewed at her from the edge of Miranda's bed.

Miranda glanced at her watch: 6:17pm. She wanted to get out of the house and think, but didn't have anywhere to go. Really, she just wanted to talk to someone who wouldn't think she was crazy. The idea of telling her dad floated to the surface, and she realized she did have somewhere she could go, and talk, and be in private.

Polly began purring and kneading the comforter, scooting closer to Miranda. As she stroked the little cat, she debated ways to ask her mom for the car without sounding suspicious. Almost everything sounded fishy even to her, being home "sick" from school, but she finally formed a plan.

Miranda stood up and stretched. She smoothed her hair and checked herself in the mirror to make sure she didn't look greenish. As she reached the living room, she heard the bangs of pots and pans getting put away in the kitchen.

"Hey, Mom?" she called.

"How are you?" her mother asked, walking into the living room holding a pan and a dry towel. "Still feeling gross?"

"No, I'm much better." She smiled as her mother touched her forehead again to check her temperature. "Really, I'm okay."

"Well, I still think you need to go to bed early tonight."

"Probably a good idea," she said. "I left my homework at school, though. Can I go over and get it? I'll be right back."

Her mother surveyed her for a moment. "Can't you call one of your friends to bring it to you?"

"I'm not in the same classes with them," she lied. "Besides, all I have to do is run in to my locker and back. It'll take five minutes."

"It's getting late, and I don't like the idea of you driving when you've been sick— "

"I'm a lot better now. Promise," Miranda insisted, picking up her backpack from the coffee table as she edged toward the door. "You just checked me. No fever. I haven't felt sick since we got home. I guess it was food poisoning or something. And the school's open because they've got sports practice and clubs and stuff."

"Well... I suppose you can go," she said. "But come straight back here."

"Thanks, Mom," Miranda said. She turned to grab her keys, but hesitated. Spinning, she strode across the living room and threw her arms around her mother in a tight bear hug.

"What's this for?" her mom asked, hugging her back nonetheless.

"You're the best, Mom," Miranda whispered.

"I love you, too, sweetie," her mom replied, kissing her cheek. "Now get going before it's much later and they lock the building for the day."

As Miranda cranked the engine, she saw her mom peeking through the slim window beside the front door. She waved and backed out of the driveway, careful to head in the direction of the school.

About a mile down the road, Miranda turned and drove in the opposite direction of the school, rolling down the windows so she could feel the cool air on her skin while her mind raced as she headed toward the cemetery.

Miranda pulled up to the front entrance of Greenlawn and parked the car. Something kept her from wanting to go inside now that she was here. She leaned on the steering wheel and bit one of her fingernails, debating what to do. As she sat, the back of her neck prickled. Her phone vibrated and began to ring. She jumped and then fumbled in her satchel for it. Her mother's number flashed across the screen.

"Hello?" she asked, breathless but relieved.

The line clicked and died. Miranda tried to call back, but the call wouldn't connect. She flung open her door and stepped out into the evening air. Her stomach lurched for the second time that

91

day, and she slumped against the car, her forehead on her arms, trying to concentrate on staying upright.

Around her, the sunset deepened to rose and purple, with orange streaks reaching across the clouds towards the west, where a few stars already winked in the gathering dusk. Miranda's vision swirled again, and she couldn't see the sky or the ground anymore. Another car rushed past her, and she felt the force of the wind push her against her own car. After several long minutes, the sick feeling faded.

She paced around the car, checking the tires and peering into the back seat to make sure everything looked normal. As it got darker, she shivered. She got back in the car, put it in gear, and headed toward home, guilt nagging at her for lying to her mom and then for not even following through with her plan. "I guess I'll have to talk to you another time, Dad," Miranda blinked back tears.

When she arrived home, all the downstairs lights glowed and the TV flickered with her mom's favorite Tuesday night reality singing show. She closed the door behind her.

"Hey, Mom! I'm home now! Sorry I took so long."

She didn't hear an answer, so she locked the front door and headed up the stairs. She glanced into her mother's empty room, at the made bed and the bedside table lamp, left on from the morning. She found herself gazing at the giant portrait over the bed of her mom cuddling her as an infant. She looked around the rest of the room but didn't notice anything amiss, so she turned off the light and walked back downstairs to the kitchen. She grabbed a slice of leftover pizza from the refrigerator and settled in the living room to watch TV until her mom got home.

Maybe she went back to work, Miranda thought. As she finished the pizza, Miranda's stomach twisted for the third time that day and she regretted eating it. She curled up on the couch, afraid to get sick all over the living room carpet but unable to stand up and get to the hall bathroom. As a wave of dizziness swept over her, everything went black.

Chapter 6

Miranda's head felt like a knife had sliced through her temples. She was still curled on the couch, hugging one of the throw pillows to her chest. Early daylight pierced through the mini-blinds and into her eyes; she blinked and tried to swallow, but her mouth felt as cottony as the pillow she clutched. To her relief her stomach held as she sat up, covering the side of her face with one hand to shield her eyes from the sunlight. She didn't remember anything after the sick feeling.

Getting to her feet, Miranda wandered up the stairs to her mother's bedroom to borrow some pain killer for her head. Halfway up the staircase, she stopped. None of the family photos hung on the walls. Miranda turned and looked back down the stairs, but the entire length was bare, without even nail holes to show where the frames belonged. Miranda pounded up the rest of the steps and flung open her mother's room, stopping in the doorway.

Empty.

Everything in her mother's room, from the bed to the old recliner in the corner, was gone. Miranda tiptoed into the middle of the room, checking every corner, but not even imprints from the furniture on the carpet remained. She went into her mother's bathroom: also empty, from the medicine cabinet to the linen drawer. Miranda ran out of the room and across the hall to her own bedroom, flinging open the door.

Everything inside looked the same.

Miranda started pulling open all her drawers and the closet, looking through the trash can and under the bed, trying to find some change, but her things all seemed to be okay. She collapsed onto the bed where she lay for several minutes, staring at the ceiling, considering the options. Deciding to try the obvious, she pulled her phone out of her pocket and tried again to call her mother to find out what happened to the furniture. An automated voice answered.

"The number you have dialed is not in service. Please try your call again."

She started to throw the phone across the room, but thought better of it and collapsed into her desk chair. Then, she noticed the almost blank screensaver. Only the canoe picture remained. Now, the photo was just Miranda, sitting an empty boat, clutching a paddle. She was no longer looking at the camera, but to her left, a look of surprise on her face. Miranda trembled as she leaned close to the screen, trying to see what her younger self saw, but the person or thing was out of frame. She looked at the photo for a long time, and hit print. The printer under her desk hummed, rattled, and spat out the image.

Something out of the corner of Miranda's eye made her turn toward the short bookcase beside the desk. Before, the books were nestled against one another, packed tight on the shelf, but now leaned to the side as if one or more had been pulled. Miranda ran her finger along the spines. Halfway down the second row, she found one book with its pages facing out instead of its spine. She pulled it off the shelf; it was her well-worn copy of *A Wrinkle in Time* that belonged to her elementary school library. She remembered checking it out years earlier and then losing it, and her mother paid the library for it before Miranda found it again. It now lived on her bookshelf, the library stamp still inside the front cover. As she started to put the book back on the shelf, a torn page fell to the floor with a note scribbled across a margin:

Get out now.

Miranda snatched up the page and stuck it and the photo into the front of the book. She jumped to her feet, ready to bolt.

Suddenly, someone rang front doorbell. Miranda froze, her heart pounding as her grip tightened on the paperback. The bell rang again, followed by loud knocking. No one ever came to the house this early. She tiptoed out of her room and to the top of the stairs, inching forward until she had a clear view of the front door.

A silhouette moved against the door-side window, obscured by the curtain. It looked like a man with a smooth, round head. As she watched, his arm moved so that one hand was across his brow, his image sharpening as he leaned against the glass, trying to see inside. Miranda shrank against the wall and backed out of sight. The man rang the bell again, and Miranda held her breath. When she looked again, the silhouette was gone.

Miranda crept back to her mother's empty room, bent double to edge her way to the window that offered a partial view of the back stoop. She reached the window, and, careful to stay below the sill, stood, keeping to the shadow beside the glass.

Pressing her cheek against the window frame, she strained to see the back door. The shiny top of a man's bald head moved into view, as if he'd been leaning against the back window looking into the kitchen. The man wore a black, leather jacket that looked a little too snug on him, and dark blue jeans with shiny black dress shoes. He took another step back, looking up toward the upstairs windows, and Miranda sank further into the shadow.

His face looked familiar, and it struck her that this was the man she saw at the Tailor's shop two days ago. He studied the window for a moment before moving to the right and looking along the rest of the house with no indication that he saw her. As he moved out of sight again, she went back to the top of the stairs. An engine revved outside, and what sounded like a huge motorcycle rumbled away down the street.

Miranda leaned against the wall, her mind reeling as she tried to think who the man might be. The Tailor seemed worried that the man might see her, but didn't feel the need to explain anything. Resentment bubbled inside of her. The Tailor knew more than he was telling her, and she didn't like being kept in the dark. It was time to demand some answers.

Still holding the book, Miranda grabbed her backpack, her wool pea coat, and her set of car keys, but then paused before opening the front door. Even though she only saw the one man, and the engine noise sounded like he left, she didn't want to walk out the door and straight into anyone. Instead she went into the living room and squatted behind the couch to get a view through a tiny slit in the mini-blinds. To her relief, the Honda sat alone in the empty driveway, and she didn't see anyone moving except a woman walking a dog at the far end of the street. She shifted and peered in the other direction, but the street appeared empty that way as well. She dropped the paperback into her bag, ran for the car and jumped in, cranking it as fast as possible and throwing it into gear.

Miranda stomped on the accelerator, peeling backwards from the driveway. A loud scrape and crash made her brake hard; glancing in the side view mirror, she saw their big trashcan lying on its side. Deciding the busted can was the least of her worries, she pulled forward and drove away.

She squinted into the bright morning sunlight as she drove. Her heart pounded and her hands sweat on the steering wheel as she drove as fast as she dared, glancing in the rearview mirror every few seconds, though no one appeared.

Miranda pulled into the tailor shop's parking lot fifteen minutes later. The sign on the door said "Closed" but she banged on it anyway. After a few minutes, the door opened and Bridget peeked out at her.

"What are you doing here?" she whispered.

"My mother's gone and I need to know what happened to her NOW!" Miranda shouted, shoving the copy of *A Wrinkle in Time* at the other young woman.

"Shhhh!" Bridget hissed. She took the book and opened the door, pulling Miranda inside by her arm. "Don't be so loud out there. Let me get the Tailor."

Miranda sat down in the desk chair as Bridget locked the door behind them and rushed to the back of the shop, still holding the book. The chair creaked. She didn't want to take off her backpack, so she leaned against it. She bounced her feet to channel her anxious energy and cracked her knuckles until they felt sore. The feeling that she needed to do something, anything, almost overwhelmed her. After what seemed like an eternity, the Tailor emerged from the back of the shop, bringing the battered paperback with him. Bridget followed, quietly taking her seat at the desk. Miranda leaped to her feet.

"What the hell is happening to me?" she demanded.

"Calm yourself and tell me what happened." He folded his arms and blinked owlishly through his glasses.

"My mom disappeared!" Miranda shouted, stomping.

"How do you know?" the Tailor asked.

"She wasn't home last night when I got there, and this morning, all of her stuff was gone."

"And she wasn't planning a trip?"

"No!" Miranda pressed her palms on the desk to steady herself, but her anger flared in the face of his calm questions. "Her bedroom furniture disappeared, too. And the pictures. All of the pictures are GONE!"

"All photos of your mother?" the Tailor stepped toward her. "She is gone without a trace?"

"That's what I've been trying to tell you!" Miranda shouted, flinging her arms in the air. "There was a note in my book telling me to get out! And there was a man outside my house, and I know you know him. I want to know what the HELL is going on!"

"Please do not shout," the Tailor said. "I am on your side, whether you believe it or not."

"Then why won't you tell me where my mom is? Or who that guy was?"

"Go into the office and sit. I will be there soon." He held *A Wrinkle in Time* out to her.

Miranda glared at him without moving. She wanted answers and wanted to keep stomping and shouting until she got them, but knew the best way to get them probably involved playing along. She heaved a sigh, snatched the book back from him and slouched to the office door, stopping to glance back at the Tailor before going inside. He leaned close to Bridget, whispering something to her. Bridget's eyes widened, but she nodded and reached under her desk. Then the Tailor turned and walked toward Miranda, who ducked into the office ahead of him.

"What did you tell Bridget?"

"To take a Walk," he said.

"Yeah, okay," Miranda said. She took a deep breath, and when she spoke, she kept her voice steady and slow. "Now who was that guy? And what happened to my mom?"

"Miranda, I am so very sorry," the Tailor said. He sighed and dropped on his huge carved chair, removed his glasses. Miranda stayed on her feet.

"Wait, she's not—" Miranda felt the all-too-familiar panic rise inside of her. "She's not—"

"She isn't dead, no," he said, finishing her sentence. "Not exactly."

"What is *that* supposed to mean?" Miranda's body shook. She started to feel sick again, but concentrated on remaining in the moment and not vomiting on the carpet.

"Miranda, your life is being Edited."

"It's... what?" Miranda took a step backward and leaned against the door frame. Again, she felt nauseous, like the room was spinning.

"It's being Edited." The Tailor put his glasses back on and folded his hands. "I suspected as much, but I couldn't be sure until now. Please sit down and breathe through the nausea. The man you saw was an Editor, or he works for the Editors, at any rate. They are trying to change the course of your life, and they have very nearly succeeded."

"What's an Editor?" she asked as she lowered herself into the chair on the wall.

"Let me tell you a story." He held up his hands as Miranda opened her mouth to object. "I know this is hard, but it's important you understand. And do try to breathe, this may happen a few more times, and you've got to practice working through the queasiness in case it happens when you're vulnerable."

Miranda leaned back in the chair as she watched the old man straighten some bits of chalk on his desk. She thought he must be giving her a moment to compose herself, and as her gut knotted once more, she took a slow breath, letting the feeling pass. When she opened them again, the Tailor sat facing her. She nodded and he began.

"Many, many years ago, there was a group of people who postulated that the universe was, in fact, very much like a fabric. It could bend and twist and fold and tear, and was made up of many threads."

"This sounds kind of like stuff my physics teacher tried to teach us," Miranda muttered. "She said it had to do with relativity and... something. But what's that got to do with this?"

"Patience," he repeated. "They are related, yes. But it was used by these people for other purposes." The Tailor paused and looked up at the office's high ceiling for a moment, then back at Miranda before continuing.

"These people realized that space and time were connected, and that it was possible for two points of time and space to touch. And sometimes there might be a tiny hole, a place where a certain point in time is caught, like a skipping record that repeats the same note over and over. They started trying to find these thin spots, 'Snags,' as they called them. The evidence for Snags is elusive, but one does hear stories of hauntings and the like. People see things from long ago, happening over and over, or in some cases can even interact with the people on the other side."

"Wait a minute." Miranda waved her hands, her stomach settling enough for her to sit up in the chair. Her mind flew to the shadowy figure in the old house from her birthday, and to the voices she'd heard her whole life, and keeping those voices a secret with her dad. "Are you saying that this is about ghosts?"

"Not at all!" The Tailor shook his head. "I mean that what most people think of as ghosts are simply other people, but at a different point in time. They are seeing through a thin spot, a Snag, because they and that other person are both connected to the same space. Often when there is a history of ghost sightings over hundreds of years, it is because different people stumble upon the same thin spot in the fabric. But you've heard the voices, haven't you? I imagine you've seen people that weren't supposed to be there. How else will you explain it? Ghosts?" He laughed. "You can't tell me you'd rather believe in ghosts. So then, when you hear things, when you hear those voices, you are hearing other moments in time. If you've ever seen anything, it's because of a thin spot."

"Okay…" Miranda rubbed her temples. "I'm not… I mean, you believe me that they're real, right?"

"Of course," the Tailor said. "How long have you been hearing them?"

"I'm not sure," she said. "It's been happening for a while now, but I don't remember when it started. At least since I was five, but maybe it started a while before that. I don't know." She felt like a floodgate opened and the words started pouring out of her. "It used to happen a lot when I was a kid, but then it stopped, and I never knew why. I thought maybe I'd been imagining it, but now I don't think I was. It's been happening a lot more since my dad died," she said. "And I think I've heard my name. I don't want to go back to counseling because they'll just try to put me on more drugs, or try to make me change schools or something, not that it much matters anymore."

"There is nothing wrong with you, Miranda. But let us get back to our story. These people followed the stories of ghosts and found that most of them were hallucinations brought on by fear or phobia, or hoaxes for the gullible and easily frightened. But some of them, well, some of the stories rang true, and when they arrived, they found themselves peering into another time."

"They could see through the thin places?"

"Precisely. When there is a Snag, one can see the exact same spot but at another point in its history. Time passes, but the space doesn't move."

"So, if people can see through these, um, thin spots, then what have I been seeing?"

"I am getting there." The Tailor took another deep breath. "After a time, they decided that they were tired of trying to observe through the 'thin spot' and guess at what was happening. They decided to try and push through to the other side. They became Threadwalkers."

"Thread whatsits?" Miranda raised an eyebrow. She didn't want to believe what the Tailor was telling her, but the strange things in her life needed some sort of explanation, even a ridiculous-sounding one.

The Tailor smiled and shook his head. "The problem with walking through a piece of space-time is that it isn't a stable location. The very nature of it is that is shifts. The first few attempts were disastrous, as people became stranded in other times, unable to find their way back to the exact point through which they originally passed. But after a time, and with much practice and sacrifice, they learned how to Walk." The Tailor dropped his hands into his lap and gazed down at them. "And then the world grew more complicated."

Miranda looked up at him. In the dim light, he looked ancient, the creases in his face stark in shadow and wisps of hair falling across his forehead. There almost seemed to be a veil between them, and she wasn't sure if she reached out that she would even be able to touch him. Then the moment passed. He shook himself and looked back up at her.

"How did it get complicated?" she prompted.

"These people, these first explorers, learned to turn these Snags into doors they could use to visit another place."

"So, you're saying what, exactly?"

"They found a way to travel and then return to their original point in time."

"But that's amazing!" She jumped to her feet, her mind wheeling with sudden possibilities. "We could go anywhere! I could go and save my mom and dad!"

"Ah. And now we come to the true difficulty." The Tailor's face softened as he motioned her back to her chair. Miranda sat. "Yes, you could save people. You could tweak things to be better, happier. You could spend one more day with your grandmother, or keep an important leader from dying, or stop the extinction of an entire species. And therein lies our temptation and our folly."

"I don't understand." Miranda's fists curled into tight balls.

"Try to see from a larger perspective." He motioned to the tapestries around them. "The first Walkers thought as you do, as all of us do in the beginning. What a wonderful world we could have if things were just a little different! If we could edit things to improve them! But how do *you* decide what should be changed? What kind of impact will your edits have? And what if a single person's death, tragic though it may be, is the very spark that propels an entire generation to greatness far more than that person inspired in life?"

Miranda sank back onto the chair, tucking her feet behind the legs as she looked at the illustrations. "So, I can't save my parents?"

"I didn't say that, but we haven't come to that point just yet. Please allow me to finish my story."

"Sorry," she muttered.

"Don't be sorry! Your desire to save your parents is admirable, but you need to understand the consequences of changing things.

"Those first people to go into the past began as simple observers. They called themselves Threadwalkers, those who trod on a tightrope between eras on the thread of time itself. They recorded information! They crafted a library! They solved some of the greatest mysteries! And they were very careful not to stay too long, not to alter one thing, not to interact with any people outside their own circle.

"But one day it changed. A small group of them were somewhere. I don't know where, it has never been revealed. But they saved the life of a small girl. They pulled her from danger, set her on her feet and continued. And when they passed back to their own time, things were... different. Not in any huge way, but the name of the town they visited was spelled a little differently. The name of the street changed. Small things. Innocuous things. But they realized that small things could change other small things. The world could be Edited.

"They became Editors. They went into the world and began to change small things. Mostly, they prevented innocent people from dying. But they started to aim higher. If they could save these people, why not save people who might change history for the better? What kind of impact would these keystone people have?

"So, they saved a philanthropist. It was a disaster. An entire government's economy collapsed because one seemingly good man was saved and got elected when the lesser known but wiser man should have been. And then they began to blame one another. In the end, they went separate ways and didn't speak for many years."

Miranda waited for him to continue, but the Tailor sat, gazing into the corner as if he could see something that she couldn't. After several long minutes, he straightened his back, a hard look came upon his face, and his tone bitter.

"Most of those first Walkers, the ones who became Editors, continued their work. Oh, the changes were small and mostly insignificant. Some of them used their gifts for personal travel. One left himself a vast fortune and became a recluse. But none of them could stop once they knew their own power."

"But I don't understand. Don't people notice the changes? I mean, I noticed when Perkins disappeared and that other cat showed up in his place."

"People mostly never realize it because for them, it is how things have always been. Things can change, and they might have an occasional feeling of déjà vu, but otherwise minds are adaptable, and the thing they are currently experiencing becomes the real thing. No one questions. No one notices, except those who remember the difference, who have the ability to see the threads. Think of your friends, how one day they acted as if you'd never met. Only other Threadwalkers can see Edits."

"Are you a Threadwalker?" Miranda asked, choosing to ignore the mention of Jae and Abby.

The Tailor looked back at her for a moment. "One of the first Editors realized that the changes, the Edits, were causing far more damage than first thought, and tearing holes in the Fabric much larger than the original Snags, and it troubled him. He went in secret to each of the others, but they laughed at him or dismissed him altogether. They told him he was just feeling guilty about their success. That they had things under control. That he should go back to the shadows like the rest. But he disagreed.

"That Editor decided that he wanted to repair things, to reverse the Edits where he could. He began intercepting those with the gift to Walk, and training them not to be Editors, but to be Walkers as they were originally intended. And so, after a time, he became a Tailor." He smiled. "And I have taught all of the Threadwalkers since then. They are charged with nothing less than the protection of the Fabric of space and time, and the eventual defeat of the Editors."

Miranda didn't want to believe his story, but the thought of Walking to other times and seeing things as they were and how they could be sounded intriguing.

"But, I mean, that's not really *real*, is it?" Miranda asked the carpet, which was easier to look at than the Tailor. "It's just a story!"

"Isn't everything a story?" the Tailor said, smiling. "This one is still happening, though, as so many of them are. You did well to come here. We may yet be able to stem the tide and stop whatever they are attempting."

"So, you're asking me to believe that people can Walk to other times?"

"Yes."

"And my mom?" Miranda pressed.

"There may be a way to save her, but it is not without risk." The Tailor turned to his desk and opened a drawer, pulling out a stack of small bits of paper which he spread on the desk. "This will take time, and though we don't have much, I need to teach you everything I can. This is happening much too fast, much too fast..."

Miranda watched him. "Why should I trust you? I don't even know why I came here, except you seem to be the only person who knows what's happening."

"You should trust me because your father did," he said. "And I know that when he died, he was carrying a particular package with him, addressed to you. I believe you probably have with you.

"When Threadwalkers are at risk, they sometimes take… precautions, in the event they are unable to continue their job, for whatever reason. One of your father's stipulations was that the package must reach you on or near your sixteenth birthday, if he could not give it to you himself. I did not know the contents, though I believed you would follow in his footsteps, and did not press him on the matter, but it was quite a trick getting their release delayed until the right time."

"So, you did know him," Miranda said. She glanced around the room again, almost expecting her father to step out of a hidden doorway.

"Quite well," the Tailor nodded. "He was a good man, and a brilliant Walker. One of the best, actually. I was devastated to hear of his disappearance this spring."

"Oh," Miranda turned her attention back to the Tailor. "You know he died this spring."

"Yes. Your father was a good friend. I taught him when he was a little older than you, and he learned quickly. He was especially good at researching, though, and found all sorts of little Edits that might have gone unnoticed but for his skilled eyes.

"In fact, I believe he was tracking a lead on one of them when the plane crashed. I still do not know what he found, because

110

as you know most of his personal items weren't recovered. I also don't know if his research led to his disappearance, but that makes the most sense, given the state of things."

"What state of things?"

"The Editors are working on something big," the Tailor said. "We don't know what it is, but your father was following two of them in an effort to discover it. They are going to shift the balance of power in the world somehow, and your father was close enough that they eliminated him. Now, it looks as if they are trying to eliminate you, too, or at least they will rewrite your history enough to render you a non-threat."

"What does any of this have to do with me?"

"Honestly?" The Tailor paused, his expression hard to read. His lips pursed and he peered at Miranda as if he could look right through her somehow. He shrugged. "I'm not sure. We haven't been able to figure out yet how you fit into this."

Miranda waited for any sign of him continuing, but he remained silent. She decided to try another tactic. "You told me it's about money and power and how these Editors change things so they can have it."

"Yes."

"And that they save people's lives."

"Sometimes, yes."

"So, does that mean you just let people die?" she asked, her voice rising again.

"Not exactly," the Tailor said, looking back up at her. "We try to let lives happen the way they are supposed to happen, no matter what that entails."

"And what about my mom?" Miranda pressed, clenching her fists so that she felt her fingernails dig into her palms.

"If you mother is meant to survive this, we will do everything in our power to help her," the Tailor replied.

"That's not a yes or a no," Miranda shot back at him.

"Because I cannot see the bigger picture yet," he said. "Your life has been changing, but it is difficult to know for how long, and to know what is and is not supposed to happen. We can make an educated guess, but the best course of action is to find a way to a time before any changes began and try to stop them."

"How do I do that?" Miranda asked.

"That is what I am going to teach you," the Tailor said. "It's time you learn how to Walk."

Chapter 7

Miranda stared at the Tailor. He looked perfectly serious. "Right now? I mean, you're really not kidding. You think I can just, well, *walk* to another place? I mean, not down the sidewalk but somewhere *else?*"

"Not to another place; to another point in time," he said. "Come with me, and bring your bag."

The Tailor stood up and walked out of the office, so Miranda followed him, hitching her backpack up on her shoulders as she went. He strode around the desk to the front door, where the sign still read "Closed." He unbolted the door and motioned for Miranda to come stand beside him. He turned to face the closed door, his nose about an arm's length away from it, and reached for the knob.

"Now then," he began, "normally this would be a lesson for much later in your training, but I think we need to get your head where it needs to be. You need to understand what I am asking you to do so that you're not taken by surprise later."

"What's that got to do with the door?" Miranda asked.

"You will see," he said. "Look at it closely."

Miranda faced the door. It looked like a regular wooden shop door, with a paneled glass window in the top and the Open/Closed sign hanging from a single nail right in the center of the wooden crosspiece. She scanned the door frame, and took in the antique fixtures and worn hinges, along with the smooth brass doorknob and lock.

"Okay, it's an old door," she said at last.

"A very old Door," the Tailor replied. "Doors are helpful, you see. They mark places, and allow an easier mental transition. You walk through them from one place to another."

"Yeah..." Miranda looked sideways at him. "That's how they usually work."

"Yes, Miranda, but there are doors and Doors. Threadwalkers use Doors to help them Walk from one side to another through an open Snag. Hold onto my arm, please."

Miranda now turned to look straight at him. The Tailor held out his arm for her to clasp his elbow, and waited. She reached out and linked her arm through his, her whole body tense.

"Lovely. Now, we are going to step forward. I want you to move exactly with me, no matter what."

The Tailor unlocked the door with his free hand and opened it. The morning light poured into the shop entrance through the doorway, and Miranda saw cars whizzing past on the road, all without stopping.

"Now, concentrate on staying with me, Miranda," he said. She looked down at their feet, making sure she moved forward with him as they took a step.

Miranda gasped. She felt a momentary sensation of thick, icy air around her, like being pulled through a nearly frozen wool blanket, and just as quickly, she stood on the sidewalk in front of the shop under a dark sky. Rain poured from the awning. Miranda tried to wrench herself free from the Tailor, but he held on to her shoulder.

"Do not let go. I want you to concentrate on what you felt, and on what you see."

"It's raining! How did you make it rain?" she demanded.

"Look at the sky, Miranda!" he said. "It's dark! It is night!"

"What does it mean?" she asked, turning to look at him without letting go.

"It means we are in another time, but at the same place. Now step with me again, this time into the shop."

Miranda let the Tailor pull her back through the shop door, and felt the sensation of being pulled through ice cold wool again, and suddenly they stood back in the entryway to the shop, looking out at the sunny morning.

"What just happened?" she whispered, dropping his arm. She stepped through the door and onto the sidewalk, then back inside, but nothing changed. No rain, no darkness. She stepped back onto the sidewalk. "How did you do that?"

"I Walked us to a night a long time ago, on this spot," he said. "A night when it poured rain, and people came to the shop who weren't supposed to find it."

"What do you mean, Walked?" She backed away from him. "You can't mean that we…"

"That we what?" he asked.

"That we just... traveled..."

"Please come back inside, Miranda. I promise I will explain."

Miranda didn't move. Every instinct in her told her to run, except the part of her that still wanted more than anything to simply understand.

"I'm not going to harm you," he said. "You are safe here, but only inside. Please come back into the shop."

"I don't understand," she said.

"I know that, but they can see you out here."

At this, Miranda flung herself through the door. She didn't know what to think of the Tailor yet, but he certainly didn't frighten her the way the bald man in the leather jacket did.

"Okay, explain," she said, once the Tailor closed and locked the door behind her.

"Doors are helpful mental markers," he said. "A few highly skilled Walkers do not need them, but for most, they provide a way to allow the mind to accept what is happening, and pass along the thread."

"And when a Snag is near a physical doorway, it is easier mentally to Walk."

"It still doesn't make sense," she said as she followed him back to the office.

"Remember what I said about space and time being like a fabric?"

"Yes..."

"Try to imagine all of space and time that we perceive as a huge piece of cloth, like a bed sheet." The Tailor took a white handkerchief out of his pocket and held it up in front of her. "Usually it lies flat on the bed, and the corners are far away from one another. The individual threads are in their set place and go in their set directions, all at lovely perpendicular angles to one another. You can follow one thread in a straight line from one edge all the way across the sheet. But flat on the bed isn't the only position for that cloth to lie." He folded the handkerchief into a smaller square. "It can be folded in the closet; it can be left in a heap on the floor; it can be torn and pulled so that the pieces once side by side are stretched three times the original distance from one another.

"Now if we think of space and time in this way, the question must arise: What happens when the cloth is folded and two points touch? What if a particular thread gets, well, a Snag? What if the threads perpendicular to it keep moving, but it remains? And then you must ask yourself: What if you could see through this tiniest of gaps, or even push through it to another point along the same thread?"

"So, when we just traveled, it was through a gap?"

"A Snag. And we didn't travel, we stayed in the same location. We Walked *into* another point in time."

Miranda shook her head. "I don't believe you."

"You don't believe what your own eyes told you?" he asked.

"This can't be right."

"Why?" he asked.

"Because it doesn't make any sense!"

"Just because it is new, doesn't mean it is nonsense." He pointed toward the shop door. "That is just the first time you've experienced it. But I would hazard that you've been looking for this your whole life."

"But why can I see this stuff?" she asked in a small voice.

"Because it's who you are. You father was one of our best Walkers, and you are his daughter. You need to learn how to Walk, and you need to do it now because your life is in danger, and possibly a lot of other people's, too. So, what are you going to do, Miranda?"

Miranda stood motionless for several minutes, trying not to blink too much as the Tailor watched her. Her mind whirled with everything he'd told her, and yet somehow it made as much sense as anything else she'd experienced. Edits certainly explained her friends' strange behavior and her mother's mysterious disappearance. The thought of her mother lost somewhere, or missing, pushed her. She nodded.

"I want to learn," she said.

"Excellent!" The Tailor beamed at her. "There isn't time for complete instruction, but we'll do the best we can. You must at least learn to recognize the doors so you can use them, but also so you don't get stranded anywhere."

"*Stranded*?"

"When a Threadwalker cannot find her way back to her point of origin, she is stranded and must enact the Hermit Protocol. But we'll put that particular lesson off for now. At the moment, I want you to try to use a door, just as I showed you."

"How am I supposed to do that?" she asked.

"Stand here," he said, pointing to an open spot in the middle of the office floor. "And listen."

Miranda stepped forward to the center of the narrow office. The Tailor watched her, so she concentrated on listening, like she did when she heard the voices. She strained to hear anything, but for a long time, all she could make out was the beating of her own heart, throbbing in her ears. Miranda focused on her breathing, in through her nose and out through her mouth, but visions of shadowy figures leaping through open doors and the man in the leather jacket kept swimming into her thoughts. She rotated on the spot, but didn't hear anything at all. She shrugged.

"Nothing."

"Try focusing on the physical doorway. Remember, it will help you visualize."

"How do you even know this will work?" she asked.

"The entire shop is a hot spot, if you will. Please concentrate."

Miranda tried to listen in the general direction of the doorway. She wished they could go to her own house, where she heard things more often, but the thought that the whole exercise was silly kept distracting her. She forced herself to stop that train of thought and tried clearing her mind. After several long minutes, she heard a whisper.

"Hello?"

"Yes?" she asked, turning to the Tailor.

"I didn't say anything," he said. "What did you hear?"

"Just a hello." She scanned the room, goose bumps rising on her arms. "Are you sure this is what I'm supposed to do? I'm kind of freaked out right now." She rubbed her arms a bit. "I guess it's kind of a relief, though," she said.

"You aren't alone, Miranda," he answered, smiling. "Now try again. Reach out and find the thin place."

Miranda hesitated, and instead stepped toward the office door. She concentrated on the doorknob, staring at it, trying to see past it and letting the little sphere fill her whole focus. Reaching out, she grasped it; the knob felt cold as ice. She dropped it.

"The handle, it's..."

The Tailor put a hand on her shoulder and nodded. "Try again."

Miranda focused on the knob, the rest of the office fading from her perception, until she again felt the urge to reach out and turn it. With the Tailor's hand gripping her shoulder, she wrapped her fingers around the cold, metal knob and turned. As she pulled the door open, she felt herself propelled forward, and then the cold sensation followed by the feeling of being pushed through a thick blanket. She blinked and realized she wasn't holding the doorknob anymore.

Miranda stood behind the counter of an old drug store, its fixtures covered in drop cloths and a thick layer of dust covering every surface. An old oil lamp hung overhead, cobwebs draped across its arms. Across from where she stood, most of the wooden shelves were empty, save for a couple of broken glass jars, long emptied of anything they once held. Miranda started to take a step forward, but the Tailor held her firm.

"Do not move," he said, and she froze. "Look down at your feet, and look back at where you traveled."

Miranda gazed down at a dusty wooden floor, and her feet side by side, as if she hadn't even taken a step. Then she turned to look behind her, and was very glad of the Tailor holding her still: the office had vanished.

"Where did the door go?"

"As I told you, they are good mental markers, but unnecessary. Now, we must go back." He gave her shoulder a gentle squeeze. "Concentrate on where you want to be. Focus on going back through the door, even if you can't see it right now. The doorway is still there if you focus."

Miranda tried looking for something to hold her concentration but she couldn't stop looking at the empty shop, wondering where she might be.

"Focus, please," the Tailor repeated.

Miranda looked back down at her feet. The dust on either side of them looked undisturbed, and she thought about the dark carpet of the Tailor's shop. "My feet haven't moved," she thought. "Not really. I just need to go back."

She focused on her shoes, and tried to picture the floor in the Tailor shop beneath them, and to put them back in front of the office door. Just as she thought they might be stuck in this new place, she felt it: the momentary cold and then the push through the thickness, and she leaned back until she stood once more in the open doorway, the velvety blue carpet once more under her feet.

"Excellent!" the Tailor said, letting go of her. "You did it on the first try! Very exciting!"

She turned to look at him, shivering from the lingering cold sensation. "What just happened? How did I do that?"

"You have just taken your first step toward becoming a Threadwalker." He beamed at her, his hands pressed together in front of his smile. "Now sit. I will make you some tea to help you cope with the shock."

Miranda sank onto the little chair, letting her bag drop to the ground. She leaned forward so that her head almost touched her knees. She didn't feel sick, per se, but she was disoriented, and her legs wobbled like jelly. She stayed that way while the Tailor rummaged in a desk drawer, then began banging around the back of the long, narrow room. When she lifted her head, she could just see him leaning over an electric kettle with a pair of teacups sitting on an end table beside him. After about a minute, the kettle sang. Miranda forced herself upright as he poured boiling water into the cups. She wrapped her hands around the steaming cup a few minutes later, and realized that her entire body felt chilled.

"Thank you," she said.

"Let it steep a bit before you drink," he replied, setting his cup on the desk. "How are you feeling?"

"A little better now," she said, leaning into the steam and the gentle spicy aroma of the tea. "That was weird."

"It can take your body a bit to adjust to things," he said, nodding. "But with practice you will be able to step across those thresholds with little ill effect."

"Why wasn't I allowed to move?" she asked, taking a tiny sip of the scalding tea.

"If you move, you might not find your way back," he said.

"I'd have been stuck there?" she asked.

"Not while you had me with you, no," he said, laughing. "But until you are confident going from one side to the other, you need to be very careful. There are most certainly ways to move around, and to spend longer periods of time. How else would things be changed? But you need to learn to Walk before anything else."

"But how do you come and go?" she asked, sipping the tea again. It tasted like apples and spices and she breathed it in.

"It has to do with how you mark and your Snag. Remember where it is," the Tailor replied. "But really, being in the same shop, you'd have found your way back if you were an experienced Walker."

"What do you mean, the same shop?"

"Just what I said. We were still in this shop, just at another time."

"It looked different," Miranda said. She looked around the small inner office, at the long side walls and the narrow entryway.

"This room was indeed added later, but when I acquired the location, it had been vacant for some time after a series of traumatic events took place in the pharmacy that once occupied the space."

"Oh." Miranda didn't know what to say to this. Instead she pointed at the door. "So even though that door isn't always there, it's still kind of... there?"

"Correct." The Tailor took a long drink from his own cup. "The physical door may help you to see that you are going from one spot to another, but it is wholly unnecessary."

"So, I could be in the middle of nowhere and still do that, that Walking thing?" she asked.

"Yes, though it would be extremely difficult to find your way back to where you began," he replied. "Landmarks and visual cues are your best defense against being stranded, but they aren't the only way. There are other markers to show you where the Snags are."

"So, what was that Hermit thing you mentioned before? I mean, what happens if I do get stuck?"

The Tailor looked down into his cup for a long time, then back up at Miranda. "If you are stranded, you are on your own. You are trapped at that point in time."

"But wouldn't you just be able to keep living then? I mean, if you went back to the 1920s or something, couldn't you just be a flapper or something?"

"It is not so simple." The Tailor sighed and set down his cup. "The problem with Editors is that they change things in a way that affects the future. They wreak havoc with people's lives, and with history itself. It creates chaos. So, imagine if you were to insert yourself into a life at another point in time. Where would you go? What would you do? And what if knowledge you took with you of future events changed your behavior, or what if someone else found out you knew about things that would happen? You could live well, make money, yes, but at what cost? Or you could be in serious danger if someone thought they could glean information from you.

"Everything that changes could have catastrophic results later on. If you make friends or form relationships with people, it might prevent them from participating in events they might otherwise have been part of, or you could unintentionally change the outcome of something small that turns out to be a keystone event in someone's life."

"Then what happens if you're stuck?"

"The Hermit Protocol is enacted. In the event that you are stranded, and have no way to return to your point of origin, you must disconnect from the world as you know it."

"Disconnect?" Miranda shifted in the chair and watched him.

"Completely remove yourself from it. Find a remote location, have no contact with anyone, and create as little impact on that place as possible."

"But how do you even start to live like that?" Miranda too, set down her cup. "I couldn't ever do that. I'd lose it!"

"It isn't easy," he agreed. "Isolation is difficult. It has not happened many times because most Threadwalkers are far too careful, but sometimes it cannot be helped in the case of an emergency. Occasionally, the Walker finds his or her way back again, but usually... Well, we wait a designated amount of time and then complete their final requests."

"Oh." Miranda glanced at her backpack, slouching beside the chair with the copy of *A Wrinkle in Time* still inside, along with the carved wooden box. A thought struck her. "So, did my dad get stranded?"

"That I don't know," the Tailor said. "And I'm sorry about. Your birthday gift was separate from any other request he might have made. It was to be delivered at a designated time regardless of your father's status."

"Did he make any other... requests?" Miranda swallowed hard.

"I'm afraid not," the Tailor said, looking down at his hands. "Not everyone does. Most don't believe it will happen to them. But you had your mother, and there were no other affairs to be put in order."

"So, you knew about me and mom?"

"I knew about you, but I had never seen you until you walked into my shop two days ago," he said. "That is why we had to be certain you were who you said you were, and that your life had not already been so edited that you could no longer tell the correct from the altered."

Miranda didn't respond. She felt the shock of her mother's disappearance starting to surface, but didn't want to cry in front of the Tailor. Instead, she concentrated on the tapestries, the carpet, and on her backpack, anything that might distract her. All the pain and frustration of the last week overwhelmed her and she couldn't hold back anymore.

"If you knew about me, why didn't you do anything about it?" she whispered, tears beginning to brim over her bottom eyelashes. She blinked to try and stop them, but they began running down her reddened cheeks. Her voice shook as the words came pouring out of her. "My friends don't know who I am. My mom is gone, and my dad is gone, and even my cat is gone, and I don't have anywhere to go and I don't want to BE HERE anymore!"

Miranda's voice rose to a scream. She was on her feet even though she didn't remember standing. "This isn't fair! I didn't ask to be here. I just want my life back, and you're telling me there are these people screwing with my life and I can't do anything about it? What the hell?"

"Miranda, please— "

"And DON'T tell me I need to calm down because this is NOT OKAY, do you understand? I am not okay. I shouldn't even be here!" She flung her arms in the air and turned to gesture to the entire room. "I'm not even sure I believe any of this, except that nothing else makes sense. What am I supposed to do now? I can't go back to school, and I can't even go home...." Miranda fell back into her chair as quickly as she'd stood, her face in her hands as hot, angry tears spilled into her lap.

Threadwalkers

Chapter 8

"You're right," the Tailor said, and his face looked so sad it made her cry harder. "This isn't okay. But we cannot make it right without you. You know what your life needs, and you'll have to go and find whoever is doing this to you. Only you can put a stop to it and bring back your family." When she looked up he was kneeling in front of her on the carpet, his face even with hers. He took her hands in his. She sniffed hard as he pulled her to her feet. "Now get hold of yourself."

"I'm so tired," she said.

"I know you are," he answered. "And you're going to get a chance to rest. But before we do that, I need to teach you how to find your way back when you've gone Walking. There may not be much time, and it is vital so that you don't end up stranded. Do you understand?"

Miranda nodded.

"Let's try this one more time."

Miranda lifted her bag and slung it across her shoulders. She hooked her thumbs under the straps and centered them, feeling the weight of the box and her school things bounce against her. The Tailor put his hand on her shoulder again and steered her back to the doorway. This time, she moved almost instinctively, reaching out for the knob, feeling the momentary sensation of cold and pulling them both to the other side. The Tailor let go of her shoulder this time, and she looked around to see why.

"Now, do you think you could stand exactly here again?" he asked.

"I guess so," she said.

"Good."

The Tailor gave her a gentle but firm shove, catching her off balance so that she stumbled forward against the long, wooden counter. She spun to face him, horrified.

"How can I get back now?"

"Find where your feet belong, and look for the Snag," the Tailor said.

Confused, but unsure what else to do, Miranda turned to face the spot where he still stood. At first, she didn't see anything, but as the longer she looked, the more something came into view. The something was thin, almost like a gossamer veil, hanging in the space where she was certain the office doorway had been.

"What do you see?" the Tailor asked.

"I think I see… spider web. Or something like it." She reached out to touch it, but found that it vanished if her fingers got too close.

"Think about where you need to be," the Tailor said, "and picture where your feet were when you Walked."

Miranda looked from the pale golden veil to the old man and back again. She shrugged, stepped right to the center of the space, so that whatever it was seemed to disappear all around her.

"You see the Snag, don't you?" he asked.

"Is that what the weird stuff is floating right here?" Miranda leaned in and out of the spot, looking at it from both sides as the Tailor nodded. "So, if I can see this, I could leave and come back?"

"Yes. But for now, we should get you to a safe place to sleep. Come, take us home."

Miranda hesitated, but her exhaustion weighed on her and all she wanted was to lie down in the dark, by herself. She reached out and linked arms with him, focused on going back to the office, and pulled them both forward and into the familiar room.

That evening, Miranda stayed at Bridget's apartment. The young woman lived a few miles from the shop, and Miranda drove there with directions on a small piece of paper. It felt strange to have nothing but her backpack with her, but she didn't feel safe going home, and the Tailor agreed. She also didn't know if home even existed anymore, as everything had changed so rapidly, and somehow not knowing for sure was better than showing up and the house being gone. Miranda parked in a guest parking spot and climbed the stairs to the second floor and unit 8. Bridget opened the door before she even knocked and, to Miranda's shock, gave her a big hug.

"I'm so sorry for what's happening to you," Bridget said. "Come on in, I've got lasagna cooking, and you can pick a movie."

Miranda stepped through the door, while Bridget closed and locked it behind her. A large overstuffed sofa dominated the living room, facing a small TV that stood on a low table. A peach crate sat beside the couch, tipped on its side, full of movies and books. A mirror hung by the front door, the only wall decoration in the whole place. Bridget disappeared through the open doorway at the back of the living room, and Miranda dropped her bag by the couch.

"Can I get you something to drink? All I have is water, and maybe a Coke," Bridget called.

"Water's fine," Miranda said, following her into what turned out to be the kitchen.

The warm room smelled like Italian seasoning and marinara sauce. The counters were smooth and brown and Miranda went to perch on a stool along one of them. Bridget pulled the lasagna from the oven and put it on the stove top to cool while she flitted around pulling out plates and glasses. A square aquarium on the counter contained two goldfish, drifting between the spokes of artificial coral while bubbles rose from the gravel bottom. A bowl with a handful of apples sat on the counter beside the aquarium with a stack of old books, their pages fading to yellow and green, sitting on top of a Cosmopolitan magazine. It occurred to Miranda that Bridget couldn't be much older than her.

"Are you a Threadwalker?" she asked.

Bridget grinned at her. "Kind of. I don't do much. Mostly, I just manage the paperwork for the Tailor and keep the shop running." She spooned a large square of lasagna onto a plate and pushed it along the counter it to Miranda, along with a glass of water. "Why don't you grab a spot on the couch, and I'll be right there."

Miranda took the plate into the other room, glancing around before she settled on the couch, sinking into the cushions with her plate balanced on her knees. She set the glass on the floor, and Bridget joined her not long after, bringing forks. The other girl flipped on the TV and changed the channel a few times, before stopping on a reality show about people searching for ghosts.

"You never know what you might find," Bridget said, giggling, as she took a bite of the steaming pasta.

Miranda laughed, too. "This has a whole new level to it now." Her desire to be alone evaporated, replaced with relief to have someone to talk to who understood.

"Doesn't it? It's so weird how things that don't seem to mean anything suddenly do. Your whole perspective changes."

They ate in a comfortable silence for a while, watching the people on TV shine flashlights on each other and take photos in the dark hoping to capture orbs and the like. Hanging out with Bridget reminded Miranda of her friends, and she enjoyed the amicable quiet. They both burst into laughter when one of the guys on the show went tearing out of the house, shedding his hat and camera mount as he ran. When it got to a commercial break, Miranda put down her fork.

"Can I ask you some stuff?"

"You can ask, but I may not answer," Bridget said, winking. She muted the TV and scooted around on the couch to face Miranda, her feet curled under her.

"Fair enough," Miranda said, laughing. "Okay, so how long have you been a... y'know?"

"Walker? I guess it's been about six years. I found out I could Walk when I was about thirteen. That's supposed to be way too young to Walk, but it was a total accident. I was trying to get away from these girls at school who were chasing me. They wanted to... well, it's not important. But I wanted to be someplace else, and suddenly I *was* someplace else. I freaked out about it, and all I wanted was to be back where I belonged. Then, I was back!"

"Were the girls gone?" Miranda asked.

"Well, no, but it scared the ever-living daylights out of them when I disappeared and came back right before their eyes! They never did bother me again. So, when I was seventeen, the Tailor sent me a message. He's really good at that. I don't know how he does it. But, I wound up coming to the shop. It was in a different place then." She took a bite of lasagna and chewed for a moment before continuing. "So, I guess my actual training started then, and I can't tell you what a relief it was to know that what happened to me didn't make me a freak, that it was just a gift I could be trained to use properly."

"I know what you mean," Miranda said. Even though everything the Tailor said seemed impossible and completely overwhelming, at least it gave her an explanation, and even a way to try and fix everything. Hope, and not being alone, helped. "Do your parents... Walk... too?"

"I don't know," Bridget said. "But I think my mom must've. She died when I was little, and my dad never wanted to talk about it. I spent most of my childhood with my grandparents, and if either of them Walked, I couldn't tell you. They're all gone now."

"Did someone, y'know, Edit them away?"

"I don't think so. Some people run into Editing, and that's how they find out they can Walk, but since I figured it out by actually doing it, my journey was different. I guess it's different for everybody. The Editors try to be careful not to fiddle with things that people will notice, though. In any case, somehow the Tailor finds all of us and teaches us. But no, my parents are just dead. They have been for a long time."

"I'm sorry."

"Oh, it's all right. The funny thing about this is you realize that time is all relative anyway. So somewhere they're still around even if I can't go see them, and that's okay.

"Why can't you go see them?"

"Part of the rules. I mean, unless they're Walkers for sure, I can't risk going and scaring the jeebies out of them or changing something about their lives without maybe changing my own. See what I mean?"

"Yeah," Miranda said, looking down at her plate. "It doesn't seem fair, though."

"Look, I know it doesn't make sense, and some of these rules sound arbitrary, but they're all for our safety, and they keep bad things from happening to us. If we messed up our own lives, we might disappear, too. Like your mom? If you messed up your own Thread and disappeared, there wouldn't be anyone to fix it. How would we even know where to go find you?"

"Oh," Miranda said. "I didn't think about that."

"It's okay. Listen, I've got an air bed that I can set up out here, or I can put you on the floor in my room if you'd rather have some company."

Still uneasy after having her own house cased that morning, Miranda thought for a moment. "I don't want to be alone."

"You've got it," Bridget said and smiled. "We'll get some clean clothes for you, too. You're nearly my same size."

After they finished their dinner and did the dishes, the girls set up a spot for Miranda in the bedroom. They inflated an air bed and Miranda curled under a well-worn quilt made by Bridget's grandmother, listening as the other girl fell asleep. She couldn't believe that just that morning, she woke up expecting to find her mom and tonight she wasn't even sure the house still existed. She drifted off into uneasy sleep.

At some point in the early morning hours, Miranda woke to what sounded like a huge drum, beating against her temples. As she came to, she realized it was someone pounding on the apartment door, alternated with someone leaning on the bell. She rolled over and poked Bridget's arm, dangling out from the covers beside her.

"Unhh?" Bridget mumbled.

"Someone's at the door," Miranda hissed.

"Wha—?" Bridget started mumbling again, but when she heard the pounding, she sat straight up in bed. She looked at Miranda and turned on the bedside lamp, then glanced at the window. "Something's happened. Stay here."

Bridget pulled a thick robe over her shorts and tank top and dashed out of the bedroom. Miranda heard her open the front door and say something, then yell. Miranda started to dive behind the bed to hide, when Bridget reappeared in the doorway, her face ashen.

"Grab your stuff. We have to go. Now." Bridget's wide eyes shone in the lamplight. Miranda jumped up.

"What's wrong?"

"The building's on fire," Bridget said, voice trembling. "It's not here yet, but it's moving fast. We have to get out."

Adrenaline coursed through Miranda as she grabbed her up backpack and pulled on her tennis shoes. Still wearing a pair of Bridget's sweat pants and a t-shirt, she stuffed her own clothes into her bag with the extras from Bridget, and put her coat on over the sleep shirt. Bridget gathered the quilt in her arms, then reached under the bed and pulled out a small black duffle bag.

"Always have a go bag," she said to Miranda's questioning expression. "Come on."

They ran out of the apartment and down the stairs to the parking lot. People streamed out of the building on all sides, huddling in the grassy median between parking spaces as fire crews tried to douse the flames leaping from the far side of the roof. As Miranda watched, the fire shifted and began devouring the apartment next to Bridget's. She glanced at her new friend, and saw her cuddling the quilt, her eyes shining. Bridget reached out and gripped Miranda's arm, her fingernails digging into Miranda's skin.

"Do you recognize that guy?" she whispered, glancing over her own right shoulder. Miranda leaned back to see around the quilt, and felt her heart in her throat. The firelight reflected on a shiny, bald head, and made the all-too-familiar black leather glow. She nodded.

"Then we need to go," Bridget said. Miranda started for her Honda, but Bridget pulled her the other way. "Leave it."

They wound their way through the parking area, ducking between cars, and trying to stay hidden from view as much as possible. The quilt slowed Bridget down, but Miranda saw no point asking her to drop it. She had a feeling it was just as likely she'd leave her wooden box somewhere. When they reached the other side of the building, Bridget pulled a car key out of her pocket and led Miranda to a small dark colored SUV. As they started to climb inside, Miranda heard a familiar sound: a motorcycle engine revved.

"Get in!" Bridget shouted.

Miranda didn't need to be told. She hauled herself into the passenger seat while Bridget cranked the engine. Miranda pulled her door closed as Bridget pealed out of the parking lot, the motorcycle right on their tail. Bridget flew down the empty streets, turning a few times trying to lose the bike, but it stayed right behind them. Miranda looked in the side view mirror. Even though he wore a black helmet that covered most of his face, she recognized him. The same fear she'd felt in her house crashed over her like a wave, and she felt herself getting dizzy.

Bridget cursed under her breath and made another sharp turn. Miranda gripped the seat cushion, suddenly aware of the road again. "Hang on!" she said. "I'm going to get on the highway!"

"Just get us away from him!"

She swerved hard to the left and turned down a side road, then pulled to the right to take an entrance ramp to the interstate. The bike fell behind, and she merged into a group of other cars, drove two miles down, and exited again. As they pulled onto the off-ramp, Miranda checked the mirrors, but the bike wasn't anywhere in sight.

"Did we lose him?"

"I'm not sure. He might have seen where we went, so we need to keep going. And we should get out of sight, at least for a while," Bridget said.

Even in the dark, this street looked familiar to Miranda, and it nagged at her. Bridget kept glancing in her rear-view mirror, but didn't say anything else. She seemed to know where she was going. They drove through an older residential area, most of the homes were dark, save for a handful of porch lights. Bare tree branches reached over the road, leaning toward the car in the moonlight. It began to dawn on Miranda why the street looked so familiar. As they passed a wooden fence with a large, twisted metal gate, Miranda realized where they were.

"Are we headed where I think we're heading?"

"Could be," Bridget said. "But let's not talk about it. I need to concentrate."

Miranda felt her stomach drop. She didn't want to go where she thought they were headed, but she didn't want Bridget to think she was afraid. She chewed on the back of her lip and looked out the car window. They drove in silence for several minutes, each of them checking the mirrors, but the motorcycle never appeared.

After a few more miles, the road came to a T-intersection and turned left. They drove as quickly as they dared down the winding road. The tree line drew close to the road here, and the houses spread out from one another. After about a mile, they passed a familiar large farm house, shrouded by the trees growing a little too close to its front porch, the driveway cracked and covered in leaves. Miranda tried not to look at it, waiting to see a familiar entryway just past it.

Miranda put her hand on Bridget's arm. "I know those gates."

"There's someone I need you to meet here." Bridget said. "There's a reason your dad is buried in this cemetery, and not in the one in town."

Bridget pulled up to the gates, which stood open despite the fact that it was past midnight. The wrought-iron archway over it read "Greenlawn Cemetery." Bridget parked to the left of the gate and turned off the engine. She was quiet, and she kept scanning back and forth in the darkness that pressed over the hills. Miranda couldn't tell if there was anything out of the ordinary to see.

"Who are we meeting?" Miranda asked.

"A friend," Bridget said. "But I think we should go visit your dad's grave first."

Miranda's stomach sank. "I don't think that's a good idea."

Bridget turned and looked at her, and set her jaw. "Listen. Your dad isn't really there. You know he isn't. It's not like with my folks. When I visit their gravesites, I know they're gone, but their bodies are really there. Dead." Her eyes shone, and Miranda looked away, not wanting to see her new friend cry.

"Okay," Miranda said quietly. "I'll go. You're coming with me, though."

"Go on ahead," Bridget said. "I want to try and hide the car, but I'll be right behind you."

"Promise you won't be long?" Miranda asked. She didn't want to be alone in this cemetery at night any longer than necessary.

"I promise."

Miranda turned and walked into the cemetery. Rolling hills spread on either side of the narrow drive, and the long shadows of the gravestone reached toward her as the moon hung low in the sky. She kept glancing over her shoulder where Bridget's car had reversed back onto the road and pulled away, listening for the sound of another engine, but she didn't hear anything except the wind rushing through the leaves.

Before long, Miranda veered to the right on a footpath that opened from the main drive. Letting her feet move without much thought, she trudged the path she took only once before, the day of the funeral. Papery leaves crunched and shredded beneath her, leaving brown confetti footprints in her wake. She shoved her hands deep in her coat pocket, curling her cold fingers into fists, her cheeks still warm with adrenaline. The walk lasted about five minutes, though it seemed much longer on her last visit. Still, Miranda found herself all too soon standing in front of the little stone. She used her phone to illuminate the text:

Samuel M. Woodward

She couldn't believe six whole months slipped away since the plane crash. Six months ago felt like an eternity. Her mother was still at home. Her friends still knew her. She didn't know about Threadwalkers or the people trying to change her whole life or have strange men chasing her.

"And I had a cat named Perkins," she said aloud. "What happened, Dad?"

Miranda stared at the stone she helped her mother choose, looking at the date carved into it, the date that everything changed. March 19. Miranda sank to the ground, sitting in front of the stone that marked nothing but dirt.

At the time, Miranda didn't understand her mother's insistence on having a gravestone with no body to bury. She even had nasty thoughts about the cost of the burial plot, and how it might be keeping them from doing other things, like Miranda getting her own car. But now, as she sat in front of it, she started to understand why her mother pushed so hard for it. It felt comforting to sit there and imagine that this random piece of rock somehow connected to her father. In a way, she almost believed he could hear her. Almost.

Miranda sat there a long time, her forehead pressed against the cold, smooth surface. Then, a gradual chill crept over Miranda as she felt someone watching her. Her breath caught in her chest as she strained to hear footsteps, a voice, or any indication of who or what it might be. She forced herself to inhale, screwed up her courage, and stood.

She didn't see anyone.

Miranda pivoted. She looked in all directions, but saw nothing but gravestones—rows and rows of them, like uneven teeth jutting from the ground in the moonlight. The thought that there might be someone behind any of them made her shiver. Turning back to her father's stone, she jumped, stifling a scream.

On top of the stone lay a tiny pair of scissors, glinting in the moonlight. Miranda wheeled around, but no one else was in sight. The cemetery stretched a good distance to the surrounding trees, and she didn't see anyone running for them. She turned back to the stone and the scissors.

"Come out here right now!" Miranda hissed, trying to use her peripheral vision to see as much at once as possible. Nothing moved. "I know you're there! Show yourself!"

She turned and squatted with her back pressed to the stone, bracing herself, trying to stop herself from trembling. "I'm not afraid of you!" she called.

Miranda's pulse slowed until she felt well enough to stand. She paced around her father's stone, keeping her eyes on the scissors and straining to hear, though the sound of the wind in the leaves made it difficult.

When she got to the back of the stone, she noticed something: her mother left that side blank to save money, but now it looked like it had something carved on it, visible beneath a pile of leaves. She knelt in front of the leaf litter, shoving away the built-up debris until she saw it. She traced her finger over it—a small oval with a straight tail coming down from it, and a long thin line spiraling around it. The whole design was inside a perfectly round circle. She didn't recognize it.

Hands trembling, she pulled her phone out of her pocket, careful not to drop it in the leaves now heaped around her ankles. She took a picture of the carving, emailed it to herself, and shoved the phone back in her pocket before standing again. The scissors still sat on top of the stone. She hesitated, then snatched them and started back toward the main driveway to look for Bridget. Now that she thought about it, she wondered why her friend hadn't caught up to her yet. Maybe it had taken longer than she thought to hide the car.

Miranda turned the scissors over in her hands as she walked. They felt lighter than she expected, and were perfectly smooth. As she reached the main drive, she paused and pulled out the small wooden box from her backpack. Opening the box, she saw a faint glow coming from the golden spool of thread.

"These must go together," she muttered. "It can't be coincidence."

She set the tiny scissors inside the little box, where they nested beside the spool. Miranda looked again back toward her father's grave, then closed the box and dropped it back into her bag. Just as she pulled the zipper, she heard a noise that almost made her heart stop: the grumble of a motorcycle engine. Miranda dropped to her stomach and rolled behind the nearest upright gravestone, her backpack sliding up to rest between her shoulder blades. The engine sounded close, but she couldn't tell if it was inside the cemetery or not. She inched to one side to see around the base of the stone, and peered down the driveway.

Under the gates, Miranda made out a dark, hulking shadow. The shape was much smaller than Bridget's car, which was nowhere to be seen. The motorcycle didn't have headlights turned on, but she heard it idling as the driver sat there, leaning from side to side as if scanning the cemetery. Miranda tried not to move, hoping she'd gotten behind the stone in time. A rock on the ground dug into her shin, but she was afraid to shift her weight in case it might draw attention to her. Her whole body felt tense, like a compressed spring. She felt like she was in one of her nightmares, except this time she couldn't escape by waking up. Miranda felt cold and sweaty at the same time, crouching in the leaves, hoping the motorcycle would just leave.

After what felt like an hour, the shadowy figure pulled the bike forward, glancing to the left and right along the drive. Miranda ducked behind the gravestone to stay out of his sight. She heard the motorcycle roll down the pavement, until it stopped even with the footpath that led up the hill and to her father's empty grave. Concentrating on not breathing loudly, Miranda pressed her body as flat against the ground as she could manage, grateful for the leaf litter that piled around the gravestones to make body-like heaps.

The engine stopped. Miranda heard a heavy step hit the ground, then become muffled as it got to the dirt. She watched the silhouette of the figure in the moonlight pace down the footpath, looking left and right. Miranda felt her leg twinge where the rock was slowly stabbing her, but she couldn't move her toes to help the prickles now surging up her leg from her shin. The figure continued past her, and she thought that if only this person would go over the hill, she could make a crouching run for it, but just as she started tensing her arms, the figure froze. It turned to face her, and she caught a glimpse of the man's face in the moonlight: he was looking right at her.

In panic, Miranda sprang to her feet and bolted in the opposite direction, down the slope toward the main entrance, hoping against hope that Bridget was back already. The man came thundering after her, his footfalls heavy on the path. She saw a glimmer of gold like the one from the thread in her box, and she felt herself drawn to it almost instinctively. She scrambled toward the pale glow in the darkness, though she didn't have enough clarity of mind to think much beyond what she'd do when she got there. She stumbled. Pain shot up her leg from her ankle, and she fell heavily against a gravestone. The man was twenty feet away. Then fifteen feet. Ten. Miranda screamed and flung herself around the stone toward the faint, golden glow. She felt a sudden icy sensation, then a thick press over her whole body, and landed hard on the ground beside the stone, expecting to at any moment to be caught by huge hands. No one touched her.

Miranda scrambled to her feet and looked around. It was as if the man had vanished, but her sense of space felt muddled. The darkness, too, was different; she looked up and saw the moon much higher in the sky, a thin crescent shape. She could have sworn the moon was bigger before. The icy thickness of her fall hit her and realized what must have happened.

"Shit."

She'd accidentally Walked. The motorcycle wasn't on the driveway anymore, and the man had vanished. Miranda twisted, looking all around her, trying to get her bearings in the cemetery. She hobbled away from the stone on her twisted ankle, heading toward the entrance, trying to keep out of sight.

When she reached the main entrance, Miranda paused and peered up the driveway. She still didn't see anyone. She leaned out and looked up and down the road, but it was all clear. No Bridget, but also no motorcycle anywhere, or any other vehicles for that matter. Not that she honestly expected to see Bridget. She leaned into the tall hedge beside the gate and rubbed her calf as the tingling subsided. She looked again up at the moon, and thought how strange it was that, for her, it had been fuller when her night started.

The thought made her pause, and a small thrill somewhere between excitement and terror ran up her spine, like the feeling she always got at the top of a roller coaster. She looked around her again, but there was no clear way to tell anything about when she was. She retrieved the wooden box and slowly opened it, looking down at the still faintly glowing golden thread. It certainly looked like the stuff she'd seen by that gravestone. Surely it couldn't be that easy. She shook her head, put the box back in her bag, and tried to focus on her options. She could stay hidden for a while, but not all night. At some point, she needed to move.

After a while, Miranda checked her phone to find the screen black. She tried several things to make it respond, but it seemed the battery was shot, or the phone was just frozen. She stuffed it back in her pocket and adjusted her backpack so that the weight sat higher on her shoulders, wondering how long she should wait before looking for a way back to Bridget. She didn't like just standing and waiting, but didn't want to stray too far, either. After several more minutes, she grew impatient and began walking along the interior of the hedge, where she could listen for traffic and keep a clear view of the gate.

When she reached the edge of the forest, Miranda glanced up at the trees to her right and behind, and back to the cemetery, then turned again to look at the trees.

Their branches were covered in thick, full leaves.

Though she couldn't see the color in the dark, she was almost certain that these leaves were bright green. The autumn smell of musk and mold was gone, and in its place, she detected something light and floral. She walked around to the front side of one of the gravestones, but it didn't have flowers on it. The trees bent in a gentle breeze, and the scent grew stronger. Miranda realized that she was standing in the cemetery in spring. And then she remembered what the Tailor said about carefully marking your Snag, and her stomach dropped into her feet. She might be stranded.

Miranda turned and ran back along the hedge, no longer worried about the man with the motorcycle on the other side. She needed to find her way back. When she reached the driveway again, she made a sharp right turn to head back up to the footpath, but could no longer tell the gravestones apart. She scanned the ground, looking for any clue to show her the way back, but everything looked the same. She had no way to find the golden threads that marked the way home. Miranda turned and marched off in the direction of her father's gravestone to retrace her steps.

Miranda walked back to the stone. She slowed when she got near to the spot. She approached quietly at first, but broke into a run as the area came into view.

"Where did it go?" she said, standing on the bare patch of ground. Her father's stone was gone. "Don't you change on me, too, Dad," she whispered. Miranda turned on the spot, but couldn't see any other differences in the cemetery. She hadn't exactly been paying close attention to the details on the other stones the last time she stood here, and now irritation surged through her.

She walked away and back again a few times, hoping that somehow, she'd just gone to the wrong place, but the stone never appeared. She sat down on top of one of the other gravestones and scanned the area. With her elbows on her knees, she leaned forward and concentrated.

"This is springtime," she said to herself. "But other than that, you don't even know when this is. Maybe you went backwards and maybe that's why Dad's grave isn't here yet." She sat up straight and looked around. Maybe it wasn't there yet because her dad was still out there! The thought shot through her like fire. Of course, there wasn't going to be a big sign to tell her the date, but surely it was possible. The Tailor's voice drifted into her thoughts just then, with his warnings against changing the past. But would just going to *see* her dad really count as a change? She didn't want to admit it, but right then she didn't care much about the Tailor's rules.

The wind shifted and she felt a chill; the night deepened. Crickets chirped in the tall grass around some of the less maintained areas, and the trees rustled. Miranda listened to them for a while, but couldn't pick out any other sounds apart, and stood to go back to the main driveway, intending to at least try to find the way back to the Snag, even if she didn't want to use it just yet. She just needed to keep looking for it. After a few minutes, she arrived where she thought she might have hidden from the bald man, and she crouched down to check the stone.

The graves in this part of the cemetery seemed to be much older than the ones where her father was supposed to be. She could just make out a few of them in the moonlight, though most were in too much shadow to see at all. Most of the dates were from at least one hundred years earlier, many of them even older than that, worn down by exposure to wind, rain, snow, and everything else that erodes even the memory of life. Miranda meandered through them, but didn't see anything familiar. She reached the point where the path split from the pavement, and she planted her feet, studying it.

Walking around every single marker in a wide swath, Miranda made her way from stone to stone, trying to jog her memory. When she thought she reached the rough distance, she knelt to try and recreate her view. Unfortunately, most of the stones just here were all the same low rectangular shape, so she couldn't quite figure out which one had been her hiding spot.

Drumming her fingers on the top of a stone, Miranda surveyed the rest of the cemetery from this vantage. The hill where her father was buried, or where they marked him anyway, rose higher than the others, though the footpath leading to it stayed on low ground. That explained why the man hadn't seen her right away. She might have been visible on top of the hill, but not in the shadow beside it.

"I don't want to be stranded!" Miranda cried, flinging herself onto the ground in frustration.

She leaned against a gravestone. "How could this happen?"

Suddenly, a shadowy figure appeared just up the hill. Miranda squinted in the darkness, but the dim light masked the shape. The person seemed to be fumbling around in the dark. She leaned around the gravestone to get a clearer view.

The tall, thin man paced in front of a gravestone about thirty feet away from her. He carried a jacket that he didn't need in the warm night air along with a flashlight, and rubbed at his nose a few times, sniffing hard. He kept clicking the flashlight on and off, as if he was checking something. After a few minutes, he sneezed again.

Geez, take a Claritin, Miranda thought, watching him as he moved back and forth.

The man stopped pacing and scanned the cemetery. Miranda remained motionless, glad she stopped before she went up the driveway; otherwise she'd have run straight into him. Of course, from here she had nowhere to go, but being momentarily stuck far outweighed being caught. It almost looked like the man stood guard over the spot. After several passes, he leaned back against the gravestone and sighed, folding his arms across his chest.

She stayed still for several more minutes as the man began pacing again, stopping every so often to check the surrounding area. The longer she watched, the more she was able to make out some of his features. His shaggy hair fell over his forehead, and he had a goatee trimmed close to his face. His shoulders slouched a little, and he rocked back and forth on his feet when he paused.

After a while, he seemed to get tired of waiting. He stopped walking, and began running his hands along the side of the gravestone. He stood, turned around, and strode back over the hill toward the edge of the cemetery. Miranda counted to five, then pushed herself to a crouch and followed at a distance.

The tall man slipped out of sight for a moment, and then she caught a glimpse of him again at the crest of the next hill past her father's plot. He paused with just his shoulders and head visible behind the slope, then sank out of view. Miranda followed, ducking low when she reached the hill. She dodged from stone to stone, hoping he wouldn't turn around and see her. When she crested the hill, the man was out of sight, and she'd recovered her breath enough to try and figure out what to do next. Who visited a cemetery in the middle of the night?

"People looking for ghosts," she said, laughing to herself. "This whole thing is ridiculous. And I'm not going to be stranded here."

"Well, you might be," said a voice behind her. She jumped and wheeled around to find the tall, sneezing man standing on the footpath. "You don't know where you're going, do you?" he asked.

"Who are you?" Her heart pounded in her chest and she started to back away. Who was this strange man? Her thoughts raced to her mom and the pepper spray she'd insisted on putting on Miranda's car keys before they went to the DMV, and wishing she'd dropped them in her bag. Every warning she'd ever gotten in an email or seen on TV was flashing red across her thoughts. Should she scream? Should she run?

"I was just... out for a walk," she said.

"I see," the man said. He straightened his shoulders a bit. "What sort of walk?"

"The sort where I go where I want," she said, taking another step back as goosebumps rolled across her arms, the hair on the back of her neck standing up. The running option won her internal debate. She turned and bolted, trying to put as much distance between her and the strange man as possible.

"Where are you going to go?" the man shouted after her. "Wait! Miranda!"

Miranda froze in her tracks, nearly stumbling over a low-lying gravestone. She spun to face him. "Excuse me?"

"Please wait!" the man called, holding out his arms and jogging after her. "I saw you fall through. I don't know why you're alone, but I want to help you. That's why I'm here. I wanted to make sure you got through okay, that you don't get stuck," the man continued. He stopped about twenty paces in front of her.

"That's not your business," Miranda snapped.

"Where is Bridget?" the man asked. "I thought she was bringing you with her. Where is she?"

Miranda felt herself relax a tiny bit at the mention of her friend. "How do you know Bridget?"

"I know her the same way you do," the man said calmly, taking a few steps toward her. "As for what I'm doing in a cemetery in the middle of the night, I could ask you the same thing."

Miranda inhaled quickly, and gripped the straps of her backpack. Now close enough for a slightly better look in the dim moonlight, she saw that he was older than her by at least ten years, though she couldn't quite be sure of how much. His forehead and the sides of his eyes were creased but he didn't look as old as her parents. If she had to guess, she thought his hair looked light brown and his goatee was neatly trimmed. Something about him looked familiar.

"What do you mean?" she asked, shifting her feet, ready to take off running again.

"I mean that if you're willing to trust me, I might be able to help you."

"Why should I trust you?" she asked, taking yet another step backward.

"Because you're Sam Woodward's daughter, and I think you're in trouble," the man said. "That's the only reason you'd be here, especially alone."

Miranda's jaw dropped open. She tried to speak but couldn't find the words. She managed to sputter, "Go—go back to the thing, the thing about me being stuck. Am I—am I *stranded* here?"

"Well, no, not really," he said. "But I imagine that you wound up here under, well, unexpected conditions, and that not enough time has passed for you to go through safely. It might even take all night for it to be safe enough for you to go back."

She flung her arms in the air. "What am I supposed to do? I told Bridget I'd be back."

"Bridget is probably in more danger than you are, but there's nothing we can do about it at the moment unless you want to get caught. So, what about it? Are you staying here until things quiet down, or are you going back now and risking the both of you?"

"Well, I..." She looked left and right, in a last effort to get her bearings.

"Yeah. You don't know where you came through." He shook his head. "Come on, I'll show you, and then you can decide." The man walked toward Miranda, but gave her a wide berth as he passed. She followed him down the footpath and several yards further down the driveway than she expected. He stepped off the path and moved about four stones to the right before stopping and pointing. "You popped out from behind here. And you were on the ground, so it must've been a low one."

Miranda approached the spot and knelt, checking it while keeping a close eye on the man. He stayed at a respectable distance, which made her relax just a bit. The gravestone in front of her looked like all the others in this section, faded and covered in lichen. "I guess that looks like it."

"Look harder," he said.

Miranda glanced at him, then back to the stone. She ran her hands along it, trying to remember if she'd touched this particular one before, and wondering how he could be so certain. And then she noticed it: minuscule and pale and spider web thin, a sheet of gossamer threads fluttered in the air. The Snag! It wasn't glowing as brightly as before. She looked up at him.

"Now you see it," he said.

"See what?" she asked, wondering if he could see it, too, or if he was trying to trick her.

"Seriously?" he asked, and sighed with exasperation. "That's the Snag you fell through earlier. It's probably harder to spot because you had more moonlight on your side, reflecting. It's good you found one so low to the ground; whoever was chasing you probably won't be able to find it."

"You found it," she pointed out.

"Well, yeah, I saw you come through it, didn't I? And I know how to spot them. This area is full of them, you know," he said pointing to the hillsides all around them. "These places don't change much."

"Cemeteries?" she asked. "You're telling me that cemeteries are full of... these spots?"

"Of course they are. Nowhere else mixes up time like a cemetery does. They hardly change for years and years, sometimes for millennia depending on where in the world you are, so it's easy for Threads to get Snagged here. Of course, it's hard to use them, what with the lack of actual doors and all. That's probably why no one has followed you through yet."

Miranda looked back up the hillside and shivered. Then she looked back down at the strands around the Snag and wondered what would happen if she just rolled through it and away from this guy. Before she could make up her mind, he spoke again.

"That's enough talking for out here. What are you going to do? Either you need to go back through, or you need to get out of sight. I really don't want to attract extra visitors. There's a safe place not far from here where you can wait for them to leave," he said.

"Yeah, I appreciate your offer and all," she replied, "but I don't even know who you are. I need to figure this out on my own."

"Look," he reached out to put his hand on her shoulder, but Miranda stiffened and backed quickly away before he could. He quickly dropped his hand again. "I'm sorry. It's just that I feel like I already know you. And you may not know me, but I knew your dad, and I know Bridget and the Tailor. I'm sure that things are confusing right now, but trust me when I say you need to lie low for a while. I don't know where you'll go from here, but you're still in danger. The more we stand out here and talk, the more attention we'll draw to this Snag. You've heard the voices, right?" Miranda nodded. "Don't *be* one of those voices."

Miranda looked at the wispy threads again, this time with some alarm. She hadn't even considered her own voice drifting through might attract people to the spot, and backed away from the stone. "How can I trust you?" she whispered. "Prove you're a friend of my dad's."

"As I said, I've known your father a long time. And he wanted you to trust me." The man took several steps away from the Snag and this time Miranda followed him. "Tell you what. How about I give you a token. Something that'll let you know you can trust me." The man reached into his pocket and pulled out a small, folded black and white photo, handing it to Miranda. She peered at it in his flashlight's beam; it was a picture of the man and her father, both in tuxes, arms around each other's shoulders, laughing at something off camera. It looked like it could have been taken at her parents' wedding. She handed the photo back to him and he slid it into his pocket.

"Why didn't you show me this first?" she asked quietly, glancing down at the Snag.

"I thought you had to be Woodward's kid because he could do that thing, too, where he didn't need a door. He just popped up sometimes. But I needed to make sure. I had to talk to you." He studied her for a moment and then said in a low voice, "I also know your favorite book as a child was *Alice's Adventures in*

Wonderland, and I know your dad got you your cat Perkins for your sixth birthday. You named him Perkins because you wanted a Cheshire Cat, but you thought he looked more like a butler on a TV show your mother watched than like the Cheshire Cat. And your own copy of *Alice* has been missing since you were ten."

"How did you know all that?" Miranda asked.

"I told you. I've known your dad a long time."

Miranda took a quick step closer, the small bubble of hope that had first formed earlier when she found the gravestone missing now buoyed by this man's tone. "Do you still know him?" she asked.

The man looked down at his feet. "He isn't here, Miranda," he said.

Disappointment washed over her, though she tried not to show it. She should have known it wouldn't be that easy, but her chest ached all the same. She clenched and unclenched her fists several times. *You got your own hopes up,* she told herself. *Now figure out what to do.*

Once she composed herself, Miranda looked up at the man. Something about his face looked familiar, though she couldn't place why. He no longer looked frightening, and since so far only the Tailor and Bridget had known about her cat, she decided to trust him, at least for the time being.

"So, what do we do now?" she whispered

"Well, now we go back to the Library and see if you can get some sleep. In the morning, we'll reassess the situation and decide if you can get back through then. And my name's Jake." He turned and began striding across the grass, stepping around stones as he went.

"Nice to meet you, Jake," Miranda said. She followed Jake back across the cemetery grounds. She wondered how many times she walked across the same strip of ground tonight. When they reached the area close to her father's future plot, Jake veered to the left and over a hill. At the bottom of the hill, in a little valley before the ground rose again, was a small building. It looked like a mausoleum except only about the size of a garden shed, with tall, gothic columns on the side nearest her, flanking a stone door. Jake stopped in front of it and looked sideways at her.

"I'm going to show you this, but don't share it with anyone else, all right?"

"Isn't this a crypt?" she asked. He didn't answer.

Jake ran his fingers along the edge of the door until he got to a particular spot and paused, reaching out for her hand. She lifted her hand and he gripped it, then pressed her palm against the piece of stone. Miranda gasped as the stone seemed to compress ever so slightly around her hand, and the wide stone door popped open an inch. Jake slid his fingers to the open side and pulled hard; after a moment, the door pivoted on a huge hinge.

Jake led the way into the little building. He hauled on the wrought iron handle inside the door to pull it closed again. They stood on a narrow ledge in front of shallow, earthen steps, leading underground. Lit by flickering lights, the walls were smooth and narrow.

Miranda glanced at Jake, more visible in the light of the tunnel. His goatee covered a narrow chin above a long neck that sprouted from a sweater vest. He wore a long sleeve shirt under that, and brown pants similar to the color of the dirt floor on which they walked. His hair was slightly thin on top, but still mostly a sandy brown color with just a few lighter silver patches over his temples. It made him look a bit older than his face, which she now guessed looked like he was in his late twenties or maybe early thirties. The laugh lines around his eyes gave him a look like he'd seen a few things in his life, but he was a lot younger than her dad in any case. In fact, he looked exactly like he did in the wedding photo, but that was taken twenty years ago. The man in front of her looked no older. How far back had she Walked? And how did he know her father was gone?

While she pondered how Jake could possibly have known about her father, he led the way down the stairs and into darkness. Miranda had no choice but to follow. She hitched up her bag and made her way down the shallow steps behind him. When they reached the bottom, it opened into a passageway wide enough for three people to walk side by side, lit every so often by a single bulb electric lamp. Slate pieces lined the floors and the walls were smooth dirt. The passage seemed to go more or less in a straight line.

"Come on," Jake said. "We'll be at the Library in no time."

Minutes later they reached the end of the passageway and another set of steps. These were wood like in an old cellar and led up to a door in the ceiling. Jake turned the handle, pushing it open. He vanished through the door and Miranda came on his heels. She stepped out into a cramped, dark space. Jake opened another door and as light poured in, she realized where they stood: in a small coat closet. There were even winter coats hanging on either side of her.

"See? And no one saw us coming," Jake said.

Miranda stepped out of the closet and walked into the room. Along the wall to her left a fire crackled in its fireplace, and the room was full of comfortable looking antique furniture.

Something about the room felt familiar, but she couldn't quite place it. She glanced over the bookshelves along the wall opposite to the fireplace, and at the wide doorway out to a foyer. She turned in time to watch Jake reset the hidden doors, the one to the passageway vanishing into the floor once closed, perfectly camouflaged with the wood.

"So, what's this?"

"It's a safe place," he said. "Not many people know about it."

"I feel like I've been here before…" She walked out into the foyer, Jake right behind her and suddenly she drew in a sharp breath as she suddenly recognized where she was: they stood at the bottom of the flight of stairs, carpeted and flanked by polished banisters. Firelight danced in the parlor to the right where Miranda last saw empty bottles and graffiti, and little tables lined the walls, supporting curios and framed photos.

She was in the haunted house from her birthday night.

Chapter 9

"I was just here!" Miranda said. "Except… it didn't look like this." She wondered how far in time she'd traveled, looking at how well-put-together the house looked. *Jake must be way in the past for the house to look so good*, she thought.

"Why don't we sit down and talk?" Jake suggested, drawing her attention back. "You can ask me anything you like."

Miranda followed Jake back into the fire-lit room. Her steps didn't creak on the well-varnished wooden floors beneath their feet, and she noticed the intricate wallpaper in the living room they entered, now bright instead of dull. The burgundy upholstered sofas looked nothing like the dingy stuff she expected. Jake pointed for her to sit, and she settled onto the very edge of a cushion. His hand had a massive scar from the thumb all the way up his wrist, and Miranda had to pull her eyes away from.

She looked past Jake at the huge mirror on the wall, in an ornate carved frame. A few oil paintings hung on either side of the fireplace, under which stood a pair of bookshelves with leather bound volumes lining them, and she felt the heat from the fire warming her right cheek. She didn't like the idea of being alone with a stranger, but her curiosity overpowered her fear. He sat down on the large, overstuffed sofa across from her.

"So how exactly do you know my dad?" she asked.

"Reasonable question," he said. "I was your father's Librarian for years."

"That's...weird."

Miranda eyed Jake curiously. His knees stuck up slightly as if his legs were a bit too long for the chair, and he leaned forward as if studying her, too. She felt very aware of the fact that she was still wearing Bridget's sweats and had been lying in the dirt and leaves. She glanced down at the sofa and tried to be subtle as she brushed away some leaf bits. Jake burst into laughter.

"Don't worry. It's easy to clean," he said. "Really, I already knew you'd been having a rough night when I told you to sit."

"So, you're a librarian," Miranda said. She wanted to make sense of why Bridget had intended on coming here.

"Your father's Librarian, yes," Jake replied.

"I have a book," she said. She reached into her backpack and pulled out *A Wrinkle in Time*, which was stuffed beneath the clothes. She handed over the paperback with the photo inside the front cover, minus the torn page, which she left in her backpack under the wooden box. "That's from my house. Everything else disappeared."

"But you got this out?" he asked, turning the book over in his hands and examining the spine. He looked at the old photo. "That's quite a trick. Usually everything disappears once it starts to go."

"That was my dad's favorite book to read to me a few years ago," she said. "How do I know I can trust you?"

"You don't," Jake said, handing her back the book. "You need to know that you aren't safe anywhere you go right now," he continued. "And you shouldn't trust anyone you meet, especially people who are friendly to you."

"So what about you, then?" Miranda wondered. "Should I not trust you?"

"I don't know how much more I can do to gain your trust," he said. "But you don't have much choice, and I'm probably a better option than the guy you're running from, am I right?"

"Well, yeah…" Miranda tucked the book into the bag, sliding the torn page in with the photograph. Something else occurred to her. "What time is it? I lost track when I… Walked." She relished using the word. If Jake believed she was good at this, then she would have to sound like she was good at it.

Jake checked his watch. She touched the smooth face on her own wrist, and her mother's face swam into her mind's eye. "Well, here it's about eight-thirty at night. Dark, but not too late. You've been running," he observed.

"Yeah. It feels like I've been running all night."

"Do you know who you're running from?"

"Not really," she answered. "Do you?"

"Not per se."

"Okay…"

"Look," Jake said, "I don't know who he is *exactly*." He swallowed. "But I know who he represents, and we are much safer waiting in here until we're certain you weren't followed."

"How could I be followed?" Miranda glanced toward the front door, half expecting the bald man to burst through it. "I thought, I mean, I hoped they couldn't find the Snag."

She fidgeted on the cushion and shook her head. The thought of more than one motorcycle following her through the dark was not something she'd considered and the thought gave her chills. "What's happening to me?" she murmured.

Jake leaned forward, his hands folded just past his knees. Miranda raised her gaze to meet his. "Your life is being Edited," he explained.

"That's what the Tailor said," Miranda answered. "But that doesn't really tell me anything. Who's Editing me? How are they doing it? How do I make them stop?" She felt her frustration growing again, and wanted to scream at this man sitting calmly across from her.

"I'm so sorry, Miranda." Jake's face fell. "I don't know how they're doing it. I don't know how to stop it. I just know that it's happening, and that I want to help however I can."

"You're not much help, then," Miranda said. The pained expression on his face made her regret her bluntness for a moment, but she didn't know what else to do. What good was someone who wanted to help but couldn't answer her questions?

"I wish I could do more."

Jake was looking down at his hands, and for a moment he looked older. It suddenly occurred to her that he might start crying. Trying to change the subject, she pointed at the bookshelves along the wall. "What are all these for? Do you just sit here and read all day?"

"Sometimes," Jake replied. "But that's part of my job, so of course I sit and read."

"Oh." Miranda tried to look anywhere but at him, though there wasn't much else in the room. After several minutes of silence, Jake got up and began pulling out various books, replacing most of them but keeping a few in his hands. Soon, he turned around again, setting several on the coffee table between the sofas. His expression had relaxed a little and his eyes were clear.

"So how long have you been doing this?" he asked.

"Doing what?"

"*Walking*," he said, throwing his hand in the air. "Come on, I'm just trying to make conversation and you are not helping in the slightest."

"Well it's not like you've been very specific about what's going on," she shot back. She sighed, and softened her tone. "I only got here a little before you saw me, so however long that's been."

Jake blinked at her. "I meant in general, but I guess that's answer enough." He went back to the sofa and sat down again. His legs were so long that his knees stuck out, and he tucked his feet under the furniture. "But Bridget thought you needed something, or she wouldn't have brought you here so soon after you started."

"And what do I need?"

"Well that's the question, isn't it?" he asked. "Most folks need information of some sort. And I have information. All sorts of information." He pointed at the books between them.

"I don't think books can help me."

"I think you should look anyway," he said. "There are more, if you don't find what you're looking for down here." He put his hands on his knees and stood. "I'll go check the grounds and give you some space to look around. Take your time." With that, he strode to the front door and went outside. Miranda heard the lock click and his footsteps going down the wooden steps.

After sitting for a few moments longer, she paced the perimeter of the room, looking for anything that might tell her more about *when* she was, and what Jake's relationship with her father might be. The only thing she found was a small opening into a secondary room, which turned out to be a closet. Nothing else caught her eye, and she soon stood in front of the bookshelves again.

With time to examine them, she was able to see what sort of books Jake had. Most of them seemed to be textbooks, particularly world history, though some were novels and a handful were autobiographies. Many of them looked old, and several had gold leaf lettering on the covers. They reminded her of her father's collection, though she didn't particularly recognize any of the titles.

Maybe Dad sold books to Jake, she thought, running her finger along the leather spines. *He called himself my dad's librarian, though this isn't much of a library.*

"There doesn't seem to be anyone else out there," Jake called from the entryway. She started and backed quickly away from the shelf as he walked back into the room. "Which is weird, because I thought for sure… Anyway, did you find anything of interest?"

"Not really." She felt frustrated that she hadn't gotten more time to look around, and she must have shown it on her face because Jake asked, "Why don't I show you the rest of the house? There's even a guest room for you."

Miranda's curiosity about this place before it became "haunted" was thoroughly piqued. Jake led her back to the foyer and up to the second floor. Miranda half-expected one of the shadowy figures to cross in front of her again, but the hall seemed quiet. Jake led her past two open doors. She peeked inside one of the rooms. Hundreds of books lined the walls, floor to ceiling. Several large chairs grouped around a heavy wooden table in the center of the room, its carved legs as thick as Miranda's own. Jake leaned over her shoulder.

"Told you there were more books," he said. "And the guest room is over here across from this one."

"But… where did this all come from?" she asked.

"Oh, I've been building my collection for years," he said. "I'm a Librarian, after all."

"No joke," Miranda said. "What are they for?"

"They're for reading," he said.

"I'd never have guessed."

"Look," he said, "I don't know what you've already discovered, or what your current task is. You know I can't tell you too much, so all I can do is provide *specific* information for the questions you ask me."

"And I don't even know where to begin asking." Miranda was starting to feel truly anxious about leaving Bridget behind, and wondered where she could have gone. She hoped her friend wasn't still waiting in the cemetery for her, but also kind of hoped she was.

Frustrated, Miranda walked over to a small shelf filled with paperbacks. She picked up one of them and turned it over to read the cover. It was a copy of *Peter Pan*. In fact, it looked remarkably like her own copy of *Peter Pan*. "My dad read me this one," she said.

"I'm not surprised," Jake said. "Most of these serve a purpose." He pointed at the book. "That one, for instance, is the story of a kid who took a bunch of other folks Walking when most of them got stranded."

"Seriously?"

"Sure! Think about it—only Peter could come and go, but the other kids and the pirates and all the rest were stuck in this other place. He kept trying and trying until he managed to figure out how to get people back to the other side. Otherwise, Wendy would've been stranded, too."

"So, what's Neverland supposed to be, then?"

"Just the impossible. It's more fun for kids to think about visiting fairies and mermaids than to visit empty battlefields and graveyards." He shrugged.

"So, this whole book— "

"Was written to start introducing the idea to children," he finished. "Most kids read it as a fairy tale. A few try to go to Neverland. Even fewer succeed."

Miranda put the book back on the shelf, aware of Jake watching her. She tried not to be self-conscious as she skimmed the titles, but no others jumped out at her until she got to the biographies, which took up most of a wall. Then, she pulled out one on Elvis.

"My dad had this one, too," she said. "Why are there so many biographies here?"

"Biographies are useful as a way to track what happens to specific people over time. Autobiographies and memoirs are best, but if there's been any kind of change and the person doesn't know their life was Edited, accurate ones are hard to find once you go back a few decades. The longer the time since an Edit, the more impact it can have."

"Oh."

"Your dad was an Elvis fan, you know," he said, smiling.

"Yeah, I know," she said. She put the book back on the shelf with the other biographies.

"Maybe you should get some rest," Jake said.

They went back out in the hallway where Jake stopped in front of a blank wall. He pushed on a seemingly random spot and the wall shifted, sliding open to reveal another door. Miranda opened it and walked into the guest room, setting down her backpack by the door. The small room had a cot and a low table with a lamp, an old book, and a round, silver clock. She went back into the hallway, then stepped through the door again. This hidden opening was roughly where the figure had vanished the night of her birthday. Thinking back to that night with Jae and Abby made her breath catch for a moment. She wished she could call them to talk through every terrifying thing that had happened to her.

"I know it's not much, but you can use it as long as you like," Jake said, watching her. "I've had a fair number of guests, and it's relatively safe and quiet, especially if you want to be out of sight. Plus, we can always close the entrance, and poof! You're gone."

"That's ingenious."

"It's necessary," Jake replied. "There's a black metal panel to press just here that will open this door from the inside, and the bathroom is down at the end of the hall. Now, try and get some sleep, and we'll see if I can help you more in the morning, all right?"

"Right."

Jake disappeared through the bedroom door, and she heard him close the hidden wall panel. She tossed her coat over the wooden chair, then sat on the foot of the cot. She rummaged in her backpack, pulling out the tattered paperback and the photograph inside of it. The picture still looked like it had when she printed it, her younger self staring out of frame at something Miranda couldn't see. She flipped through *A Wrinkle in Time*, but didn't find any other loose pages.

She could faintly hear Jake moving around downstairs as she stuffed everything back in the bag. She yawned, wondering if jetlag applied when you weren't even in the same year anymore. The thought made her smile. As Miranda lay down, she glanced at the book on the little bedside table and saw it was *Alice's Adventures in Wonderland*. Scooping it up, she turned to the inside of the front cover where careful six-year-old font spelled out "Miranda Jane Woodward" in pencil. Clutching the book, she curled onto the bed, pulled the blanket over her shoulders, and fell asleep.

Miranda woke suddenly, unsure of the time except that it was still dark and she was lying on a strange bed. She sat up a little too quickly and nearly fell off of the cot before she remembered that she was in a hidden room inside the old Henley House. Miranda reached for her phone, remembered that it didn't work, and groaned as she flipped on the little bedside lamp. The round clock read a little after 5am. Her back hurt where she'd fallen on it, and her legs ached from all the sprinting the night before, so she lay still on the mattress, letting herself adjust to the lamplight. Her *Alice* book lay on the floor where she'd dropped it sometime in the night. She sat up and pulled on her shoes. According to her watch, it had been about nine hours since she first fell through the Snag.

Grabbing her backpack, Miranda made her way downstairs, still amazed at the change in the house since the night of her birthday; in the lamplight from the landing, she could see striped purple wallpaper lining the stairwell, and the banisters felt smooth and freshly polished. The stairs creaked in a friendly way, like the house was wishing her a good morning. She smelled coffee and followed the welcome aroma into the kitchen.

Jake sat at the little table, reading a large book that looked like an atlas. He looked up at her and smiled. "Sleep well?"

"Yeah, I guess," she said. "Did you even sleep? It's way early."

"Yes, but I'm an early riser. Plus, someone needed to check and make sure we didn't have any visitors last night. The Snag looks totally undisturbed, by the way."

"Oh." She put her hands in her pockets and rocked back and forth on her feet. "How'd you tell?"

"I've got little, well, alarms that go off if certain Snags are used, and that one's been quiet since you came through. There's breakfast on the counter," Jake said, turning back to his atlas.

"Thanks," she said. It was strange—having a normal breakfast in what her classmates all thought of as a haunted house, with a friend of her father's that she'd only just met. Miranda picked up a banana and a bagel, poured a cup of coffee. Jake closed his book.

"If the snag was silent, I guess that means Bridget never came for me, either," Miranda said. Jake shook his head, and she thought he looked a little worried as well. "What do I do now?" she asked.

"Now we wait until daylight," he said.

"Then what?"

"Then you decide what you're going to do because I can't do it for you." He peered at her through his glasses as she carried the bagel and coffee back to the table.

"I thought you said you were going to help me," she said, plunking down opposite him.

"I am helping you," he replied. "I've given you shelter and advice, and I will give you more if you let me know what you need."

Miranda peeled her banana and ran through the list of things she needed. She needed her parents. She needed to be home. She needed to figure out what was happening to her. She needed to figure out why her dad had vanished and the only thing the Coast Guard found was a box with a spool of what looked like stuff from Snags. At this, she sat up straight, nearly choking on her banana in her excitement. Jake could see the Snags. He might be able to see the thread, too.

"Actually, there might be something you can help me with, since you're a friend of my dad's and all." Miranda reached under the table and pulled out her backpack, rummaging inside until she pulled out the little wooden box. "Do you know what this is?"

Jake leaned back in his chair, eyes fixed on the small object. "It's a box."

"Yes, but I think it was my dad's. It's got stuff inside, and I can't figure out what to do with it. I thought maybe you might know, since you're a librarian."

She pulled out the spool and the tiny scissors and set them on the table in front of him. She picked up her banana again while Jake looked in silence at the objects. He started to reach for them, but pulled his hand back quickly and didn't touch them. His face held a strange expression.

"Do you know what they are?" She turned the thread so that it shone a little in the overhead kitchen light.

"It's a sewing kit." Jake's voice sounded strained, and he hadn't taken his eyes off of the little objects.

"Yeah, but I don't think it's a regular sewing kit. I mean, look at the color of the thread."

"It is distinctive." He could see it, too! Jake finally looked up at her, and she had the distinct impression he was sizing her up, deciding just how much to say. He sighed. "Now, hear me out."

She raised an eyebrow at him. "So you *do* know something about them."

Threadwalkers

Chapter 10

"It's like this," Jake began. "Like I said before, I was your dad's librarian for years. Not just his librarian. I am his Librarian, capital L. I don't know who he had before, but I've managed his collection for a long time."

"What do you mean by Librarian? I mean, like what kind of librarian are you?" she asked.

"I maintain one of the research collections," he said. "You'll need them when you start looking for Edits, if you haven't already. You can look for inconsistencies in the books. Changes to stories or timelines. Sometimes changes are small, but if you see something you know isn't true, or shouldn't be, then you might have spotted an Edit."

"So I could look for changes in the books," Miranda said. Jake nodded. "And you have my dad's books, don't you? My mom wouldn't tell me what happened to them." Miranda looked back at the shelf over her shoulder.

"I managed his collection, yes, but most of it is gone, other than a handful of books that he left with me. I'm not sure what happened to it. It may have been one of the edits. But my collection always needs to have balance. If you take a book, you've got to leave a book behind. Pay it forward, so to speak."

"But what about—"

"Just listen," he said, shaking his head and holding up one finger. "I still don't know how much you know, but I doubt they'd have sent you Walking without some sort of knowledge. And you didn't completely lose it when you wound up here, so I've got to give you credit for that. Good job."

"Uh... thanks?"

"I'm not sure what your father found, but it had to be something big. He had a whole group of *them* after him. And they wanted whatever it was, or to stop him from using it. He came here, you know, right before... Well, he was looking for a place to stay for a while, to escape. He asked me to keep an eye out for you if anything happened to him, and he made sure I knew enough about you to recognize you. I thought he was being paranoid. I mean, everyone's had run-ins at some point or another, but he feared for his life.

"He had that box with him and told me, 'Miranda might be lost, and she might be scared, but she's smart and she'll figure it out.' And here you are. No you've got that stuff, and I think your father was right about you. I think whatever he was doing cost him everything, but that he intended for you to have that box.

"And I do have one more thing you may find helpful. At least, I hope it is." Jake opened one of the books beside his chair and pulled out a single white envelope. It was sealed and had no markings other than a single "M" on the front in her dad's boxy script.

"Is this...?" Miranda asked, holding the letter while her hands began to sweat.

"It is from your father. Open it in private; it's for you and only you."

They sat in silence for a moment as Miranda clutched the letter from her father, desperate to open it but also aware that she'd just been instructed to wait. Why did everything have to be so cryptic? The overhead light flickered off the scissors on the table, and she was struck by how they didn't seem to show fingerprints. The spool of thread was reflected in tiny form along the scissor blade.

"What's the thread for? How do I use it?" she asked.

"I have no idea," Jake said. "Your father didn't tell me how to use it. He was pretty vague about what exactly he'd found, to be honest. I think he was worried someone might come and try...but that's not the point. The point is, you need to figure out what your dad was doing. And you need to be careful who you trust. And wherever you go next, you shouldn't linger. I can't give you much help otherwise, except to say I had the utmost respect for your father, and if you need a Librarian, well... I have an opening." He looked at Miranda, his brown eyes intensely focused on her, until she had to look away, feeling herself flush.

"I need to go back," she said at last.

"I think so, yes." Jake looked up at her and nodded. "You've got a big job ahead of you, Miranda. "

Feeling a little shaky, Miranda gathered the spool and tiny scissors, placing them back into the box. She set it back into its spot in her backpack, and zipped it shut, keeping the letter in her sweaty hand. She wasn't going to wait another minute to read it.

She strode into the front room with all the bookshelves and sat down, trying to hold her hand steady while she tore open the envelope. It was short, and dated from a month before the plane crash. Seeing her father's handwriting again was like a fresh gut punch. Still, she read the message hungrily.

Dear Miranda,

I hope you are well on your way by now, though what I truly hope is that I have taken this back from Jake and you never read it. If you're receiving this, then things aren't going as I'd planned. Come to Oakland. You'll know where to find me. Look for our mutual Friend.

The past is present and future.

Love in all times,

Dad

Oakland? Why would he father send her to Oakland? She didn't know anyone in Oakland, but she had wanted to go there for a long, long time, for a very specific reason: the Oakland Aviation Museum. It had a whole exhibit about Women in Aviation, and Oakland was also where Amelia Earhart had left for her failed trip around the world in 1937. Her dad had promised to take her there someday so they could walk where the famous pilot herself walked. She had no idea what any of that had to do with her father or her current task, but if her dad wanted her to go to Oakland, the museum was as good a place to start. She folded the letter and slipped it into her backpack.

Jake appeared in the doorway. He didn't say anything, and she thought he looked far more worried than before; his eyebrows pinched together, and he kept picking at his sweater like a little kid. She turned away from him, looking up at the oil paintings for a moment before crossing to the closet that hid the trap door and passageway back to the cemetery.

"Follow the tunnel to the end, and you'll see the door from the inside," Jake said. "You should be able to find your way from there. I'll check from the front to make sure the coast is clear."

"Thanks, Jake," Miranda said.

Before she could turn the doorknob, Jake reached out and gave her a tight hug. "Please be careful," he said. She stiffened for a moment, then reached up and returned it, glad to have found a friend.

Miranda nodded, and pulled open the closet door. With Jake's help, she hauled open the trap door and descended into the tunnel, retracing their steps from the night before. Soon, she stepped through the mausoleum door and into a rosy sunrise, just beginning to show over the treetops in front of her. Miranda took a slow, deep breath, and headed back to the Snag.

As she walked the path, she pondered everything Jake told her, about her dad finding something that got him killed and about the people coming after her because of it, but the only thing he left her was, as Jake said, essentially a sewing kit.

What am I supposed to do with this? Does it have something to do with the Snags? Why wouldn't Dad tell Jake? Miranda wondered. *Surely some thread isn't worth dying over.*

Before long, Miranda stood in front of the gravestone that Jake showed her the night before. In the morning sunlight, she could still make out the spider-web thin strands that indicated where she Walked. She got down on her hands and knees and tried to see through it, but found herself staring at stone and grass and dirt. Feeling a little awkward even though no one could see her,

Miranda sat in front of the spot and tried envisioning the other side of the space. Nothing happened.

This is why they use actual doors, she thought.

Miranda knelt in front of the gravestone one more time and strained to listen for voices that might tell her if anyone was on the other side. She didn't hear anything, but with the birdsong coming from the forest, she wasn't sure that she'd be able to. In exasperation, she closed her eyes and took a determined step forward.

Her body squeezed through the cold thickness. She found herself standing beside the same gravestone, the sun setting on the other side of the cemetery. Ducking behind the stone, Miranda scooted along the ground in a crouch until she was about twenty feet away, then stood to check the entire area. The cemetery looked empty.

The sunset was rich with oranges and purples across the thick clouds, and Miranda walked across the crunching leaves toward the front gate, keeping an eye out for any movement. Still, it felt comforting to be back "home" in a way, even if she didn't have a place to go anymore, and she felt proud for getting herself back, too. When she reached the front gate, she pressed her back into the hedge and leaned around the corner, looking for Bridget's car. Her phone vibrated. Startled, she pulled it out of her pocket. The battery was almost dead, but she had about a dozen messages on the screen.

Where are you?

You should have been back by now. I'm coming to look for you.

Think I see company. Have to take off for a bit. Be back as soon as I can.

Seriously, where are you?

The last message was time-stamped at nine o'clock that morning, hours earlier. Had Bridget been waiting that whole time? Miranda quickly tapped the keyboard to reply, hoping her friend would be able to come get her.

Had to take a short Walk. Ready for pickup.

There wasn't an immediate response, so Miranda pulled on her coat and sat down with her back to the hedge. She knew it might take some time for Bridget to get there, especially after not hearing from her for most of a day. She didn't want to think about Bridget not coming, but the idea kept nagging at her. There wasn't a plan beyond "find Bridget," and Miranda didn't know what else to do. She considered walking over the hill to see her father's empty grave, but as she made up her mind, her phone buzzed again.

Be right there.

Miranda stretched and got to her feet as a car came into view. It wasn't Bridget's car. She pressed herself into the prickly hedge, ignoring the branch digging into her back, as a dark sedan cruised into the cemetery. She could barely make out the driver and a passenger, and they seemed to be looking from side to side along the driveway. Feeling grateful for her dark coat, she hoped that they would back out again; if they turned around, the headlights would be right on her. As the car got almost level with the footpath, her phone vibrated again. She punched the button to silence it, but saw the message.

Where are you? Don't see you.

She sank into a squat as the car started to pull around the circle at the top of the hill. Bridget couldn't be in the dark sedan. She'd have rolled down the window, or told Miranda that she'd be in a different car. So where was Bridget? Something must have happened. What if these people had caught Bridget and taken her phone? Miranda felt her chest tighten, but she knew she ought to get further out of sight.

Keeping as close to the hedge as possible, Miranda began inching back toward trees on the other side of the cemetery, trying not to make any sound. She reached the low fence at the corner just as the car swung around to head back out the gate. For a heart-stopping moment that sent her heart into her throat, the beam came within a few feet of her, and then was gone.

Taking a deep breath, Miranda hoisted herself over the fence and dashed into the forest. She heard voices from the cemetery and huddled behind a fallen tree. The voices sound like two men, and she peered through the branches of the downed tree as they walked right up to the fence with flashlights. Miranda ducked, hoping they hadn't seen her, and held her breath. The footsteps retreated, and she heard the slamming of two car doors. After a minute, the car turned left out of the cemetery and barreled down the road.

Taking a deep breath for the first time in several long minutes, Miranda pulled her phone out of her pocket and reread the messages. She'd assumed they were all from Bridget, but Jake had told her not to trust anyone. Seized by an impulse, she popped the back off her phone and pulled out the battery, then shoved the phone back into one pocket, the battery in the other. She'd read online that killing the power to a phone made it impossible to use the GPS to find it, even if you could turn it on remotely. Hopefully, that would stop anyone who might be tracking her.

The forest was already dark, with the night shadows clinging to its roots. Crickets and frogs chorused, though before long, the nighttime temperatures would be too cold for them. As she walked along the fence line and away from the road, Miranda wondered what she ought to do next. With Jake back in the past and Bridget gone, she was alone, and the thought terrified her. She didn't know how to get to Oakland without any money, and she didn't have any food. Gathering supplies seemed to be the next most obvious choice while she figured out transportation. But where could she go without being seen?

Chapter 11

Drawing level with a gap in the trees that overlooked a low place in the cemetery, Miranda looked down at the mausoleum. Maybe it was still an entrance to the old house? After all, how long ago could that have been? She strained, looking for movement in that direction, but the grounds were too dark to see anything. Still she waited as long as she could, thankful for the breakfast with Jake but wishing she'd eaten another bagel. Once she decided that the vehicle wasn't coming right back, she hopped the fence back into the cemetery.

A few minutes later, Miranda stood in front of the small marble building, staring at the thick, sealed stone door. Dropping her backpack, she pressed her hand against the stone Jake showed her, but it didn't move. Shoving her fingertips into the minuscule seam, she tried to pry it open, but with no luck. In frustration, she kicked it, regretting her impulsiveness almost instantly, as the stone sent a shock of pain through her toe and up her leg. Miranda leaned against the door. How did Jake make it work? Why hadn't she paid closer attention?

The air grew chilly, and Miranda wrapped her coat tighter around herself, shivering against the cold marble. The stone felt good and solid against her back while she considered her next move. Without knowing for sure that Bridget was safe, she couldn't risk texting or calling. She didn't have transportation, and she didn't know where to go. Feeling overwhelmed, she pounded her fists against the door. Still nothing.

"There's got to be a way in there," she muttered.

Miranda took a step back and examined the wall again, but knew that in the darkness there was a good chance she wouldn't see anything at all, and that she might have to wait out the night. The thought made her skin crawl. Just as she was about to scoop up her bag and head back toward the road, something caught her eye. It was the tiniest wisp of something, like the thin strands coming from the Snag where she'd fallen through earlier, but these were coming from the wall. They looked like streamers coming from a very tiny spot about shoulder-height from the ground, exactly where Jake put her hand. Miranda walked slowly up to it. Trying not to hope, she raised her hand to the spot and pressed. The door swung open about three inches. Miranda grabbed her bag, and pried the door open the rest of the way, ducking inside and pulling the handle to close the heavy door behind her.

For a moment, she stood in complete darkness, but then one of the overhead lights sputtered to life, and she was able to see the steps in front of her. It was dim and cobwebs covered the walls. Taking care not to slip, Miranda made her way down. The light grew dim until she was in near darkness at the foot of the stairs. Instinctively, she reached for the wall, and after feeling around a bit came across a light switch.

Old bulbs lit up the passageway. Miranda blinked in the light, then set off down the tunnel toward the house, hoping the other end of the passage was still in one piece. After several minutes, she reached the wooden door. She pushed the handle and stepped into the darkness as the passageway light turned off behind her. Careful to close the trap door behind her, she stepped through the closet and into the living room. It looked just as it had the night of her birthday, one sofa upended and worn, and broken bottles piled in the fireplace. She shuddered and walked down the hall to the kitchen.

The place was a wreck. Huge cracks ran along the black and white tile floors. The table lay on its side, its pedestal leg snapped in half. The appliances were gone, leaving gaping holes where they once stood, loose wires dangling from abandoned and stripped outlets. Most of the cabinet doors were missing, and the few left hung crookedly. She left the kitchen and headed back to the entryway.

Miranda crept up the bowed main stairs to the library and swung open the door. Inside, the room looked like a disaster. The curtains lay in piles on the floor, a few tattered bits dangling from the rods. Most of the shelves were empty, the books either ripped apart or half burned. The armchairs were on their sides, one of them slashed open in the seat with bits of stuffing spilling onto the floor. The whole place smelled stale and damp.

Miranda stood in the doorway for several minutes. She wondered how long it had been like this; she didn't think anyone had been there in a while. Without going inside, she turned to face the guest room. The hidden panel hung on its side, the room wide open. The bed was flipped and the mattress lay in the corner, covered in dust. The chair was broken into several pieces, and otherwise the room was empty. Miranda sighed and walked back into the library.

She flipped the armchairs onto their feet. The one with the missing stuffing seemed to be pretty much destroyed, but the other chair wasn't in bad shape, and Miranda sank into it, debating her next move. At least up here she was out of sight and warm. She hoped no one else had a reason to come there that night, and wondered if the people in the sedan knew about the house. How long would she be stuck inside before she could make a break for it? She also wondered what happened to Jake. Of course, it could be a decade or more since she'd seen him here, but what would make him leave the place like this? The destruction made her think it had been searched at some point, though it was hard to tell how long ago.

While taking stock of her options, Miranda carefully rehung the library curtains, sealing off the windows before trying the lamps. To her surprise, one of them turned on, and she smiled to herself. In the lamplight, she picked up the nearest books. They were the first things she wanted to check, to see if any of the books might be of help. Jake told her that they were for research, but she didn't really know where to begin. Miranda scanned the book covers, but most were the atlases and old history books. The paperbacks were almost all gone, other than a few pages of *Peter Pan*, and the biographies were nearly all missing. She soon had all the remaining books on the shelf, though it made her sad to realize so few were left.

In the far corner, she found one of the blankets from the guest room. It smelled a little musty, but didn't seem to have anything wrong with it, so she shook it out and carried back it into the room. She flipped the bed frame into place and hauled the mattress back on top of it, then made the bed before heading back into the library.

Finally, Miranda carried the last two books to the shelf between the chairs. The shelf stood out a little from the wall, and she started to shove it back into place, but something kept the shelf from moving. She looked behind it and saw a small wooden door wedged open. Curious, she pulled the bookshelf forward to expose it.

It turned out to be a cabinet. The small, cubical space was empty except for a single, thin paperback book in the very back. She pulled it out. It was a kids' biography of Amelia Earhart. Scrawled across the inside cover she saw:

Just in case. --J

Remembering what Jake said about leaving a book if you take a book, she grabbed her backpack and retrieved the copy of *A Wrinkle in Time*. She set it on the shelf beside the pages of *Peter Pan*, and stepped back to look at it. She felt a bit better. She then carefully closed the cabinet door, and sat down in the remaining chair, clutching the little biography. She opened the book and started skimming, but everything inside seemed just as she'd remembered it. After several minutes of increasingly forceful page turning, she snapped it shut in frustration. She already knew to go to Oakland, so why had Jake left her this biography? Why couldn't anyone just give her a straight answer?

Miranda looked around the room. Other than the odd charring on some of the books, she couldn't figure out what happened to the library, or to Jake. She thought for a moment about going back through the Snag to warn him, but she didn't relish the thought of being exposed at night again so soon. It also occurred to her that telling him might count as an Edit, too. The thought of being hidden was comforting, and she didn't want to risk anything unnecessary.

Miranda yawned. She didn't know what time it was, or how long she'd been awake, but now that she felt somewhat safe, the last few days were hitting her hard, and exhaustion turning her body into lead, but more than anything, she was dying of thirst.

Miranda went downstairs to the kitchen, making sure carrying her bag with her. She leaned over the sink, reaching for the faucet. Now, she wondered whether the water would even be on, and if it was, whether it would be safe to drink from.

"Miranda?" a woman's voice asked behind her.

Miranda screamed and pivoted, almost falling into the solid countertop. A middle-aged woman caught her by the arm with a firm grip. "Steady on there, girl. You don't want to get a concussion. We don't have a lot of time."

Miranda eyed the woman. Her short, silver hair looked like it might once have been very dark because her eyebrows were still striking and prominent. Her clothes looked like an old uniform, with pressed black pants and a matching shirt, the sleeves rolled to her elbows. Her black boots were caked with mud, and as Miranda watched, she put her hand on the wall as if to steady herself. Miranda's heart pounded.

"Miranda, I need you to listen to me. My name is Hestia. I'm a friend of your father's, and you need to get out of here."

"Why? What's wrong?" Miranda asked quickly.

"They're coming," the woman said urgently, glancing toward the front door. "They'll be here soon."

"Who's 'they'?" Miranda asked.

Before Hestia could answer, someone knocked on the front door. Hestia put her finger to her lips and motioned for Miranda to follow before walking out to the hallway. When they reached the living room, Hestia pointed her inside. Miranda ducked to the side of the living room door where anyone at the front porch wouldn't see her. She heard Hestia's footsteps stop, and then a soft gasp. The woman came back into the living room.

"We've got to go. *Now.*" Hestia snatched up what Miranda assumed must have been her satchel from the living room floor and strode to the closet and the trap door that would take them back to the mausoleum.

"Who's out there?" Miranda whispered.

"Someone neither of us wants to see," Hestia hissed. She yanked open the trap door and moved for Miranda to climb down the stairs first. "Just walk straight to the end, and be quick."

Threadwalkers

Chapter 12

Miranda's feet hit the dirt floor in the dark passageway, but she stepped to the side to pull out her small flashlight as Hestia pulled the trap door shut and dropped beside her. Silently, with heads bent to give them clearance, the two of them made their way through the narrow tunnel. Miranda kept her free hand on the wall to help her footing, and they soon reached the shallow stone stairs leading to the exit and the cemetery.

"Go on. I'll catch up, but I want to try and seal this a little better first," Hestia murmured. "We'll be followed, but maybe I can delay them. Meet me at the far side gate, past the old section of the cemetery."

Miranda opened the mausoleum door. It had rained at some point, leaving the ground slick with pools of murky water in the low spaces between hillocks. Miranda didn't hang around, but tromped across the muddy ground, heading toward the little metal gate on the edge of the forest. She had seen this little gate earlier that morning, when the sky was still clear. Now she lifted the latch and slipped through, ducking into the cover of the thick underbrush on the other side. The wind began to pick up and water droplets shook from the trees, making the woods sound like they had their own private shower. The air smelled like it might condense into another downpour at any moment, and Miranda flinched as a droplet ran down the back of her neck.

Just then, Hestia came over the rise. She was panting and kept glancing over her shoulder. When the older woman got to the gate, she leaned on it, catching her breath. Miranda moved closer to her, but Hestia shook her head, waving away any offer of help. After a moment, she got up and stumbled under the tree cover, heading farther into the woods. Miranda looked back into the cemetery, expecting a shadowy figure in black leather to appear at any moment. She thought of the phone and its battery sitting in her pocket, but decided not to mention it for the time being.

"We need to get out of sight," she said.

"I know," Hestia answered, nodding. "Do you have any idea where you're supposed to go next?"

"No.... Well, maybe. I'm not sure. But I feel like I need to find out what happened to my dad. What really happened?" Miranda took a deep breath. She wasn't ready to tell anyone else about Oakland.

"Then let's go find out what happened to your dad," Hestia said. She took Miranda's elbow and led her toward the front gate of the cemetery. Failing to see any cars, they started on the road back toward town.

Hestia led them to a small house on the very edge of Henley. Miranda hadn't noticed it before, and if she had, would have assumed it was abandoned, but Hestia pulled out a key and, with a last glance down the house's empty driveway, opened the door. Miranda followed her inside.

The curtains to the house were heavy, drawn tightly across the windows, and there wasn't a sliver of sunlight coming through them. Hestia turned on a couple of lamps, and Miranda found herself standing in a tiny sitting room with a small folding table and narrow door through which she could see a counter with a sink and a fridge along one wall.

"It's small, but it's home," Hestia said.

"Thanks for helping me," Miranda said. "I don't really have anywhere else to go right now."

Hestia shrugged. "I'm just here to do my part of this job so I can get back to being dead."

"You don't look dead," Miranda said.

"How kind of you!" Hestia laughed. "No, I'm not dead yet, but I've managed to make almost everyone think I am for quite a while now. Living beyond my own Thread and all of that." Her laugh stopped abruptly and she looked serious again. "Now then, we are limited in what we can do at the moment. You know by now there are people looking for you. Before too long they will track you down again, so we can't stay here. They've got your whole Thread monitored."

"My what?"

"You Thread. Everything associated with you, your history, your timeline. That's what we call it. And at the end of your Thread, well, you end up back there somewhere," Hestia said, motioning to the far wall, though Miranda knew she meant the cemetery they'd just left.

"But how could they find me?"

"They weren't far behind us, and I wouldn't trust that they don't know about my house. And then there's the other thing--you're Samuel Woodward's daughter! You're likely to go where he went, and believe me, they put a lot of effort into finding out where he went."

"Why?"

"He's valuable," Hestia said. "Now then, you're already good enough at Walking, though I suspect you have to work quite hard at it still."

Miranda didn't mention accidentally going through Snags like she had when she found Jake, and tried to keep her expression blank. Hestia must have taken it for agreement because she nodded.

"Normal. It takes a lot of time and practice to be able to pass through without much effort. I've even heard the occasional Walker claiming to have fallen through by accident and then needing to find their way back! Ha!" Hestia shook her head, and Miranda tried her best to look incredulous as well. "Now, you were about to get a drink when we had to vamoose. Let me get you a cup of water and see if we can find you something to eat around here."

Hestia stood up and marched to the kitchen where she started rummaging in cabinets. Miranda shivered, her rain-dampened clothes letting the chill into her so that her skin felt clammy and her shirt stuck to her. In a few moments, Hestia gave her a glass of water. Going back into the kitchen, the older woman produced a pan and a lighter from the back recesses of a cabinet. She quickly lit a single burner and dumped a can of condensed chicken soup into the pan. Still shivering, Miranda walked back to the main room and curled up on one of the chairs. After a while, Hestia came into the room and handed her a steaming mug.

"Have some soup."

Miranda took the soup and felt her hands warm. When she took a small sip, the steaming, oniony broth scalded the roof of her mouth, but she didn't care. It tasted wonderful as she felt its warmth blanket her insides. Hestia reached into a satchel sitting on the floor beside her. She pulled out a lightweight sweater and tossed it over to Miranda. Miranda took off her jacket and pulled the sweater over her head. Between the soup and the sweater, Miranda's shivering started to subside.

"Now then," Hestia said, settling into the chair opposite with her own mug of soup. "I know you can't be far into your training, but clearly it's enough that you're traveling on your own. Don't look at me like that," she laughed. "Some things are always the same. You sought out help for the things you were seeing, and now you're trying to sort things out on your own."

Miranda didn't say anything, but took another sip from the mug. She desperately wanted to seem as confident as this woman. Hestia's easy manner, the way she acted like she owned the room, chair, or whatever space she occupied, was fascinating. Miranda started envisioning herself as an experienced Threadwalker, lounging on a chair and explaining things to the new kid. Her thoughts came back to the present as Hestia continued.

"The important thing is to figure out where you are and how I can help. I know you need help."

"Can you really help me?" Miranda asked. Her hope soared. Maybe Hestia would give her actual answers instead of riddles. Maybe she they could go to Oakland together!

"I have experience, I have contacts, and right now I'm probably the only person in your life who knows who you are and what you're going through. There's more, of course, but what else do you need?"

Miranda considered this. She watched the older woman stir her soup with a large spoon and taste it, then shrug to herself and start eating, unaware or uninterested in Miranda watching her. Help was more than she could have dared to hope, considering she had no real plan yet on how to get to Oakland.

"Have you given any thought to the problem?" Hestia spoke, and Miranda jumped.

"What problem?" she asked, wondering briefly if this woman might already know that she needed to get to California.

"Of where to go next?" Hestia asked.

Of course, only Miranda had read the letter. Not even Jake had read it. She was the only one who knew where her dad wanted her to go. Maybe that was how it was meant to be? She felt confused, and a little bit torn. Part of her wanted to just confide everything to Hestia and see what ideas the woman might have. But, part of Miranda believed she was supposed to go alone.

Hestia got up and took the empty mugs to the kitchen; Miranda heard water running in the sink. Curious about the experienced Walker, Miranda stole over to the other chair, where Hestia's satchel lay. The initials HL were pressed into the front of the leather. With another quick glance to make sure Hestia wasn't coming right back, she flipped it open.

File folders crammed into the narrow bag, their tops bent from the bag's flap over them. The labels seemed to be in some kind of chronological order, though the dates weren't specific, mostly just "Before the company started" or "During the drought" and the like. She pulled out a file from the middle of the stack. The selected file turned out to be a collection of newspaper clippings from the 1980s. They didn't seem to have much in common, but one had a grainy picture of the author, an older man with a thick mustache. Miranda glanced at the other articles and noticed they were all written by the same man. They were short, maybe three or four paragraphs apiece, and covered innocuous events in the man's local community.

"School's Fall Festival Raises $3,406"

"Record-breaking Rain Bad for Pumpkin Crop"

"Local Scouts Build Bat Houses"

Miranda skimmed the last article about bats, and how encouraging bats to house in the neighborhood would cut down on the mosquito population, but she didn't see how anything like that might be important. She skimmed the others, too, but they didn't seem to be connected, except by the author. Miranda studied the photo, but the details were fuzzy. She kept thumbing through the articles. Then, at the bottom of the pile she found a single photograph. It was a faded picture of the writer. He had silvery hair and a prominent mustache, and he stood in front of a boxy brown car wearing very short shorts and a striped shirt. A teenage boy stood with him, grinning at the camera. Miranda studied it for a moment, then flipped it and found that someone had scrawled the date on the back: November 2, 1986. She closed the file and slid it back into place, as near to where she pulled it as she could guess, and closed the satchel.

"Finding anything?" Hestia asked, making her jump.

"You snuck up on me!" Miranda snapped. She felt herself go hot with mortification at being caught snooping through someone else's things.

"Maybe you should have better situational awareness," Hestia said. "You'd know what's happening around you."

"Maybe you shouldn't try to scare the crap out of me all the time," Miranda shot back, her embarrassment making her defensive. "You did that on purpose."

"The files are from my own investigations," Hestia said, ignoring the comment as she opened the satchel herself, "and won't make much sense to you, but you've got the right idea about looking into things. After all, investigating everything around you is how you find the good info. Though I recommend this file here, in the back. You'll find it much more... contemporary."

Miranda took the offered file and went back to her chair while Hestia pulled out another file for herself. They settled across from each other once more. As she turned the folder over to open it from the front, her heart leaped into her throat: her father's name, "Samuel Woodward," was scrawled across the top of the blue folder.

Miranda opened it. On top of the stack, she found a copy of the obituary, and a copy of the photo that her mother submitted for it. Looking at it was like a gut punch and she inhaled sharply, then set aside the pieces aside and looked at the next piece of paper. It was a shopping list for one of their camping trips. She recognized it because her father always got the same things: powdered eggs, jerky, tortillas, and peanut butter. At the bottom he'd scrawled "Pop Tarts," and she smiled knowing that this list was written to include her younger self.

The next entry in the file was a little stranger, a page torn from a book. Miranda read it through, but didn't recognize it, so she kept flipping. The rest of the folder contained old notes in her father's handwriting, jumbled phrases like he'd been taking down messages to remind himself of things later. She found a few more photos, including one of her old school photos that came from his wallet and one from a camping trip when she was a little girl. There were a couple of newspaper clippings, including a version of the article about the crash that she'd read online, but the date hadn't been included in the clipping. Then in the bottom, she found one more photo. This one she knew well; it hung in the hallway for years until her mother took it down the day of the funeral. It was her parents' wedding picture, strange and somehow more real outside of its usual frame. Her mother's long hair tumbled around her beaming face, and her father was clean-shaven and looked a little scared but excited. Miranda smiled at them, took it and lay it in her lap.

"Can I keep this?"

"If you must," Hestia said.

"Where did you get this stuff? And why?"

"I collected it."

"Okay..." Miranda watched Hestia, but the woman's face was inscrutable. "That's it?"

"That's it. I collect information that might be useful. There's not much about your dad left anymore, but that's what I've got. I don't need it anymore, either."

"Why not?"

"Because I've found you," Hestia said.

"Oh." Miranda looked down at the file in her lap. The swooping excitement she'd felt was replaced by the familiar leaden knot. She still didn't know what to do, and she didn't want to disappoint Hestia. Maybe she would tell her about Oakland after all...

"You'll figure out what you need to do," Hestia said. Miranda looked up, and for the first time, she saw Hestia's face soften. "I am sorry you lost him."

Hestia stood and beckoned for Miranda to follow. She led the way to a small bedroom behind the kitchen, and left Miranda there to change into dry clothes. As soon as Miranda was in dry jeans and one of Bridget's sweatshirts, she spread everything from the folder with her father's name on it across the double bed, wanting to look at them without Hestia watching her.

More than anything, Miranda to find a clear connection or message that might tie to Oakland, or to anywhere else he might have left a clue. She looked at the camping photo and the notes, but she didn't remember much of anything about that specific trip. The obituary and the other clipped article she placed on the left, the scraps of notes on the right, and the photos all in the middle together. After staring at the photos for a few minutes, she decided to start by reading the newspaper clipping she hadn't seen before.

*New Earhart Exhibit Opens at the
National Air and Space Museum*

A new exhibit of artifacts all relating to Amelia Earhart is set to open on Friday. Earhart, famous for being the first woman to circumnavigate the earth and known for her celebrated Flight Academy for Women, is to be featured in next year's focus on aviation of the last century. The collection is partly on loan from a private owner who has been collecting the objects for years, and wants to share his own findings with the public for the first time.

Artifacts include clothes, flight gear, and even a journal kept by Earhart herself where she recounted the lead up to World War II and the fight to allow female pilots a chance to serve alongside their male counterparts.

The article continued, but Miranda fixated on the last sentence. She knew Amelia Earhart vanished while flying around the world. Everyone knew that. That and the fact the pilot didn't have anything to do with World War II was one of the first things she'd ever learned about Earhart.

Miranda plunged her hand into her backpack and pulled out the little biography that she'd found in the library. Flipping to the last chapter, she found what she was looking for. Sure enough, the biography confirmed what she knew to be the case: Amelia Earhart had vanished on July 2, 1937. The article didn't match. *She'd spotted an Edit.* A thrill ran up her spine, and she almost squealed with excitement. Her father must have been working on something with the pilot's disappearance!

Miranda remembered her father had taken her to the National Air and Space Museum in Washington, DC when she was eight because she wanted to look at the old space shuttle on exhibit in the giant hanger. He walked her around to all the other planes and rockets as well, explaining as much history as her attention span could handle. Of all the things he told Miranda that day, the story of Amelia Earhart stuck with her the most, and it was the start of her fascination with the famous pilot and her own flying ambitions.

As a kid, she liked to picture Amelia living the rest of her life on a tropical island somewhere, though the older she got, the more she thought the theory about the small plane crashing into the ocean might be closer to the truth. But what if there was more to her father's story than that? Was it like Jake said about reading kids' books like *Peter Pan*? Had he been telling her about the Threadwalkers, even back then? Strange to think her dad had disappeared with a plane crash, too. Maybe it wasn't so much a coincidence after all.

Miranda reluctantly set down the biography and turned to the four photos: the photo of the camping trip, the wedding photo, a picture of her with both of her parents at a miniature golf place she didn't remember, and her third grade elementary school photo. She checked the back of each. Living with her mother taught her long ago that notes on the backs provided dates and maybe even the location a photograph was taken. Sure enough, the school photo read "Miranda, Age 9" and featured her own jagged signature, one of her first cursive attempts. The miniature golf photo was blank on the back, and the wedding photo had the date stamped in red ink, which made her think it was a photographer's proof. The camping photo, though, had a date that placed her at age five, with "Peaks of Otter" on the back. In it, she stood in a creek, grasping her father's hand.

Miranda remembered a little bit about the trip, though she suspected the memories might be more from stories her parents told her and the fact they'd camped at Peaks of Otter several times during her childhood. It was along the Blue Ridge Parkway, not too far of a drive from where her family lived, and doable in a weekend. The whole family used to wade in the icy creek at the campground, and she remembered eating cold Pop Tarts for breakfast while her dad scrambled eggs and her mom made instant coffee for them. Those mornings were some of her favorite memories, and she smiled as she touched each of their faces. But these didn't get her closer to figuring out the task at hand.

This much was clear: her father had left a task for her to finish. Having that knowledge was keeping Miranda calm, and giving her what determination she could muster. A mission meant direction, and direction felt better than sitting alone in an old house, hiding from people she didn't even know.

"What were you trying to tell me, Dad?" she whispered. "What's out there?"

Miranda gathered all the paper and photos back into the file folder and slid it back into her backpack with the Amelia Earhart biography. A question was bothering her, and she thought Hestia might be the one to answer it, or to at least point her in the right direction, if she could ask directly. With a deep breath, she headed back into the living room, where the older woman sat, leafing through yet another file folder.

"There's something I want to know," Miranda said, trying to match the older woman's straight, confident posture.

Hestia closed the folder and sat up. "And what is that?"

"How do you see an Edit?" It was the thing she'd been wondering about since the Tailor first mentioned that it was happening to her, and she wanted desperately to know why nobody else in her life noticed the changes happening.

"What do you mean?"

"I mean, if someone Edits something, how can you be sure? Unless you see them do it?"

"Well, most people don't notice, for one," Hestia said. "Why are you asking?"

"Academic reasons," Miranda said, waving her hand. "But what if you *do* notice something change?"

"Then it's probably something that directly affects you," Hestia replied. "Seeing an Edit that doesn't directly affect your own Thread is very rare. Almost unheard of."

"But possible?"

"Possible."

"And how would you stop someone from Editing something?"

"That is the tricky part. First, you'd have to make sure that you were the one in the right and that they were, in fact, in the wrong. It's possible, for instance, that whatever they changed was meant to be."

"So, you're saying... sometimes it's okay to let people Edit things? That's not what... everyone else has said." She studied Hestia's face with some interest. The Tailor had made Edits sound like they were completely wrong, but Hestia made it sound like more of a gray area. Maybe it wasn't so clear-cut after all. And Hestia would know; from the sound of things, she'd been out there actually Walking. The Tailor seemed to spend all his time in his shop.

"I'm saying it's important to know how things are supposed to happen, and then to let them take their course," Hestia continued. "Not acting is as much a decision as taking action, and you need to learn to recognize the difference." Hestia set down the file she'd been holding. "Incidentally, it's very hard to know what to fix in your own Thread, or to do anything about it if you think there's been a change."

"Why?"

"For one, your past self might see you, or notice a change, and panic. It's against the rules. Don't interfere in your own Thread."

"But then how am I supposed to fix my Thread?"

"You keep someone else from interfering," Hestia said. "Or if that doesn't work, you get someone to help you fix it. You make sure things happen the way they're meant to, and things should work out fine."

"But how will I know?"

"You know your own life, yes?"

"Yeah...."

"Then you know how it's supposed to go." Hestia stood. "I hope that answers your question. But now I have one for you: what happens if you *can't* see an Edit in your own life?"

Miranda's hadn't even thought of that. She started to panic. "So this whole thing is impossible?"

"Not impossible. You've just got to be cleverer than other people. Don't believe what people tell you. They might be lying or they might not know something has been Edited. You've got to see things for yourself, always." Hestia shrugged. "That's both the easiest and hardest thing about all of this, that you can only trust your own eyes, your own research. And your instincts."

Miranda wanted to say that her instincts were confusing at the best of times, and hadn't been quite right since losing her dad. But she knew Hestia was right about one thing—they needed to keep moving.

"I have an idea," Miranda began. Her thoughts were on the contents of her father's file, and the supply list and the photos. "We need to get out of here and go someplace they wouldn't really expect. What if we go camping?"

Miranda sat with her cheek pressed against the cold glass of the car window, picking at the bar code sticker that marked the car as a rental. Hestia hadn't said anything for the past few hours as they drove across the northern part of the state toward Virginia. Fading autumn leaves blew across the road, blending into an amber-red patchwork as they flew past. She shivered despite the car's heater turned toward her and folded her arms across herself, tucking her hands beneath her elbows.

Miranda felt relieved she'd made a habit out of carrying her bag everywhere with her, even when she expected to stay somewhere. The weight of it comforted her, settling onto her shoulders as she walked or ran. She glanced down at the bag sitting on her feet, glad that the little box inside remained secret.

Hestia didn't look at Miranda much while she drove, and Miranda would have felt more comfortable with at least some random conversation, but she couldn't think of anything to talk about. How do you make small talk with someone who has spent an unknown amount of their life stepping through thin places in the fabric of space-time? "So, have you ever been to a classic World Series game?" didn't get much response. Even more oddly, Hestia seemed to know where they were headed, but she hadn't given Miranda anything but vague answers when pressed on where this knowledge came from.

"We'll get to the park late tonight if we drive straight through," Hestia said as they climbed into the car rented using I.D.s and credit cards for someone named "Susan Goodwright." Miranda kept expecting someone to burst into the room to try and grab them, but the rental agency handed Hestia the keys to a little white coupe, and they drove away without incident. Now, Miranda glanced every so often at the woman whose silver hair was mussed, her eyes hidden behind large sunglasses, wondering if she'd made the right decision.

"So, do you know anything about your father's death?" Hestia asked, her eyes flicking toward Miranda for a moment.

"Not really," Miranda answered. "When he disappeared, the Coast Guard just sent us back his wallet." She wasn't ready to tell Hestia about the box and the spool, not yet. "How long were you friends with my dad?"

"Oh, for a very long time. Right up to the end," Hestia said. She glanced at Miranda. "I know this is hard for you." She fixed her gaze once more on the road ahead. "You're on the run, and you're not even sure who you're running from. Your family is gone, and I can't give you any answers because if you aren't ready for them, it could ruin everything. You've got to learn as you go, I'm afraid."

"Ruin everything?"

"Your training, of course," Hestia said. "There's a lot at stake, but I don't want you to get in over your head before you fully understand everything about the Walkers and Editors. You've got to be ready to act, but you need time to process, to wrap your mind around it."

"I'll never wrap my mind around this," Miranda muttered. To her surprise, Hestia laughed.

"That's probably true," she said, glancing at Miranda with the kindest smile she'd seen yet from the woman. "I am sorry about all of this."

Miranda shrugged. "I wish I could do something about it."

"You are!" Hestia motioned to the car. "We're going somewhere. You're taking action! Even if you don't know where it'll take you yet, doing something is always better than doing nothing."

"I guess so."

"We'll figure this out together, Miranda. You'll see." Hestia reached out and put her hand on top of Miranda's, giving it a gentle squeeze before letting go and returning to the wheel. Miranda found the gesture comforting, like something her mom might do. The sudden thought of her mother's disappearance hit Miranda like a brick wall, and she struggled to take a deep breath. She'd been running so much in the last few days, she hadn't thought much about her mom, and guilt pulsed between the surges of grief, but she tried to fight both feelings back. She needed to stay strong, to stay alive, to rescue her mother. Her father might be gone, but if she could just fix her life and get her mother back, things might be kind of okay. Things had to be okay.

"Is there anything else you want to talk about?" Hestia asked, again reminding Miranda forcibly of her mother.

Miranda thought about all the things that went through her mind over the last several days, about the letter and the spool with the thread only other Threadwalkers could see, and all the strange things she'd experienced and sighed. "I don't know."

Hestia went back to driving, looking straight ahead, but every so often glancing at Miranda and at the backpack sitting on the floorboard.

It took them more four hours to get to the Peaks Lodge in Virginia, and by then, it was well past sunset and the temperatures outside were already dropping. The lodge's lobby had a high, open ceiling with exposed wooden beams and a wooden desk with two women working off a single computer. While Hestia approached the desk, Miranda ducked into the gift shop beside them and wandered through it, looking at the bear figurines and sweatshirts. After a while, her lack of sleep began to catch up with her and she felt herself fading. She wandered back into the lobby and leaned against the counter beside Hestia.

"I'm sorry, but we're all booked," one of the women was saying. "I think we might have an opening tomorrow."

"And there's nothing you can do for us?" Hestia pressed. The woman behind the counter shook her head.

"That's okay," Miranda said. "We'll just go back to the car and try somewhere else."

They walked back outside, and Hestia sat on the hood of the car, taking out a map to look for somewhere with a room available. Miranda kept walking, trying to decide what to do next. They hadn't picked up camping supplies, and the night was getting colder. She took the little side trail beside the lodge that led to the lake and a walking trail there.

The moonlight reflected on the still lake surface. Sharp Top Mountain left its triangular silhouette against the sky behind it. Miranda walked along the lake edge, watching the occasional ripple in the water from a breeze or animal, though the cold air ensured a still and quiet night. About a quarter of the way around the lake, she drew level with a side path that turned toward the mountain. Miranda thought she saw movement out of the corner of her eye. She stopped and peered into the darkness, hoping her vision would adjust and she'd be able to see whatever it was. When nothing happened, she kept going around the lake.

A few minutes later, she saw the movement again. This time she whirled to face it, taking a step closer and straining to hear anything. Still nothing appeared, but it looked like there might be a trail head just there, or that the same trail curved along the foot of the mountain. Glancing around at the empty lake path, she ducked into the trees and toward the spot.

The ground was soft and leaves crunched under her feet as she turned in place, looking up and down the trail. She didn't hear any animal sounds, not even a late cricket, but she thought there might be an odd smell. Thinking of skunks, she moved a little further down the path, making sure she could still just see the lake through the trees. A pale patch of moonlight shone on the ground at her feet.

Miranda shoved her hands in her pockets. Memories from childhood bubbled up as she listened to the sounds of the forest, slightly muted for the autumn, but still there, singing the chorus of night. She wondered if it was a good idea, coming here. Maybe the Editors would think to come here. Should she just break down and tell Hestia about Oakland? Miranda leaned on one of the trees, listening to the rustle of leaves and the gentle lapping from the lakeside. She froze as she heard a voice hiss.

"Miranda?" Hestia stepped out of the shadows. Miranda relaxed and stepped toward her. "Where have you been?" the older woman asked. "I saw you go down this way, and then you disappeared. I thought... It's not important. Find anything?"

"Not really," Miranda said, shrugging. "I don't know. I just don't think this is right. It didn't feel right."

"We can leave again in the morning." Hestia patted Miranda's shoulder.

Miranda followed her back to the car. Something in Miranda's gut told her she shouldn't tell Hestia about the letter. She liked Hestia more and more as they spent the day together, but she kept coming back to the idea that this was really a journey just for her. The letters were for her eyes only, and not even Jake had opened the envelope he'd been keeping all that time. She wasn't going to tell Hestia or anybody else about her father's gift unless she absolutely had to.

For now she'd wait and see how much she could learn from this other woman. Then, when she had a chance, she'd cut loose (and maybe take a credit card) and book a flight to Oakland. Or maybe Hestia would just take her to the airport and not ask questions. *And in any case,* she thought, *this has to have thrown any of those Editors off my track. So, either way it's good.* Satisfied that she was in the right, at least on some level, she turned to Hestia who put down the map.

"Any luck?" she asked.

"Well, there are a whole bunch of campgrounds along the Parkway. It's just a matter of picking one."

Miranda took the map and peered at it under the car's overhead light. Hestia watched her for a moment, then leaned back in the seat. *I guess we're both tired,* Miranda thought. She spotted a little mark on the map indicating a campground a few miles north of the Lodge, situated right on a curve of the river. She ran her finger over it and traced the blue line for a while, but it didn't come near any other campgrounds in the Peaks of Otter area.

"How about this one?" she asked, handing the map back to Hestia and pointing. "Look. It's right by the water, and it's not far from here. We can at least sleep in the car." Miranda didn't much

213

like the idea of sleeping in a car, but then again, what choice did they have?

"Worth checking out, then." Hestia nodded. She cranked the car, and they turned north.

As they drove, Miranda watched the trees as they came into view in the headlights and vanished just as quickly into the darkness behind them. Her thoughts turned to Bridget, and she wondered where her new friend might be, and whether she was okay. Bridget was the closest thing to a friend Miranda had found since things started to get scary, and she didn't want to lose anyone else. At the same time, it had been days since she got any messages or had contact.

The Tailor hadn't given her any specific instructions, and she still didn't know how she was supposed to fix things without her father, but the longer it took to find him or what he was working on, the more her optimism dwindled. And Hestia had said all those things about how Threads were "supposed" to be. How was she supposed to really know how things were supposed to be? The Tailor really hadn't prepared her for anything, and Miranda resented it. Why hadn't he given her more information? Why hadn't he just told her everything?

The car passed within fifteen feet of a pair of deer, which looked up from grazing to watch, turning back to the grass as soon as it became apparent no-one was stopping. Soon, they reached the entrance to the campground. Hestia pulled the car toward the slat-rail fence and tiny ranger booth. The park ranger wore a wide-brimmed park hat and a thick mustache.

"Hello," he nodded to Miranda. "It's a bit late in the season for camping."

"Oh, we know," Hestia answered. Miranda turned her face away from the ranger, not trusting herself to play it as cool as the other woman. "We're just taking a long weekend away. Mother-daughter thing, y'know?"

"Do you have a site reserved?" the ranger asked, leaning into the little booth and pulling out a large binder.

"Not yet. Do you have openings? We have cash."

"Perfect," the ranger said. "Like I said. Bit late in the season. We've got a lot of room. Tell you what. Take a site at the back and come tell me which one it is in the morning. That'll be $27."

"Thank you so much!" Hestia said, handing over the cash.

They followed the loop to the back of the campground where Miranda thought the little river might be. She recalled wading on its smooth stones in cheap white sneakers her mother called her "creek-walking shoes" whenever they'd go wading. The shoes kept her from getting cut on anything sharp, though most of the river rocks here were so smooth, slipping was a bigger concern. She heard the water ahead and saw one or two cars pulled into campsites along the road, most with regular tents and one with a big pop-up over their picnic table. Children laughed as they ran through the trees between the sites, playing with new-found friends and waving sticks in the air like swords or magic wands.

As they reached the back of the campground, Miranda saw fewer cars, which made her feel a little safer. There might be some security in being around other people, but she didn't want them to attract any more attention than necessary. She thought about their lack of camping gear and wondered again what it was like to spend the night in a car.

Hestia pulled into the little gravel parking space at the adjacent empty tent site, and Miranda hopped out of the car. She glanced to either side at the nearest campers, but they were several hundred yards apart.

The campground was well-maintained and lacked underbrush, leaving wide open space between trees. Miranda decided to walk a little way into the forest, and Hestia followed her. As they climbed over the little rise behind the tent pad, they came on a little footpath that Miranda assumed led to the bathhouse. She stopped. From what she recalled from camping as a child, the bathhouses around here had running water, and maybe even hot water. The idea of a hot shower was tempting. She wanted so much to be clean and to get some rest. It occurred to her that no one would think twice about them sleeping in the car this late. She turned toward the bathhouse, but Hestia stopped her.

"Hold on. I've got something you might want," she said, jogging back toward the car. She returned a minute later with a little bottle of soap and a comb. "It's not much, but I picked them up at the rest stop just in case."

"Thanks!" Miranda took them and nearly skipped to the bathhouse, looking forward to her first shower in days.

She got to the low building and turned on the faucet, intending to wash just her face if the water was as cold as the creek's. After a few seconds, the water began to grow warm, and she almost let out a whoop of excitement. Forgetting everything else, Miranda dashed into the open shower stall and pulled the little door closed, hanging up her bag and clothes on a provided hook. She hesitated, then pulled off her shoes, too. Warm, clean feet later were more important than worrying about bare feet now. She turned on the faucet, huddled in the corner until it got hot, and basked in the warm water, enjoying the feeling of being clean for the first time in a week. She had to use one of her t-shirts as a towel, but she didn't care as she bundled back into her remaining clothes and tied her shoes. Miranda was clean, and in that moment, she felt like she could do anything.

As Miranda walked back into the quickly-dropping temperatures she regretted the wet hair a bit, but tried to concentrate on the fact that at least her wet hair was *clean* hair. She pulled the hood of her coat up and stood, looking toward the fires at nearby campsites. She could smell the wood smoke blowing between the tree trunks and imagined sitting with her back to the fire as her hair dried in its heat, letting her back get so warm it prickled and she had to shift. The children at the campsite nearest to theirs huddled near their fire as they roasted marshmallows. Miranda had to turn away, stomach growling.

Back on the footpath, she passed a couple of guys, not much older than her, setting up camp. They had coolers and a huge tent for just the two of them, but as she got closer, she discovered a whole group of people sitting and laughing on the other side of their vehicle. She edged close to them so that she could feel the edges of the fire's heat and held out her hands.

"Hey! Can I help you?" one of the guys called. Miranda didn't realize how visible she must be.

"Oh, I'm just... never mind," she said, hurrying away.

She walked faster, shoving her hands deep into her coat pockets. Her wet hair now stuck to the side of her face in stiff chunks. She reached the site and, to her surprise, found Hestia sitting in front of a small fire, with a tent set up in front of the car. Miranda ran to the fireside and sat down on a little stump, reaching toward the flames. Hestia smiled and handed her a sandwich.

"Where'd you get this stuff?"

"The ranger station at the top of the road has a little supply section. You just have to know how to ask nicely." They ate their sandwiches in amiable silence and Miranda enjoyed feeling the warmth of the fire while her hair dried. She was relaxing more and more around Hestia, despite the unusual way they'd met. After all, she'd met Jake in a pretty unusual way, not to mention Bridget and the Tailor. Pretty much everything in her life right now was an unusual circumstance after all.

The next morning, Miranda woke curled in a little ball inside the tent, a blanket wrapped around her feet so that she couldn't move at first. While not exactly warm, the tent did hold her own body heat well enough. She felt stiff but rested as she pulled on her coat, smelling the smoke in its lining. Hestia wasn't there, but the tent was zipped shut. She pulled her hair into a ponytail and unzipped the tent door.

Outside, a little fire burned low but was still crackling. Miranda saw the car was gone, but figured Hestia went out for more supplies. She prodded the fire embers with a stick and saw it flare, so she leaned close to it, blowing gently and slipping tiny bits of twig and leaves to it, feeding it breakfast. Soon, Miranda had the fire dancing again, and she sat as near to it as she could, her feet on either side of it to keep her legs warm. She glanced around at the other quiet campsites and wondered whether Hestia might also be picking up breakfast. After her legs felt warmer, she decided to make a trip to the bathhouse.

Hitching her backpack onto her shoulders (the idea of leaving it behind made her nervous), Miranda headed back downstream toward the main campground. In a much shorter time than she'd realized the previous night, she was back at the main area. The large group wasn't stirring yet, though one young woman sat by the fire drinking from a mug. She wore a charcoal gray sweater and a pair of black running pants, with heavy boots, her blonde hair cut short. She glanced up at Miranda but quickly looked away again.

When Miranda got to the bathhouse, she found it empty. She walked up to the sink, set down her bag, and studied her own face in the spotted mirror. In the daylight, she saw dark circles under her eyes and flyaway bits of hair sticking out of her ponytail, which scrunched to one side from using her arms as a pillow. She took down her hair and combed her fingers through it. It felt cold, and while not damp anymore, she decided against washing it again. There was no reason to spend another day colder than necessary. Instead, she turned on the faucet and washed her arms, trying to help herself wake up a little more. Cupping her hands, she scooped water and splashed her face, then rubbed soap on her forehead, nose, and cheeks.

As she rinsed her face, she heard movement behind her. Looking into the dingy mirror, she saw four or five of the group campsite people standing in the open doorway behind her, not really looking at her, but leaning on the cinderblock walls without saying a word. Besides the woman from the campfire, the rest were hard to distinguish, standing in the shadows. They each had on a pair of jeans and a sweatshirt, and it struck her that they seemed to be waiting for something.

Miranda grabbed a paper towel and dried her face and hands, making sure she wiped any vestige of soap from her face.

Without turning, she picked up her backpack and slung it across her shoulders, watching the group in the mirror. Her eyes met one of the guys', and he lunged.

Miranda dove to the side and the guy slammed into the sink, but she didn't hear him make contact because all the others were now scrambling toward her across the slick, polished cement floor. Miranda fell back against the shower wall, trying to get away from them, but some instinct screamed at her not to get boxed into the stall and she hurtled to her left, toward the entrance. She felt someone grip the top of her arm, and she wrenched it free as someone else hauled on her backpack. Miranda spun, ripping her backpack strap but still clinging to it as she fought her way to the open air. She kicked out and made contact with someone who grunted and fell. Then, she dug her elbows into another person trying to make another grab for the backpack. She reached the doorway, but the woman stood there, waiting. Miranda tried to backpedal, tripped over her own feet, and fell on top of the woman, who yelled "Shit!" as they tumbled onto the gravel.

Miranda scrambled to her feet, kicking gravel onto the woman as she tried to run, stumbling on protruding roots. Miranda didn't stop; she raced down the path and when she saw a large tree down beside the path, she dove behind it, peering out from behind the trunk, gripping the straps of her bag. Sure enough, three of her attackers, including the woman, appeared on the path moments later, looking around.

"She probably took off down the trail," the woman said. "You, go that way. I'll head for the creek. You, check the other direction of the trail. She can't have gone far."

Miranda watched as the two tall figures took off opposite one another, down the footpath. The woman waited, watching them disappear, then turned back toward the bathhouse. Miranda thought she heard footsteps on gravel. The sound of stall doors slamming on their hinges came through the trees. The woman reappeared on the path not long after, but still didn't go to the creek. Instead she peered into the trees, her back to Miranda's hiding spot. After several minutes, Miranda's legs were starting to shake from crouching so long, but she knew that any movement might betray her position. Satisfied that Miranda wasn't around anymore, the woman took off toward the creek.

Miranda counted to one hundred, just in case the woman turned around or was still within earshot, then she got to her feet, still clutching her backpack. Other than the torn strap, it looked intact, and she breathed a sigh of relief.

She didn't know how they'd found her, and she had no way to tell how big that group was. She remembered way more than five or six from the previous night. She also wasn't sure how far she could get before one of them found her.

As she looked toward the lake, trying to decide what to do, Miranda heard a car, and looked up through the trees. The little coup was pulling down the dirt road. Not giving herself time to second-guess it, she made a break for it, waving her arms as she approached the car. Hestia slammed on the brakes and Miranda flung herself into the passenger seat.

"Drive!" she shouted, looking over her shoulder. The blonde woman and her friends might break cover any moment.

"You okay?" Hestia asked, putting her foot to the gas pedal.

"We've got to go! They found us."

Hestia kept her gaze straight ahead, dirt flying behind them as they flew down the narrow road, the car jittering over potholes so that Miranda's teeth chattered. The ranger tried to wave to them to go slower, but Hestia peeled onto the Parkway and headed north. Miranda kept turning to look behind them, but didn't see any other vehicles turning onto the road and after a few minutes she began to relax.

"Sorry about all your stuff back at the site," she said.

"It's not a problem. Sometimes you've just got to cut your losses."

They drove in silence for a while down the winding two-lane road, the bare tree branches reaching overhead while the pines interspersed in the forest created a dark green backdrop. The temperature had fallen a lot overnight. A few snowflakes landed on the windshield, and Miranda hugged her bag to her chest.

Soon the snowflakes grew larger and fell on the road in front of them, melting on the pavement, but coating the dried grass on either side until the whole road began to look like the sugar drizzle on a fresh glazed doughnut. They passed a rest stop with two cars in the lot and a light on in what looked like an information hut with a large map out front, but Hestia kept driving.

"How far are we going?" she asked.

"Far enough," Hestia said. "This was too soon, too early," she muttered to herself.

"Where were you this morning?" Miranda asked.

"I was running errands."

"What kind of errands? Did you get breakfast?"

"We'll find something."

Miranda sat, watching the large snowflakes, while Hestia kept muttering. She looked irritated, but Miranda didn't know what could have happened to make the woman annoyed. She felt scared herself, and relieved to be away from those people, even if just for the time being.

"...don't know what they were thinking..." she heard Hestia murmur.

"Are you okay? Where were you this morning?" Miranda pressed again.

"I told you, I was running errands."

"Yeah, I know. But I can tell you're upset about something. What's too early? You said something was too soon."

"You ask a lot of questions," Hestia said. "Too many, now I come to think of it."

Miranda felt a chill run down her back that had nothing to do with the temperature. She looked at her companion, the woman she thought was her friend, and at the woman's hands gripping the steering wheel. Miranda's heart jumped into her throat as a wave of anxiety washed over her. Every part of her body was telling her she needed to get away, immediately. Miranda glanced from the door handle to the speedometer, just visible in the gap at the top of the dashboard. Without looking at her, Hestia's face curled into a thin smile.

"I wouldn't try it," Hestia said. "You might not survive, and even if you did, I know how to find you, and you don't have anywhere to go." Her face head snapped toward Miranda and she looked right into her eyes. "You broke the first rule: You Must Not Be Seen. You broke that rule, Miranda Woodward, that and many others, and you are going to face the consequences."

223

"I don't know any of the rules!" Miranda shouted, leaning away from the woman. "How was I supposed to know? Aren't you supposed to teach me?"

"The second rule is You Must Not Be Captured. You have broken that rule as well, and it will cost you the most." Her eyes blazed and she gripped the steering wheel tighter, accelerating on the icy road.

Miranda felt the tires spin beneath them, struggling to get traction, and the back end of the car fishtailed back and forth, but Hestia kept control as they flew faster down the Parkway. They went around a sharp turn in the road and a group of deer loomed in front of them. Hestia swerved and the car spun into the grass on the side of the road. Miranda's seat belt pinned her in place. As the car stopped, she managed to jam her thumb onto the seat belt latch and fling herself out of the car. She took off for the forest, as Hestia struggled to get free herself. Miranda didn't stop when she reached the tree cover but kept going, diving behind another fallen log. She wedged herself into the narrow space beneath it, and tried to keep from gasping for breath.

Hestia came tromping into the woods, her leather coat disheveled and her face twisted like a mask. Miranda saw the woman stop about thirty feet from where she lay, hoping that the cold air would keep any bugs from getting on her. Hestia's head swiveled left and right as she began moving forward again, inching her way closer and sniffing, as if she could find Miranda by scent. Something tickled Miranda's leg and she bit down on her exposed forefinger, fighting the urge to twitch.

"I know you came in here, Miranda Woodward!" Hestia called to the trees. "Your tracks in the snow went straight in here. You can't stay in the woods forever or you'll freeze, and you can't

Walk again because you don't know where you are. You're trapped. And before long, the rest will be here and we'll comb these woods until we find you. Come along with me now, and I might be lenient with you."

Miranda's nose was starting to sting from the cold air. Her finger was so numb she no longer felt her own teeth digging into it, and was surprised to taste blood. She released it and balled her fingers into a fist against her mouth. She didn't dare move otherwise; Hestia stood a mere matter of feet away, but she knew the woman couldn't be certain she wasn't still running.

Except there's no noise, she thought. *She'd hear me in the leaves.*

She knew there wasn't anything she could do about the quietness of the woods except hope that some animal would take off and distract the woman's attention, but of course none did, thanks to Hestia's shouts. Miranda turned her head just enough to be able to see her once-trusted ally. The woman leaned against an oak tree, her left arm hanging at her side as she massaged that shoulder with her right hand. Her dark eyes searched the underbrush, her mouth pressed into a thin line. After what seemed like a small eternity, she turned and went back the way she came.

Miranda stayed still, listening. She heard the engine fail to turn over three times. On the fourth try, the little car sputtered and then caught, coughing under its hood. She heard it roar away, but couldn't tell which direction it went. She sat up, brushed away the twig poking her leg, and tried to take stock. What Hestia said was true enough. She didn't know where she was or how to get back without following the main road. She couldn't bring herself to stand, much less to head into the woods with some unknown destination. The campground was swarming with enemies, but

Miranda hadn't found what she came for and didn't want to give up on her father yet. She thought of the other Thread Walking rule she knew, the one that Hestia hadn't yelled at her in the car: Don't get stranded.

Miranda stood. She clenched her jaw, reminding herself to be silent, and set off through the trees, determined to make it back to the campground and to find whatever her father left there. It occurred to her that they all expected her to run. Her instinct always took her away from danger, and not into it. Well, this time she'd go back toward the danger, and find a way to face it.

She reasoned that following the road still made the most sense, but she couldn't walk along the shoulder without getting caught, or without her tracks in the fresh snow giving her away. There was still just enough cover from the trees where she was however, that the thick flakes hadn't found their way more than a few feet into the woods. By staying within sight of the road, Miranda figured she could stay on course and under cover. The more she considered this group, the less they seemed like how she imagined Editors. When the Tailor told her about Editors, she figured they were more rogue agents, living on their own somewhere. But this group seemed huge and well organized. She wondered just how far this conspiracy went.

When Miranda reached the road, she paused, looking up and down the stretch of pavement in the bright sunlight. She squinted and tried to listen for any sounds of a car but didn't hear anything, so keeping to the edge of the trees, she turned to go back down the road. Someone stepped out of the trees behind her. Miranda tried to scream, but a cloth pressed against her mouth and nose. She thrashed, but the person gripped tighter and soon her vision swirled. Miranda collapsed onto the snow-covered leaves.

Chapter 13

Miranda's head felt like it was split in half and the two pieces were being pried apart with a flat-head screwdriver. Her eyes watered and she pressed them shut, trying not to let her racing heart shake her whole body as she tried to take stock of her situation. Try as she might, she couldn't pinpoint where she was or why she felt like she was moving. Her stomach lurched and she held back vomit as she came to. She saw a car floorboard and shoes; no, boots, black combat style boots, on either side of her. She realized her torso was slumped over her abdomen, and she pushed herself into an upright position. Her vision remained a little fuzzy but a woman turned around from the front of the car and Miranda snapped to alert attention.

"Hello, Miss Woodward," the woman said. As Miranda's vision cleared, she recognized Hestia's face and silver hair.

"Where are you taking me?" Miranda asked, as her muscles tightened. She glanced to either side of her, but the two people sat there, blocking any move she might make toward the car doors.

"No questions now, though I'm sure you'll find many more to ask on the way."

"I'm not going anywhere!" Miranda said.

"This isn't an optional trip," the woman said. "Besides, you're already on it."

Miranda leaned back in the seat, while her brain muddled through the situation. She remembered the campground and Hestia and being on the road... but everything after that was a blur. She couldn't remember any of these other people or getting in the car with them. *More information*, she thought. *I need to wait for more information.* She remembered her bag and sat up again, looking around, but her bag didn't seem to be anywhere in sight. Fear twisted at her, but when she tried to move them, her limbs felt like they were weighed down with tar; she couldn't lift them more than a few inches before feeling strained. She lay back against the seat.

"That was easier than we expected," one of the men beside her said.

"We're not going to say anything else about it," Hestia replied.

"All right, all right, I'm just saying I thought we'd have to find her, or chase her, or something."

"What do you think we've been doing?" the other man retorted.

"That's enough!" Hestia snapped.

The rest of them grew silent. Miranda glanced at the two men on either side of her, but they were looking out of the windows and not looking at her. After a little while, they merged onto an interstate. Miranda almost choked as they drove under a sign pointing them toward San Francisco. She was on the other side of the country with strangers, but *she was almost to Oakland.*

They must know by now. Surely they'd found the letter from her father. Would they force her to help them fill in the blanks? Miranda tried to hold her panic in check and save her energy to break loose as soon as an opportunity presented itself.

As they crossed the bay heading toward the city, Miranda looked out at the bright blue water and all the sailboats bobbing in the marina. The sky was overcast and a mist seemed to hang over the city as they pulled off the interstate again and onto a main road. They continued for an hour through town, until they reached an older neighborhood with a road on a steep incline as they climbed to the top. Once there, the driver pulled into a short driveway blocked by a metal gate.

One of the booted men got out of the car and walked up to the gate, typing something into a little panel on the side pillar. After a few seconds, the gates pulled apart, sliding to the left and right behind a stucco wall. He got back in the car and they pulled forward.

Inside the wall stood an old, three-story house. While it was larger than many they passed on the way there, it didn't look like anything special to Miranda. She tried to see around the men to glimpse what else was inside the fenced area, but there wasn't even a garden. The place was simple house with a wide grassy space between it and the main gate.

"Out," Hestia barked.

The man on Miranda's right opened the car door and got out, motioning her to follow. He gripped her arm again, though she didn't struggle. Her legs buckled under her, and the man had to half-carry her up to the front steps of the house as the car pulled around back. Hestia knocked three times on the door. It opened, and Miranda found herself ushered inside.

From the outside, the house looked old. While not quite as dilapidated as the Henley House, it wasn't fancy or well-kept. On the inside, however, the place looked like it belonged to a billionaire. Thick carpets spread across marble floors, huge paintings hung along the entry hall, and a wide staircase led to the upper floors. Miranda looked up at the ceiling, which was painted blue and white with a large glass chandelier sparkling in the center, directly over her head.

"Bring her in there," Hestia said, pointing to their left. The men steered Miranda through a paneled door and into a drawing room. It had a tall sideboard and a curved couch flanked by a pair of high-backed chairs. More paintings hung above the sofa and sideboard, and glass cases displaying various items lined the walls. The men pushed Miranda onto the couch and departed, leaving her alone with the woman.

"Where is this place?" Miranda asked, her curiosity getting the better of her.

"No questions," Hestia said. She kept looking at her watch and glancing at the door.

"Okay, but why am I here?"

"No questions," the woman repeated.

Miranda sighed and slumped back on the couch, looking around at all the items in glass cases. Some seemed to be artifacts from different countries and looked old. Others looked like souvenirs. One case held a pair of books. Miranda wanted to get up and look at them, wondering if they were some her father might have owned, but didn't think Hestia would like her moving around. She picked at the loose threads along her coat sleeve and tried to look like she wasn't paying attention to every little thing Hestia did, the anger and hurt of betrayal burning inside of her.

After what seemed an inordinately long time, the paneled door opened and a tall man walked into the room. He had thick, gray hair combed back to give more volume in the front, and he wore a slim-cut suit. His black shoes were a little scuffed, but otherwise he could have come from a business meeting in New York. He nodded at Hestia, who left through the still-open door, closing it behind her. Then he turned his attention to Miranda, his dark brown eyes staring straight into hers.

"Hello, Miranda," the man said. His voice was deep and round, and Miranda sat up a little straighter, watching him.

"What am I doing here?" she asked.

"We've been following you for quite some time," the man said. "I'd say we've been following your work, but you don't seem to get much of that done, do you?"

Miranda's face flushed. She clenched her fists, but took a slow breath and tried to steady herself. She didn't need to be operating in anger; she needed to be smart, and smart Miranda knew she needed to get information and get out of there as quickly as possible.

"As to your first question," the man continued, "you are here because you have a certain set of skills, and we need your help."

"You need—what?" Miranda looked up at him, taken aback. "My help?"

"Yes. You see, we have some members of our organization that have gone, shall we say, off track. I believe you have it in you to

231

straighten things out for us and to fix this little, well, problem we've got."

"I don't know what you're talking about," Miranda said, glaring at the man.

"How shall I put this?" the man asked, drumming his fingers on his chin as if deep in thought. "There are people who are sabotaging us, keeping us from making the world a better place. We have the ability to make sure that good people are given opportunities to positively affect the world, but there are some who think that the good people should be pushed aside and ignored. We're looking to put things back into balance."

"And you need me to do that?" Miranda asked. "That's dumb. I mean, what can I do that one of your Organization people? What *can't* they do?"

"I have an idea that you can see things others can't, Miranda," the man said, stepping closer to her and lowering his voice. "You can guide things. Show us the way to go. Give us a chance to help people."

"You want to Edit things," Miranda said.

"Don't be absurd!" the man laughed. "That term is used by those too old-fashioned and short-sighted to possibly fathom the capabilities we have for good."

"Still sounds like Editing to me," Miranda said.

"Then you have been given a skewed view of things," the man replied. "Whose word do you trust? You don't have anyone that can help you, not if you're here."

"What's that supposed to mean?"

"I'll give you time to figure that out, and a few other things. Elroy?" he called. One of the suited men from the car appeared in the doorway. "Please take her to her room."

"Where's my stuff?" she demanded.

"In a safe place. There will be no more questions. Now, go."

Miranda stood up and followed Elroy out of the drawing room and to the stairs. The steps were wide and shallow, and her legs began to burn a little as they passed the first landing and continued to the very top floor. Once there, the landing opened onto a long hallway. The floor here was linoleum, and metal, windowless doors flanked the hall, wide studs lining their edges. About halfway down the hall, Elroy stopped and unlocked a door. He opened it and stood back.

"Yeah, right," Miranda said.

Elroy took Miranda's arm and, before she realized what was happening, he twisted it behind her and used it as leverage to shove her into the room. The door slammed shut behind her. She turned and pounded on the closed door, reaching for a nonexistent doorknob.

"Let me out!" she shouted, knowing there would be no answer. She could feel her pulse racing, and her mind zoomed down all the dark possibilities of losing everything, from her father's notes to the wooden box. What if these people figured out how to use them? Everything would be ruined. She slumped against the door, her forehead on her knees, and cried.

Sometime later, when the tears subsided, Miranda uncurled herself. She still felt scared, and lost without her bag. She was alone and unarmed, and felt helpless, but her stubborn streak was starting to gain a little ground again. She wanted to examine her situation and at least try to figure out what her next step might be, even if that just meant waiting to see what happened. She got to her feet and brushed off her jeans, though they didn't have much on them, then surveyed her current situation.

She stood in the middle of a square room with plain, gray walls, with a tile floor and a single bright light mounted in the center of the ceiling. The rest of the room was empty except for a single bed and another narrow opening. She looked inside and found a toilet and sink jammed into the tiny space. Miranda walked along the entire edge of the room, looking for anything else, even a crack, but the walls were solid and smooth and she didn't find anything. Not even a glimmer of golden thread. The physical door was still visible, but had no handle on the inside: she was trapped in a prison cell.

She knew she needed to figure out a way to escape, but also needed to recover her bag. Then again, it was possible they'd look at her scraps of paper and the photos and all and have no idea what the connection might be. Clearly these people knew things about her, but they might not know everything. Her biggest concern was the wooden box.

Time dragged in the small gray room, while Miranda paced the floor or sat on the bed, trying to come up with a plan. The trouble was, no matter how much she thought about it, she didn't know anything about the house or where she was, or even who else might be there. She needed to find out more about the place to make any sort of plan. Her stomach began to ache, and she lay down on the bed, too wound up to sleep, but knowing she should rest.

At some point, the door opened and another suited man entered with a tray of food and a bottle of water. Miranda sprang to her feet, thinking she might be able to bolt, but a second man stood at the door holding a large gun, so she stayed in the middle of the room. The first man set the tray on the floor and left again, the door clicking shut behind him.

Miranda eyed the food, fighting between her distrust of this place and her hunger pangs. The tray had what looked like a peanut butter sandwich and a red apple, like an oddly-packed school lunch. After a while, she opened the water. The drink relieved the emptiness in her stomach a bit, but not enough for her to relax. She picked up the tray and ate. Nothing weird seemed to happen, and she fell asleep some time later, on top of the bed, the tray back on the floor beside her.

This pattern continued over the next few days. Miranda tried to keep track of time and tried to count of the people she saw, but it was hard to tell how long she'd been there or how many men there were, since they all stayed only a few seconds and wore the same solid black clothes. She thought they must be feeding her twice a day, and sometimes the light turned off for a few hours. She took advantage of the darkness to sleep, or to pretend to sleep while she went over the few things she discovered.

The guards varied, but always came in pairs. One always stayed at the door holding a large gun, and the other dropped off the food, and neither ever spoke to her. She glimpsed the hallway behind, and seemed to be facing another door just like hers. The floor between them was dark hardwood, and matched what she saw of the rest of the house when they first brought her there. The food changed, but was always basic and always just enough. She lay on the bed for hours at a time, or else paced the floor or did little exercises to keep herself from being too lethargic, but then went back to lying on the bed. She knew time passed, but everything blurred together in the monotony and dullness.

Miranda also made a point of going over every piece of information from her father's file in her mind, taking the time to focus on it, to turn each item over and over in her mind, to recall every single detail in case any of it jogged an idea or brought a breakthrough. Nothing did, but still she fixated on the notes, the photos, the articles, and about the spool of thread. And she thought about her mother.

Miranda's mother. The longer she was stuck in this place, the longer her mother was stranded, or gone, or stuck, or maybe even dead. Miranda tried not to imagine all the possibilities, but she couldn't help thinking of her mother. The things Hestia said about not being sure of Edits in her own life terrified her. She didn't want to forget her mother, not after everything they'd been through together. Lying on the small bed, she thought about her bed at home, and how Perkins used to lie at the foot of it. She thought about her mother baking muffins or cinnamon rolls on a Saturday morning, and about the times that Abby and Jae had spent the night, back before everything started to change.

Miranda heard a soft knocking on her bedroom door and rolled over to face it. Jae's curly brown hair was barely visible over the opening of her sleeping bag, but Abby was sprawled across the floor, going "full starfish," as they often teased her. Miranda sat up quietly as her mother opened the door and peeked inside.

Perkins dashed around her mother's ankles and hopped up onto the bed, cranky at being blocked from the room overnight after he'd made a game out of jumping on the girls in their sleeping bags every time they so much as moved a foot. He flung himself onto the foot of Miranda's bed and curled up with his back to her, his thick fluffy tail curled tightly around him.

Miranda's mother covered her mouth to stifle her laugh at the indignant cat. She held up a cup of coffee and Miranda nodded, carefully climbing out of bed and tiptoeing around her friends' sleeping forms and out into the hallway.

"Did you girls have fun last night?" her mother asked.

"Yeah," Miranda yawned, taking the hot cup. "We couldn't decide which movie to watch so we watched all of them."

"You watched all three Lord of the Rings *movies?" her mother asked, her eyebrows shooting up. "You must really love your friend Abby."*

"Well, Jae was into it, too. She said the elf guy was hot." *Miranda giggled.*

"You are something else, Sweet Pea. Why don't you come downstairs and help me start breakfast? I'll bet the other two will be up in no time."

Now, Miranda sat in her cold cell of a room, trying to remember her mother's voice, and the way she laughed, and her face. She wanted to hold onto it for all she was worth. She had to.

One day, when the guards unlocked the door, they didn't bring food. Miranda lay on the bed watching them, not bothering to get up, having long since abandoned trying to talk to them. She sat up as they both stepped into the room, facing her.

"What now?" she sighed.

"Now, you'll answer some questions," one of them said. She recognized him from the car that had brought her here. "Come with us."

Miranda stood up and followed, glad to be doing anything else, but also eager for a glimpse at the rest of the hall in case it gave her any ideas. As they walked, she scanned the hall, but all she saw were rows of identical doors. They reached the end of the hallway, and the woman pressed a button. A few seconds later, the wall split down the middle and slid apart to reveal an elevator. Miranda was led inside, followed by the guards. The man pressed another button, and the doors closed.

After a slow descent, they stepped into a long, dark hallway. Unlike the upstairs floors, this area had cement floors and industrial lighting, and the walls were painted white with nothing on them; not even a door broke their surface. Miranda followed the woman down the hallway, half-jogging to keep up with her strides, the guards on their heels. The hallway made a ninety degree turn to the left, and opened into a large, well lit room.

The walls here were similar to those in Miranda's room, gray and smooth and seamless. A long silver table stood in the middle with round-backed chairs along each side, all empty. Along the walls were rows of shelves, many covered in books and boxes, and one with more glass cases. The man led Miranda to the table and pointed at a chair on the end.

"Sit," he said.

Miranda took the seat. She bounced one leg, trying to channel her nervousness into one place in order to keep her mind focused. She didn't feel afraid, but she didn't want to be caught off guard.

"The Board will be here soon. Answer all of their questions."

"What if I don't want to answer questions?" Miranda asked.

The man's face remained blank. "You will."

He turned and walked back through the door, leaving Miranda alone in the huge room. She wanted to get up and look at the books and other things, but assumed she was being watched, at least by cameras. No one would leave her alone without some sort of safety precaution. She didn't have to wait long. Soon, a whole group of people filed through the door, all in expensive looking business attire, and filled the other chairs along the table. Some took out notebooks, while others leaned back in their chairs. None of them looked at Miranda. She studied them, though; a few looked familiar, but most were strangers. They all looked up at once and faced the opposite end of the table. Miranda looked there, too.

The tall, gray-haired man stood at the foot of the table, hands resting on the back of his chair. Unlike the others, this chair was high-backed and leather, and he peered at them over it, scanning each of their faces. As he got to Miranda, he smiled, and she shivered. Once he'd checked with each of the people there, he took his seat, and the others turned their attention to Miranda. She meanwhile kept watching the man as another figure appeared over his left shoulder. Hestia stood just out of the main light, her arms folded and her face unreadable. Miranda quivered with rage as the man began to speak, her eyes on the woman who had betrayed her.

"Hello again, Miss Woodward," the man said. He leaned forward and set his folded hands on the table. Miranda didn't answer. "How have you been enjoying your stay with us?"

"The food's all right, but the entertainment could use a little pizzazz," she said, trying to sound like she wasn't scared out of her mind. The man laughed, though the others remained silent.

"Well answered," he said. "I'm hoping you will provide some other answers for us as well."

Miranda narrowed her eyes, waiting to hear what he wanted to know. The other people around the table were staring at her, and she felt like a lab animal expected to perform so they could evaluate her. She forced her twitchy leg to be still and planted both feet on the ground.

"Now then," the man said, reaching beneath the table. Miranda tensed, but he pulled out a notebook and set it in front of him, turning to the first page. "Where is your father?"

The question was so unexpected, Miranda's mouth hung open. She started to say she didn't know, but closed her mouth again. She didn't want to answer any of their questions, either to outright lie or to skirt the truth. Silence seemed like the best strategy until she could figure out what they already knew and what they were still fishing for.

"I'll ask again," the man said. "Where is Samuel Woodward?" Miranda still didn't answer. The man looked to the doorway behind her and nodded, then turned back to her. "You will answer before we're through. For now, we'll skip it." He flipped a page in his notebook.

After a moment, he looked up and over her right shoulder. She saw one of the guards came into the room, carrying her backpack. The guard set the bag in front of the man and left. The man unzipped the bag and dumped everything out onto the table. Bridget's clothes weren't there anymore, but the file folder, the wooden box, and her father's letter tumbled onto the metal surface with a series of clangs.

"What can you tell us about these items?" the man asked. Miranda looked at the shelves off to her left, trying not to jump up and grab all her precious items.

"You will answer me, or we will destroy these things one at a time until you have nothing left, at which point you will be useless to us." Miranda turned to face him, and felt herself grow cold. "Now, I'll ask again. What can you tell us about these?"

"They're just sentimental," she said at last.

"Not likely," the man said, unfolding the letter. "This letter specifically mentions meeting him in Oakland. Well, we are in Oakland. Where is your father? Where exactly did he want you to meet him?"

"I have no idea," she snapped, forgetting her plan. "My dad's dead, as you should know as I'm *pretty* certain you're the one who killed him. Or she did," she said, nodding her head toward Hestia.

She glared at the man as he surveyed her without comment. After a long silence, he opened the wooden box. He pulled out the spool and thread and held them up, while the others around the table watched him. Hestia started to step forward, but the man held up one hand and she stopped. "This looks very interesting. I'm sure we can just burn it, though. It's just a wooden spool. You don't need something just sentimental, surely."

"It was a birthday gift," she said, trying not to react. She dug her fingernails into the palm of her hand to keep herself from flinching. "Dad knew I liked to sew."

"You like to sew?" the man repeated. "Interesting. Especially considering the state of your clothes and bag. Unless you've already used all of this?"

"I didn't say I was good at it, just that I liked it," Miranda answered flatly, but inside her heart suddenly leapt; was it possible that none of them could see the golden thread? Did it look empty to them?

"Oh, I see," the man said. "So then the file with these old photos and notes?"

"Just what's left."

"I don't think so," the man said, holding up the camping picture and examining it. "This is a message, isn't it? When was this taken?"

"I don't remember," she said.

"I will not warn you again, Miss Woodward. Do not lie to us. Now, when was this taken?"

"It was at Peaks of Otter, Virginia. I was a little kid."

"I see that," the man said. "And we know *where* it was taken, the question is *when*." He flipped over the wedding photo, and turned to the stack of loose notes. "So, we have some random family photos and some notes. Planning on doing some camping, are we?" he asked.

"You should always be ready to improvise," Miranda replied.

"True." He slid everything back into the folder, then leaned onto the table. "Where is your father?"

"I don't know," Miranda said.

"WHERE is your father?" His eyes bulged in his face and he slammed his balled fists on the table.

"I DON'T KNOW!" Miranda shouted back at him. The glared at one another across the table for a full minute.

"Yes, this time I think I believe you." He leaned his elbows on the table. "Let's try a new version, then. What happened to your father?"

"He's dead," Miranda said. "His plane crashed. Months ago. Or I'm pretty sure it did, but I can't go check because I'm locked up in here."

"You have a lot of attitude," the man said. "You should be glad I am patient. Now for the other question. Why are you really here?"

"Seriously? Your people brought me here," she snapped. "I was just out for a walk, minding my own business, and they grabbed me."

"You know what I mean." He closed the notebook and shoved it and her other things into the backpack. "If you answer me, I will let you have these things back, but only when I am satisfied you have answered to your best ability." He looked over his shoulder once more. The guard came, picked up the bag, and left.

"I believe you have an idea where your father is, and I believe you will tell us the mission he left for you because we need to rectify a few things and try to reverse the damage you've done."

"Damage I've done?" Miranda exploded. She stood, the chair behind her sliding back several feet from the sudden movement. "You're screwing with my whole life! And for what? I haven't done anything but try to fix it back the way it's supposed to be!"

"And what gives you the authority to decide how things are supposed to be?" the man asked, raising his voice over hers. "Why is it up to you? Has it ever occurred to you that people much older and wiser than you, people with a better grasp of the *big picture*, might be far better equipped to decide how it's 'supposed' to be?"

"You're not supposed to change anything!" Miranda shouted. "You changed my life!"

"And now you're changing it even more," the man replied. "If you'd stayed put, none of this would have happened to you. You couldn't leave well enough alone, or you'd still be just sitting there, safely in your mother's house."

"It's not my mom's house anymore," she spat. "You took care of that. So, no chance I'll stay there."

"Then you will stay here instead. We don't need you ruining things, trying to interfere. All your noble ideas aren't worth the scraps of paper in that folder. Useless and unnecessary... Get her out of here," he said, waving his hand in the direction of the door.

One of the guards appeared at Miranda's side and yanked her to her feet. Glaring at Hestia, who still stood in the shadow behind the chair, she marched out of the room. No one else looked at her anymore, except one young woman who she now recognized as the driver who brought her there. The woman looked more curious than angry, but disappeared from view as they went back into the hall. The guard took Miranda back up the elevator and into her room, locking the door behind her as usual.

That night, dinner never came, but she didn't care. She lay on top of the bed, the image of her bag dumped on that silver table burning in the forefront of her mind. Anger and hopelessness came in alternating waves, and she swung from wanting to leap through the door the next time it opened, regardless of any guns, to just curling up in the corner and quitting.

Though she didn't realize it at first, seeing all the items triggered her memory of them into sharper focus than they had been before. She saw each word on her father's list, his handwriting clear. It struck her that these people thought her father was *somewhere*, and the idea of him being dead didn't satisfy them. He had to be somewhere out there and she needed to find him. The part of her that wanted to make a break for it grew bit by bit, minute by minute as the thought of finding her father burned inside of her.

The lights turned off at some point, but Miranda was wide awake, still sitting on top of the bed. Any tiredness long since faded as she readied herself for morning and a potential escape. She tried to mentally count the steps to the elevator, and strained to remember the walk up the stairs, depending on which way presented itself as an easier route. As she was about to lie back on the bed to at least rest, there was a sound at the door. She froze.

A sliver of light blossomed around the edge of the door, widening inch by inch so that it shot across the floor and up the wall, yellow and bright. Miranda watched it. Now faced with putting her plan into action, she felt uneasy; this was too simple. And then a silhouette broke the light.

"Come on, move fast if you want to get out!" a voice whispered.

Miranda jumped off the bed and ran to the door, blinking as she adjusted to the bright light. There stood a boy she'd never seen in her life, holding the door open for her. In the hallway light, she could see light brown hair and dark brown eyes that studied her face in a curios, intelligent way. He was a couple of years younger than her, she guessed, from the way he held himself, and he kept glancing over his shoulder into the hallway. It was hard not to think of him as a kid, but she also thought his eyes looked smarter than a typical kid's. He wore jeans and a band t-shirt for a group she didn't recognize. She felt like she'd met this boy somewhere before. Was he one of her younger classmates back at Henley High School?

"This way," he whispered.

The boy turned and went toward the elevator, Miranda right on his heels. She wasn't going to waste an opportunity. At night, it made more sense to her to go straight down the stairs and not further into the bowels of the Editors' building, but this guy seemed to know the place, so she followed. The boy pressed the elevator button, rocking back and forth on his feet.

Miranda leaned close to him, her voice a low murmur. "Where are we going?"

"To get your stuff," he replied. Miranda nodded, and the doors slid open. Once inside the elevator, the boy turned to her and began speaking rapidly. "There's no security backup here in the elevator. Once we're downstairs, go to the right. Find the storage lockers. Your bag is in there. Whatever sounds you hear, ignore them and get to the back of the room. I've got to go back. I'll meet up with you at the door back there."

"What if you don't come?" Miranda asked.

"Improvise," the boy said, grinning at her.

The elevator doors slid open, and they stepped into the now-dark hallway. A few pools of red light indicated security and emergency lighting, but the brightness of her interrogation was gone. The boy glided through the darkness, staying out of the red patches, so Miranda did, too. Soon, they reached the end of the corridor, and the boy pointed to the right and a pitch-black opening before turning to the left. Miranda hesitated a moment, then plunged into the darkness. She walked a few steps further in, holding out her hands in front of her. Pale green markings began to glow on the floor, and she followed them forward. Once, she thought she heard screaming and a loud bang, and she almost turned back, but remembered her instructions and kept moving.

Just when she wondered how much longer the darkness would last, she reached the end of it. The corridor curved sharply out into a well-lit room lined with tall cabinets. Pausing at the edge of the shadows, Miranda scanned the space, looking for anyone who might be waiting for her, but saw no one. She stepped into the light, expecting to hear alarms sound, but nothing happened. She ran straight to the cabinets and opened them.

Each of the cabinets contained a stack of random objects. One had a set of tarot cards and a soccer ball. Another had a whole collection of scented candles, a painting of a cat, and a huge box of salt. She opened a dozen or more, each time expecting to see her bag, and each time disappointed, until she reached the second to last cabinet. Miranda opened the metal door and there, in a lumpy pile, lay her things. She almost laughed in relief. She made sure everything was in her bag before hoisting it onto her shoulders, feeling complete for the first time in days. As she turned to look for the exit, the boy burst into the room.

"We've got to move!" he said, looking back over his shoulder. A long gash on his hand was spilling blood onto his shirt, where he cradled it against his chest. It looked like someone had nearly cut his thumb off his hand.

He led the way to where the cabinets met in a corner with a narrow gap, and he squeezed himself into this. Miranda glanced back at the shadowy corridor across the room and heard voices growing louder, so she flung herself into the little space, squeezing through with her bag.

The narrow opening led to a much wider space, big enough for both of them to stand with plenty of room, like a little nook. Miranda stood facing the boy, who was breathing hard and holding his side.

"Are you okay?" Miranda whispered, but the boy shook his head and put a finger over his lips. The voices on the other side were clear now.

"They went down here!" a female voice called.

"Search it!" replied a male voice.

The boy poked Miranda's arm and then pointed at the wall beside them. Puzzled, Miranda turned to face it, but then she saw the thin outline of another door. She didn't see a handle, but suspected there might be one on the other side. She reached out and ran her hands along the seam, feeling for a catch, but found none. The boy grabbed her elbow and shook his head, standing squarely in front of the door. Miranda mimicked him, and they stood shoulder to shoulder, staring at it. After a moment, the door shifted and the thinnest of cracks started to appear around the outside of it. The boy leaned close, his voice so low Miranda almost didn't hear it.

"This comes out into the alley in back of the building. They don't know it's there. I use it when I need to get things done."

"They don't know?" Miranda breathed.

"Small things can have the biggest impact," the boy whispered. "Now go."

"Wait," Miranda said, turning to face him one last time. "What's your name?"

"It doesn't matter," the boy said. "Now get out of here!"

Miranda looked at him and smiled, then pushed the door open a crack and stepped into fresh air. She was outside the building, and free.

Chapter 14

Miranda took off down the street, grasping the straps of her backpack and trying to find the fastest place to get out of sight. She rounded a corner and ducked into an open doorway, hiding behind a stand of postcards as a man in a dark suit strode past. Though she couldn't be sure he was after her, she'd had enough of dark-suited people for the time being. She hovered just inside the little shop for a few minutes, wondering what to do and where to go, when a voice called from behind her.

"You going to buy anything?" the girl at the counter asked. She looked Miranda's age. "Or are you just hiding?"

"Just hiding," Miranda said.

The girl laughed, "Yeah, I figured. No worries. You can hang out until my shift's over."

"Thanks," Miranda said, still looking down the street. Another suited man was walking along the other side, checking in stores. "Hey, do you have a back exit?" she asked.

"Sure. But you've got to buy something. My mom says I don't try hard enough down here," she said, rolling her eyes.

"At least you've got your mom," Miranda said. The girl just rolled her eyes again, so Miranda went to the snack aisle and grabbed some things to restock her supply of power bars. She got some fresh bottles of water, went to the register, and paid with her emergency twenty-dollar bill.

"Thanks," she said, handing Miranda her change. "This way."

She led Miranda through the back of the store and into the employee-only area. There was a tiny break room with an old-fashioned box TV in front of a gold upholstered recliner and a vending machine. They passed a closet full of cleaning supplies and a narrow door that opened onto a toilet, then reached a beaten-up back door.

"This leads to the alley. Watch out for the cat; it bites," the girl said, pushing the door open.

"Thanks," Miranda said. "Listen, if anyone comes looking for me—"

"Don't worry about it. Those guys look like total tools," the girl said.

"Thanks," Miranda repeated. She slipped through the door, closed it behind her, and took off down the alley, hoping the men weren't checking it yet.

Miranda reached the end of the block and looked out from behind a stack of empty fruit boxes. People walked up and down this street, and traffic looked heavy. Plenty of people wore business suits, but none of them looked like the people chasing her. Most were on their phones or reading tablets, and a few were talking to each other. It looked like the end of a normal work day.

Without any clear idea of direction, Miranda turned right out of the alley, hugging the sidewalk and staying in the thickest part of the crowd. She wanted to blend in, but was aware of her dirty clothes and ragged hair. A few people skirted around her, but most took no notice, as if she didn't exist at all. She made a few random turns, making her way in the same general direction but zigzagging from block to block in order to stay out of a single street. She made a turn that brought her to the top of a hill and looked out over San Francisco for the first time.

Miranda stood at the crest of a tall residential area, houses descending like giant stairs down steep streets. The sun was setting across the bay, just past the Golden Gate Bridge, and she could make out the hazy form of Alcatraz to the right. The urgency of getting out of sight was forgotten for a moment as she took in the breathtaking view. She saw trees on the other side of the bay, and wondered what might be across the bridge. The deep horn of a ship floated through the air, faint and far away, but distinct. Miranda shook herself and started half-jogging down the steep sidewalk.

Keeping her breath was a little difficult after so long in a confined space, but the fresh air invigorated her, and Miranda made good time. She stumbled on a crack pushed up by a tree root, but managed to catch herself before she rolled down the hill. At the bottom, the neighborhood ended and the street intersected with a main thoroughfare. She saw cabs along the opposite curb, but with no more cash, they were useless to her. Sinking onto the bottom step of the corner house's porch, she looked back up the hill. None of the suited men were in sight, but that wasn't too comforting. She almost liked it better when she could see them.

Miranda unzipped her backpack and started sifting through her belongings. She hadn't gotten a chance to check her bag's contents. The wooden box nestled in its usual spot at the bottom, and she sighed in relief when her fingers touched the carved pattern, though she didn't dare open it in public; she couldn't tell who might be watching her.

Satisfied, she stood up and crossed the street and headed down another steep hill, in the direction of the bay. She saw a cruise ship glide across the water between buildings, and kept moving, hoping to blend in with the crowds of tourists and maybe hitch a ride to the airport. Despite the risk, Miranda wanted to retrace her father's steps. If she could understand what he was doing before he left for that last flight, she might be able to figure out what happened to him.

The sky grew dark as the sun melted into the distant trees, and the clouds turned into molten gold above the water. Miranda reached the last stretch of residential areas as the streetlights turned on overhead, and piers stretched out in front of her. A few were still old and covered in wooden huts and stands, but most were modern versions of themselves, with huge parking decks and cruise ships flanking them, or touristy versions of bygone fish markets, with restaurants and candy shops and souvenir counters. She walked out onto one of these piers, trying her best to stay just behind larger groups of tourists to draw less attention to herself. As she cut between two buildings, Miranda noticed a sign with a large picture of a sea lion and an arrow. Curious, she followed it and found that even the sea lions were in a designated area to be photographed.

This is kind of weird, she thought, looking at the rows of camera and tripods.

Miranda wandered between the people taking photos and up to a newsstand, selling tabloids and weekly papers, along with gum and crackers and motion sickness pills. The man behind the counter was watching something on his phone, and glancing up at the people walking by every so often. She walked up to the stand and picked up one of the papers to check the date. September sixth. Same year. She shook her head and studied the paper, trying to remember what the woman told her. She'd only gone back a couple of days. But this paper implied weeks.

The man behind the counter looked up from his phone. "You've got to pay to read that," he said.

"Sorry," she muttered, putting it back. "I just wanted to check the date."

"What for?" the man asked.

"Oh, you know how it is when you're having fun on vacation," she said. The man shrugged and went back to his phone.

The cover stories were becoming easier every time she needed one, and she was pleased with how vague she managed to be with most people. Of course anyone who observed her for a while would see otherwise, but no one paid much attention to a teenage girl wandering around with a backpack. She almost disappeared into the background for most people, so wrapped up in their own thoughts that they couldn't see anyone else.

Miranda walked down the side of the road along the bay, unsure of where to go, but aware that she needed shelter at least until morning. She also wanted a place to get into the file and check it. As she meandered down the street, she thought about the people she wanted to talk to, especially her mom. Her mom! Right now her mom probably hadn't disappeared yet. She'd give anything to call her mother, but the complications of calling her mother, who would then worry about her, who would then go and check on her... other self... at school. She sighed and dismissed the idea, as tempting as it might be. When did life get so complicated?

As she walked, a dense fog rolled in from the bay, muffling her footsteps and the traffic noise that hadn't quieted down even with the sunset. The air grew cool and damp, and her coat picked up small droplets from mist that clung to the fabric, pooling in the creases where her elbows bent. Miranda paused at a corner, waiting for the crosswalk signal to change, her hands deep in her pockets as she rocked back and forth to keep moving. Across the street, the bright lights of a gas station glowed in the mist, illuminating the pumps and pavement in a globe of light, a single red sedan sitting at the nearest pump like a jeweled insect in a gauzy net. The light changed, and Miranda walked to the other corner. A voice was just audible across the gray dampness. She noticed a man standing at a payphone, mounted on the side of the gas station convenience store. He said a few more words that Miranda couldn't quite make out, then hung up and disappeared into the fog down the sidewalk.

She stopped, gazing at the payphone, surprised they still existed. The urge to call her mother welled inside of her again, and she clenched her fists as her feet took her closer, despite her internal protests. Standing in front of the phone, she stared at the quarter slot, and the instructions for dialing direct. Fear of the people chasing her, and of what they'd do to her mother to get to her kept her from dialing. She turned away and started to go back to the sidewalk, but stopped in her tracks at the edge of the light.

And an idea blazed inside of her like a beacon of hope and possibility. She swung her bag around and fumbled with the side zipper, her hands trembling as she pulled out her wallet, long forgotten in the extra pocket of her bag. Her new drivers' license smiled at her from another lifetime as she shoved her fingers behind its slot and pulled out the folded index card with the ad for the Tailor Shop, with the address and phone number on it. She wondered if this broke the "Don't be seen" rule, but decided to risk it. After all, if anyone would understand the situation, the Tailor and Bridget would.

She ran back to the payphone and shoved the receiver between her ear and shoulder, holding the card in one hand and dialing the number for a collect call with the other. She hesitated when the automated voice asked for her name and in a rush said "a customer who needs things fixed" before it hung up on her. She heard the phone ring twice and then it clicked, and a familiar voice answered.

"Stitch in Time Tailoring, this is Bridget."

"Bridget!" Miranda said, her whole body relaxing, though she hadn't realized she'd been so tense.

"Who is this please?" Bridget asked.

"You don't know me, but I'm Samuel Woodward's daughter," she whispered into the phone.

"Oh, hello, Miranda!" Bridget said. "I've been wondering when you'd call. Are you safe?"

"Oh, um..." Miranda didn't quite know how to respond. Bridget must have understood because she started filling in the gaps.

"It's all right. I know we haven't met yet, but I'm sure we will soon. Now please tell me. Are you safe?"

"Well, sort of," Miranda answered. "I mean, I'm on my own, and— "

"You sound scared. We can help, but first I need to verify some information."

"Okay," Miranda said, feeling a twinge of annoyance. This wasn't going at all how she thought it would, not that she had an idea of how a conversation with someone who knows you but also doesn't should go.

"Please tell me your mother's name."

"Colette," Miranda said.

"Your birthday?"

"September ninth, but you've already asked me all of this," Miranda said.

"I see," Bridget said, and Miranda glared at the phone, imagining the young woman making some kind of note in her Rolodex.

"Siblings?"

"I don't have any. And I don't know how much time I have. I'm being followed!"

"Which is why I asked if you were safe," Bridget said. "But you are not currently under attack or we would not be having this conversation."

"Well, no," Miranda admitted.

"I'm sorry we have to do this," Bridget said. "But if you're calling me, then you must at least partially understand the complexity of the situation. I have to see where you are and be sure that I am speaking to the real Miranda Woodward, who, as you have pointed out twice now, I haven't met yet. I'm sure I'll like you when I do, though," she added. "Now then, what can the Tailor or I do to help you?"

"Well, I'm not sure," Miranda said, and her irritation grew as she realized she hadn't called with a specific purpose. "I guess I just needed advice."

"Advice about what?"

"I'm trying to find—"

"If you have a mission, then it is up to you to complete it. Too much knowledge might compromise it." Bridget paused. "I recommend you look at your immediate situation and figure out what you need. Maybe we can help with something that way."

"Oh." Miranda clenched her jaw, then took a slow, deep breath. "Well, I'm stranded in San Francisco with nowhere to go and nowhere to stay and I need to get away from some people."

"So you need cash. That we can do. Do you have a bank card?"

"No," Miranda said.

"That's all right," Bridget said. "We don't need you being traced, or calling attention to yourself with any bank fraud. Your mother has enough to deal with right now."

"No kidding."

"What can you tell me about where you are?"

"I'm outside of a gas station. Frank's Fuel."

"Perfect! Do you see the street name and number on the building?"

"There's a number by the door, 2201, and I think I can see the street sign..." Miranda leaned away from the phone and peered down into the fog. "I think it says Bay Street."

"All right. I'm going to hang up and I want you to go inside and wait. Got it?"

"Okay, but what about— "

"You will have to figure out the next step for tonight on your own. Find a way to get to a safe place once you get what I'm sending."

"But how will I— "

"You'll know," Bridget said. "Listen, Miranda... I'm sorry you're going through this. I know it's hard, but please believe me when I say that all Threadwalkers go through this. Well, maybe not *exactly* this. But things get screwed up sometimes, even for the best ones. Most of them figure out what they need to do. And from what I know about you, I'm not worried."

"Thanks," Miranda said, taken aback.

"Now head inside, wait for your assets, and get somewhere safe before calling again."

"Thanks, Bridget," Miranda said, and hung up the phone. She didn't feel better, but still, having a next step to take lifted her spirits, and she ducked inside the warm, bright store.

A man behind the counter was ringing up a customer, and chatting about the Giants' last baseball game. Miranda wandered down the snack aisle on the pretense of checking out the candies, though her stomach was too twisted with nervousness to feel hungry. The phone at the counter rang and the cashier nodded to the customer, then picked up the phone as the other man left.

"Hello?" he said. "Oh, yeah I think I see her."

Miranda looked up at him, then back down to the candy. She wasn't sure what to do.

"No problem, ma'am, we can do that. Yes, I'll just need your credit card information. Okay, when you're ready." The man did something on the cash register, scanned a few things, and then said, "You're welcome ma'am, I'm sure she'll be on her way home soon. Any time. Goodbye." He looked down the aisle, right at Miranda, and waved. "Miss?"

Miranda glanced up at him, unsure what to do. "Me?"

"Your mom just called," he said. "Come here."

Miranda approached the counter, glancing at the door in case she needed to bolt, gripping the straps of her backpack. The man leaned over the counter and said in a low voice.

"She said your car broke down and you're running a little short, so asked me to give you this," he said, sliding two things across the counter to her. She looked down at them. One was a prepaid Visa, the other a prepaid cell phone.

"Thank you!" Miranda said, trying not to smile too much as she picked up the phone and card. "Thank you so, so much!"

"Really, it's all right. I've been down on my luck before, too, and it's good to have a mom to bail you out." He grinned at her.

"Right," Miranda said. She wished it could have been her actual mom who called, but had to admire Bridget for thinking of such a good cover. She made a note to check the balance on the card at some point, though she had an idea it would be more than enough. She turned on the phone, and as it powered itself on, she walked back down the food aisle, this time picking up an assortment of portable things, and a hot sandwich from the coffee and munchies counter in the back. She paid with her new card, thanked the cashier again, and headed back into the night, a feeling of security now building inside of her.

The phone beeped twice to tell her it was on, and even though Bridget had told her to wait, she entered the Tailor Shop number into the keypad. The phone rang once, and Bridget answered.

Chapter 15

"Stitch in Time—" Bridget's voice on the phone sounded like an angel from Heaven to Miranda.

"It's me. I got the stuff," Miranda said. "Thanks. You have no idea how much this helps."

"I have a pretty good idea," Bridget said, and Miranda could tell she was smiling. "I can't help with much after this except to make sure you've got funding, but make sure no one else gets your phone number. Got it?"

"Got it," Miranda said.

"Good luck, Miranda Woodward," Bridget said. "I'm looking forward to meeting you someday."

"I'm thinking it'll be pretty soon," Miranda said.

The phone disconnected, and Miranda slid it into her jeans pocket, feeling buoyant as she continued down the sidewalk. The fog felt like a shield, hiding her movements from anyone who might be trying to track her. Of course, it also meant she wouldn't see anyone coming, but she felt in that moment like she could do anything.

Bridget had called her task a mission, she had cash and a secret phone, and the whole thing made her feel delightfully confident. She wasn't just Sam Woodward's kid anymore; she was a real Threadwalker. She moved between Snags and was out to stop Editors. The thought of the people chasing her brought her back to reality. They still might be anywhere, and she needed to remember that this wasn't a spy novel, that the bad guys were as complex as she was and way scarier because they could be anyone.

Miranda sat in the far corner of a little diner several streets over, sipping a cup of coffee and watching the other people. No one paid any attention to her, but she still felt alert, ready to spring toward the exit at any moment, her bag sitting on her feet. She finished her waffles and hardboiled egg, then headed to the front counter to pay. The man standing behind the counter swiped her prepaid card and handed her a receipt.

"Do you need anything else before you leave?" he asked.

"Actually, I need to get to Oakland. To the airport."

"There's a bus station about a mile down the road," the man said. "They should have a shuttle that goes to the airport."

Miranda thanked the man and headed outside. She peered up and down the street but didn't notice anyone who looked like the people from the Editors' house, so she turned and set off in the direction of the bus station. Twenty minutes later, she purchased a ticket on the airport shuttle bus. Every time she used the prepaid card she expected someone to question her, or to take it away, but it worked like a charm.

Soon, Miranda was getting off the bus again in front of a huge terminal, planes flying low overhead in the early evening light and the roar of jet engines making the air thrum. She strolled down the sidewalk, hanging onto the straps of her bag, and watching for any sign of the men in the dark coats. No one approached her and she didn't notice anyone particularly watching her. Now that she was here, she didn't know what to do with herself. Rather than stand on the sidewalk and attract attention, she headed for the main doors. The glass panels slid apart, welcoming her into the airport.

She strode inside and looked up. An old airplane hung in the high beams of the ceiling. Miranda wasn't sure what she was hoping to find, but a quick study of the airport map showed her a section that seemed to be marked off, labeled the "From the Oakland Aviation Museum." She thought back to the exhibit she visited with her father in Washington DC as a child and decided to give it a look. She knew it wasn't a strong lead, but didn't have any other ideas.

Miranda walked to the little information desk by the door to ask how to get to the museum. The woman at the desk advised her to take the rental car shuttle to the building shared by all the rental agencies and walk from there. So, Miranda hopped on yet another shuttle, rode to the rental car building, and then walked the rest of the way to the museum.

The Oakland Aviation Museum was in an old metal hangar bar surrounded by static displays of old fighter jets and the like, their nose cones painted with fierce faces and their tails decorated with retro cartoons of women and animals. Miranda wandered between them, under the wings of some, and up to the museum door, only to find it had closed at five that afternoon. The museum reopened at nine o'clock the next day, so she decided to find a place to stay for the night and try it then. She walked back to the rental car building and caught the shuttle back to the main terminal to wait for morning.

Once there, she found a long low bench to lie on and wait out the night. There was also a coffee shop inside that had a small cooler with sandwiches and fruit, so she got herself some dinner and settled onto a bench to people watch for a while. As it grew later, less people were coming to the airport. A stream of people exited from the gates and went out into the night, hauling suitcases and duffle bags behind them, most on their cell phones. She watched as a woman explained three times to her small son that they needed to go stay with Grandma and would be home in a few days, but the boy wanted his toy train, left at home, and no amount of Grandma-comfort was going to fix things for him. She saw a pilot and two flight attendants leave for the night, their tiny matching suitcases rolling along behind them.

As the night continued, the airport grew quiet, and Miranda found herself alone. A security guard came up to her once to ask if she needed anything, but she told him she was waiting for a flight out in the morning and he nodded.

"Sometimes these layovers are just long enough to be annoying, but not long enough to go to a hotel," he said.

Miranda dozed on the bench, feeling more exposed than she had in a while, but grateful for the bathrooms nearby all the same. In the morning, she got up and bought herself a croissant and small latte at the coffee shop before heading back to the museum, thankful once again that Bridget had been able to send her money. At ten minutes before nine, she was waiting at the front door when a woman in a blue polo with the museum logo on it unlocked it and let her inside.

Miranda paid the admission and wandered through the exhibits talking about the history of the airfield. She learned that the building in which she now stood was built in 1939, and that

Oakland had been an airfield for a long time before that. She looked at old uniforms and plane engines as she followed the gallery around. As Miranda reached the central exhibit, though, she came to a standstill. There in the middle of the museum was one of Amelia Earhart's planes.

She circled this exhibit, not taking in any information at first. She discovered that the plane was a replica. The original was the one she saw in the Smithsonian with her father all those years ago, and read how Amelia had taken off from Oakland to begin her final journey, attempting to circumnavigate the globe. Like the newspaper clipping she'd gotten from Hestia, this exhibit showed Earhart completing her journey around the world. Miranda stopped in front of the largest sign with a diagram of the plane on it, and frowned. She already knew this wasn't right, but couldn't figure out what to do with the knowledge. As she was about to turn away and walk through the rest of the museum, something caught her attention.

On the bottom right corner, like a tiny logo, she saw a now familiar little design: what she now suspected was a needle with a bit of thread curled around it, just like on her father's grave. She reached out and touched it, looking up at the plane. The little symbol looked old, like it had been there for years. Though she thought she knew what the shape was, she still didn't understand the meaning behind it. Miranda turned and began looping the exhibit again, looking for the symbol on any other signs or objects but didn't find any more. Just then the docent who unlocked the door walked up to her.

"This is our most popular exhibit," she said, smiling up at the plane. "Do you have any questions about it?"

"No, that's okay," Miranda said. When the guide started to leave, Miranda changed her mind. "Actually, I do have a question."

"Yes?" the woman asked.

"What does this mean?" Miranda pointed at the little symbol.

"You know, I have no idea. It's been on there as long as I've been a volunteer at the museum, and no one has ever explained it. I assume it was the printing company that made the signs for the exhibit, but that's been at least twenty years ago."

"Oh. Well, thanks anyway," Miranda said, her shoulders drooping.

"I'm sorry," the woman replied. "Anything else?"

"No, that's okay. Thank you." The docent was looking at her, and Miranda felt a bit uncomfortable.

"Have you been here before?" the woman asked.

"No, this is my first visit."

"Oh, well, I must be mistaken then." The docent left and Miranda stood there, still staring at the little mark, and wondering why it kept turning up in odd places.

She strolled through the rest of the museum, checking the signs and even some of the artifact cases, but didn't see the symbol anywhere else. Seeing it made her think she needed to be here, but she didn't know what to do or where to go. She also didn't want to attract attention by spending hours and hours at the museum. The frustration of feeling watched everywhere grew inside of her, and she fumed at these strange people who kept ruining her life, from her cat to her sleeping situations.

She walked back to the Amelia Earhart display to have a last look before heading back to the airport to catch a shuttle someplace else. As she stood looking from the airplane to the symbol and back again, she felt more than heard someone come up behind her. On the pretense of studying the other side of the plane, she edged around the exhibit. As she did, a petite figure in a dark coat came into the edge of her view, then ducked out of sight again. Miranda didn't doubt who it was, though. The woman from the campground was in the museum... and probably not alone.

Miranda pretended not to notice the woman. She knew the woman could follow her through a Snag, but thought that maybe if she were quick enough, she could hide on the other side of one, provided she could find one somewhere nearby. As she circled the exhibit, the woman stayed just in her blind spot, but Miranda was able to catch occasional glimpses of her. She was also able to tell that there wasn't anyone else in direct view of her. As she reached the sign with the symbol again, she felt the thickness in the air and saw a single golden thread float by her face. Without thinking twice, Miranda stepped through the Snag and took off at a run.

She was in the museum and it looked almost the same as the way she'd left it. She ducked behind a large folding display and peered out at the Amelia Earhart exhibit, expecting the woman and an entire team to come busting through at any moment. No one did. After a while she went up to it and looked. She could see a few little gossamer strands floating in the air, but nothing else, and wondered why no one followed her. Miranda sat down and considered her options. She couldn't go back through just yet because she knew the woman would be waiting for her. She didn't want to go far because she didn't know when she was, and didn't want to get stranded. But she also didn't know where to go from here. Deciding that information was more important than a low profile, Miranda walked to the gift shop. To her surprise, the same docent was standing behind the cash register with a set of keys.

"Oh!" the woman exclaimed. "We're already closed, I thought we let everyone out already."

"I must have been in the bathroom," Miranda said.

"No matter. You can walk out the front with me," the woman said, smiling. "Did you enjoy your visit today?"

"Oh, well yeah, I did," Miranda said, taken aback. "I especially liked the Amelia Earhart exhibit. I'm just sorry no one knows what that symbol is."

"What symbol is that?" the woman asked.

"The weird one on the bottom of the main sign," Miranda explained.

"Oh, that." The woman nodded and motioned for Miranda to follow her to the front door. "Yes, it's been there for years. Sometimes people ask about it, but no one has ever been able to tell me what it is."

"Too bad," Miranda said. "Say, can you tell me the date? I've been traveling a lot lately, and I've lost track of the days."

"Oh, it happens sometimes," the woman said. "Today is Saint Patrick's day, March seventeenth!"

"Thanks," Miranda said, wondering how she could find out the year. It couldn't be that long ago, the docent looked the same down to the khaki pants and dark blue polo. She walked outside and waited while the woman locked the door.

"Heading back to rentals?" the woman asked.

"Yeah, I am. Thanks," Miranda said. The woman walked around the side of the building to the little parking lot and got in her car. Miranda headed down the road, waving to her as she pulled away, going in the direction of the rental car building.

March seventeenth. If she could just find the year, she'd know for sure, but she already felt certain that she did know. And if it was March seventeenth, then at least here, right now, her dad was still alive. Somewhere. Maybe even at this airport. The thought made her pulse quicken. Even though she had no idea how to find him, she had to try and find a way. She reached the rental building and took the shuttle back to the main airport terminal.

Once there, Miranda decided to see if she could find any information on her father's flight. She knew his very last flight number, the one he would be on in two days, but not for the one he'd taken out of Oakland, so finding him would be a long shot. She wedged herself into a corner behind an information kiosk, abandoned for the night, where she could be out of sight and a little protected while she watched the sliding doors. Every time they opened in the main baggage claim, she glanced up, expecting to see the dark haired woman or one of her associates, but no one appeared. Trying not to focus on why the woman didn't follow, Miranda pulled out the file with her father's notes, pouring over it yet again. The jotted notes still didn't make sense, and "California, but why?" was the mantra playing in her own head.

She picked up her parents' wedding photo and held it for a while, thinking how young and happy they looked, and wondering if her dad already knew about everything and if he ever told her mom about Threadwalking. She flipped it again to look on the back, but it was still blank except for the photographer's proof stamp. She was glad to have the photo, since the others in her house disappeared, and it occurred to her why these photos were special. For some reason, they still existed, even when everything else had vanished. Surely that meant something.

She pulled out the camping photo and set it with the wedding photo, along with the note telling her to "Remember." She pulled out the torn book page for the first time since leaving Hestia and read it, but couldn't pick up the context, and it didn't seem to have any names. The narrator was talking about cause and effect, the consequences of actions and of inaction. It sounded like a textbook, and didn't tell her anything new. She picked up the newspaper article about the crash and read it for what seemed the hundredth time.

A small plane crashed off the southern California coast on Tuesday, killing five including the pilot. Authorities believe the plane went down due to poor weather conditions. Wreckage has been found along the southern California coast, and off Anacapa Island, part of Channel Islands National Park. Local authorities have ruled the crash an accident, and have expressed concern for the native wildlife found on the small island.

Miranda blinked at the words "southern California coast" and began to feel a twinge of anxiety. Had she gone to the wrong place? She was hours north of that area, and it was still two days until her father's plane was due to crash. Hot tears welled in her eyes, but she looked up and blinked them back into place, unwilling to let herself cry just yet. She needed to keep her head about her to figure this out. Surely everything she needed was in this folder?

But what if he didn't leave everything you needed? Miranda's irritating inner voice whispered in her ear.

"Yes, flight 1738. It's the last one heading out tonight," a man's voice said. Miranda sat bolt upright, looking around for the source, but didn't see anyone. Her tears were gone and she strained to hear the conversation, keeping herself out of sight.

"What's the gate number?" a woman asked.

"10, I think. Terminal A. I have a little while, but I should probably go ahead through security." The man's voice made her heart jump into her throat, and she tried to keep from screaming.

"I'm not so sure this is a good idea, Sam," the woman said. "You don't know how this is supposed to go."

"Yeah, I do. It's not right, what they're doing."

"But what if something happens?" the woman asked, lowering her voice so Miranda had to hold her breath to hear.

"I have a contingency plan in place," Sam said. "I'm sure it's already been mobilized, actually. There was evidence of it this afternoon."

"But if you've already seen the contingency, that means—"

"It doesn't mean anything," Sam cut across her. "Now, I need you to go uphold your end of this. Do your job and wait for further instructions. And remember, *do not be seen.*"

Miranda leaned from behind the kiosk in time to see a woman in a pencil skirt and black heels walk toward the sliding glass doors, leaving a man in a pair of jeans and a sweater to watch her go, his gray hair shining in the overhead lights with his back to Miranda. He started to turn toward security and she gasped, though she'd known from the first time she heard his voice. Unable to stop herself, Miranda sprang forward and ran to him. She hit him at a full sprint and wrapped her arms around her father.

Chapter 16

Sam Woodward looked down at his daughter for a moment, but then enveloped her in a huge hug. After a full minute, he pulled her out to arm's length, studying her face, the long-withheld tears now pouring down her cheeks. Miranda sniffed and found she couldn't breathe through her nose anymore, and laughed.

"Miranda, you're here!" he whispered. "And you're older!"

"I've missed you," she said. "And I'm lost and I need your help and I don't know what to do without you, Dad."

"I'm gone, aren't I?" he whispered. Miranda nodded, unable to say anything. "Then you've been on the move. You must be able to… to be here…" Sam looked around them. "Have you been seen? Were you followed?"

"I don't think so. I thought this woman was going to come through with me, but she didn't."

"A woman?"

"Yeah. Short, with dark hair and— "

"Not here," he whispered. "I don't have much time. I need to catch this flight, but you obviously have questions. I can't answer them all, but I can— "

"Don't get on the flight in San Diego!" Miranda gripped his arms, her knuckles turning white. "Please, please don't get on the flight!"

"What's done is done, Miranda," he said. "And if something happens... well, if anything changes, it will have dire consequences."

"But your plane—"

"Don't," he said. "I don't want to know. I can't. Now come with me."

Miranda gathered her things from behind the kiosk and returned to her father, not wanting him out of her sight for long in case he disappeared again. They walked the length of the terminal to the ticketing counter, where Sam acquired a gate pass, allowing her to come with him through security but not to board the plane. They went through the security check, and Miranda was surprised that no one questioned the wooden box with the scissors, but she didn't mention them and collected her bag on the other side. She trailed behind her father all the way to the gate where they found an unoccupied row of chairs and sat down, side by side.

They sat in silence for a few minutes. She kept looking up at him, taking in his face. It had been months since she saw him last, but he looked just as she remembered, and in that moment it felt like he had never left, but at the same time the ache in her chest opened up again and she felt herself spiraling into fear. She didn't know how she would stop him from getting on the plane yet, but she kept running through scenarios in her mind, wondering if anything from faking an injury to actually staging one might convince him to stay with her. The fact that it was two days early was a detail she decided to ignore for the time being.

"I know what you're thinking," Sam said.

"No you don't," she said, a little too quickly.

"Miranda, I raised you. You may have grown up a lot in the past few months, but I still know how you think." He patted her knee and smiled. "You can't make me stay. If I'm meant to be on this plane, I'm meant to be on this plane. And if I don't get on the plane and whatever you're worried about doesn't happen, then you might not end up here right now."

"I'd rather be with you back at home than be here right now," she said, folding her arms.

"But now you know what we are. You know it can't be like that." He shook his head. "I wish it could be different, but it can't."

"But why? I thought the whole point of sending me on this damn quest thing was to fix things! To meet you here and save you. And if I can fix it by getting you to stay with me, then haven't I done what I needed to do?"

"If it was only that simple, we wouldn't be in the mess we are," he said. "I don't want to know details about me, but tell me what you know about...things. And how you got here."

"Well, I know you're gone. And I know there are Editors who are changing things. Things to do with me, and with mom. Things that make life difficult, and make me feel like I'm losing my mind. And I met the Tailor and Jake— "

"He's called the Librarian," her father said, beaming. "And he's a very good friend."

"I should have trusted him more," she admitted. "And then I met Hestia, and she tricked me."

"Tricked you? Hestia tricked you?" Sam looked confused. "That seems odd. She's always been a friend. She was at our wedding. She—"

"Well, I don't know that she's as good a friend as you remember, Dad. At first, I thought she was helping me but we got followed and then Hestia got scary. I got captured because of her, and I had to escape. When I got out, I was in San Francisco. I took a bus and I got to the airport, and went to the museum in the old hanger like you wanted, and then I ended up here." She sighed. "And now I don't know what to do except stop you getting on the plane so we can go home."

"You can't go home from here," he said. "I'm afraid the way you came through is the way you have to return."

"What's that mean?"

"I mean you'll have to go back through the Snag in the museum and figure things out in your own timeline."

"But I'm not IN my own timeline!" she snapped. It took all of her self-control to keep her voice even. "You told me to come here, and I can't get back through because they're waiting on me, and I don't want to be stranded!"

"Calm down, Miranda. There are things that need to happen in order for all of this to work. You can figure it out. And even if, worst case scenario, you're a couple of months out of date and you can't get back the way you came then you'll have to take the natural course."

"Natural course?"

"Wait it out. Figure it out. Take the long way around."

"What about your contingency plan?" she snapped. "I thought you already had one in place in case things didn't work, and it sounds like things aren't working."

"Miranda, *you* are my contingency plan," he said. He took her hand in both of his and gave it a gentle squeeze. "I've left you everything you need. Well, almost."

"But... but then you knew this wasn't going to work?" she asked.

"I knew it would only work if I had your help, and I knew you weren't quite ready yet when I left you at home with your mother. You had to come on your own. I'm so proud of you, Miranda. I can imagine the things you've been through, the things you've learned."

"I haven't learned anything," she muttered.

"That isn't true at all. And Miranda," he said, leaning close to her, "I believe in you."

"But what am I supposed to do...?"

"You will know what to do, sweetie," he said. "My plane is boarding soon, and I want you to promise me something before I go."

"Okay," she said, but it wasn't okay. It wasn't anywhere near okay. She was angry and frustrated and desperate to keep him there with her as long as possible.

"Promise me that no matter what happens, you'll do what's right and make sure things happen the way they are supposed to happen."

"That's vague, Dad," she said, pausing. "But yeah, I promise. I'll do my best, if I can figure it out."

"That's my girl," he said, putting his arm around her shoulder. He leaned close to her ear and whispered. "Now to the things I couldn't leave anywhere. You've got the scissors and thread, right?"

"Yeah..."

"Then this is the last piece you need." Sam Woodward reached into the lapel of his shirt and pulled out a tiny needle. It glinted in the overhead lights, and he handed it to Miranda, who took it carefully. It looked like it was made out of the same bright metal as the scissors.

"Think about what the purpose of needle and thread *is*," he said.

Miranda stuck out her chin, studying her father's expression, trying to see if he was toying with her. He looked serious, and she was reminded of the times he quizzed her on spelling homework when she was younger. She glanced down at the backpack now sitting on the floor at her feet. "Well, it fixes things."

"Yes, it repairs things. One might even say you could sew up or darn holes." He smiled. "The rest you need to figure out for yourself."

"What am I supposed to *do*, Dad? I can't just stay here."

"No, you can't. You need to get home as soon as you can. You're needed there. Your mother needs you."

They sat staring at each other for several minutes in silence. Miranda felt confused and hurt. Her father hadn't apologized for any of the pain she experienced since his death, nor did he seem willing to prevent it. She still didn't know what her task might be, and didn't feel confident in any ability to repair things, much less complete this cryptic task of his. She found comfort in being able to express all of that frustration to him, but sitting there face to face, it was like a huge wall grew inside of her, getting taller and taller with her words trapped on the wrong side.

"Miranda," Sam said. "I know you're hurt. And I know you're confused and maybe even a little angry. But know that if this all works out, it will be okay on the other end."

"But how?" she whispered. "I'm so lost, and I'm tired of being alone."

"Sometimes alone is safest," he said. "And I know that's difficult. But you're not alone. There are many others, like Jake and the Tailor, and they are supporting you. But the thing is, you've got to do this yourself. I can't trust anyone else with this. You've got to repair things, make them right, and it will be difficult and maybe even frightening, but I know you can do it."

Miranda looked up at her father and tried to smile. She wanted to be brave for him, even though her insides were like jelly and all she really wanted to do was climb in his lap like she did when she was little. She wanted him to tell her the monsters weren't real. He wrapped her in another bear hug as the announcement for his flight came over the intercom. She dropped the spool and needle back into their box and snapped the lid closed. They both stood, and he gripped her shoulders again, leaning down to whisper into her ear.

"Darn the holes and do not be seen doing it," he said. "If you can get there first, you can prevent all sorts of harm."

"Why me?"

"You're the only one who can see them all," he whispered. "That's why you hear the voices. I hear them, too. That's a rare gift, even for a Threadwalker. I wish I could tell you more, but there are people everywhere, watching and listening. We're both in danger here. Keep moving and keep out of sight as much as possible.

"And Miranda?" he said, holding her shoulders with his hands. "I love you."

He kissed her forehead and gave her one last hug, then went to board the plane. Miranda looked at the sign beside the gate and saw he was flying down to Los Angeles. He turned to wave before disappearing down the hall, and she tried to smile at him, despite the tears now streaming down her cheeks.

As Miranda turned to walk back to the chairs, something made her stomach drop into her feet: a tall, trim woman with short, spiky silver hair boarded the plane right behind her father. Hestia turned to the gate attendant to show her boarding pass. Miranda shouted, but the woman walked through the gate.

"Don't let her board!" Miranda screamed, launching herself at the gate attendant. The man grabbed her around the middle and pulled her aside. She kept flailing, trying to break free to run after her father.

"Calm down right now or I'll call security, and you *won't* enjoy meeting them!" he bellowed over Miranda's shouts. She stopped struggling, but couldn't stop her body trembling. "You can't go down there without a boarding pass," the man said. "I'm sorry."

"But you've got to stop that woman," Miranda said, trying to sound as calm and rational as possible. She blinked a few times to try and regain control of her tears and look at least a little more settled.

"I can't stop anyone boarding without a real reason," he said. "They've already closed the plane's door anyway. They're taking off in just a few minutes." Miranda slumped, giving up, and he let go of her. "Why don't you take a seat?"

Miranda sat back on the chair outside the gate, watching the plane through the wide window behind the counter. She wouldn't stop Hestia from boarding, or change anything about her father's fate, but she could wait until the plane took off, and at least wave goodbye one last time. The gaping hole in her chest was back, the one that opened so huge and raw the night the police showed up at the door to tell them about the crash, and she clutched her knees to her chest, fighting the urge to either scream or vomit.

Her whole body started to shake again, and the anger that had simmered beneath the surface for weeks burst out of her. Her father was abandoning her, knowing full well that he was going to die and all the things that she was going through, and about to go through, somewhere on the other side of the country. And the woman who betrayed her was on the plane with him. How could she let them just go?

The thought of herself existing, happy and carefree and normal, a few thousand miles away made her stop. The idea fascinated her, making her wonder if there was anything she could do for herself.

Do not change anything, her little voice whispered. "But this isn't right!" she said aloud, then covered her mouth.

Her thoughts flew to what her father said. She was supposed to darn the holes, sew them shut to fix things and keep changes from happening. And the things that changed all started when he disappeared. She stood and snatched her backpack from the floor, and marched out of the terminal as the plane pulled onto the tarmac.

"This isn't goodbye because I'm going to fix everything, Dad," she whispered, marching back to the shuttle area that would return her to the aviation museum.

Half an hour later, she stood in front of the glass doors, wondering what to do. The museum was closed, and probably had dozens of cameras around, not to mention alarms and the like. But she hoped she could find a way inside, unobserved and without triggering anything. Miranda was just about to walk back to the shuttle area when she heard a car pull into the lot on the left. She ducked behind one of the larger plane's wheels and peeked around the flat tire.

An SUV idled in the parking lot with its lights off, but several figures sat inside of it backlit by the runway behind them. She saw them shift. The front passenger door opened and a man got out of the vehicle. He wore a flat-topped hat and flicked on a large flashlight, illuminating his security guard uniform. He walked around to the front door of the building, passing within a few feet of Miranda but never turning in her direction, then continued around the side of the building. Miranda glanced at the other people still in the SUV, but they didn't show any sign of following him. Crouching low, she scooted around the static display plane to follow the guard at a distance.

The man stood at a side entrance marked "Deliveries Only" and examined the lock. He glanced over one shoulder, then fiddled with the knob, which swung open. Miranda took a deep breath and ran for the door as he disappeared inside, catching it with the toe of her sneaker just before it latched. She put her eye to the crack and looked through, but the place was dark, so she pushed the door open just enough to slip inside, then let it close behind her.

She found herself in a large storage room, wall to wall with cardboard boxes, lit by a bright green exit sign above the now-closed door. Another door across the room was outlined in dim light coming from the room behind it, seeping through the crack where it hadn't closed behind the guard. Miranda crept forward, listening for anything that might let her know which way he went. Just as she was about to open the other door, she heard footsteps outside and ducked behind one of the large boxes. The guard came back into the storage room, ran his flashlight around it, before leaving again. Miranda heard the door lock behind him.

Miranda sat on top of the box and considered her options. She didn't know if the inside of the museum had cameras, but figured it was best to assume it did. She also didn't know what time it was, though it had to be late at night. Still, she had the whole place to herself, which helped with her dad's instruction to not be seen.

Don't be seen.

Miranda repeated this to herself over and over as she stood and went to the door that led into the museum. She thought about lying down and trying to see under it, but didn't much want to put her face on the floor, so instead, she opened the door as small a crack as possible and peeked through it. She could just make out the tip of a plane and the velvet ropes that surrounded it, but nothing else. The lack of screaming alarms encouraged her, though, and she opened the door a little wider.

The storage room opened onto the main gallery, about halfway around the walkway from the Earhart exhibit. Miranda looked up to the corners and along the seam between the ceiling and walls, but didn't see any cameras, so she stepped into the room. The plane in front of her was one from World War II and had bullet holes in its tail. She remembered seeing it when she toured the museum before. Or she'd seen it later. She almost laughed at the funny way time was twisting for her, and worried someone would hear, and went about her task.

Miranda walked along the gallery until she reached the now familiar Amelia Earhart exhibit, complete with replica plane and the huge sign with the map of her last flight, the little symbol at the bottom corner. She looked at it for a while, then turned her attention to the flight path, which took the pilot and her navigator from Oakland to Miami, and then to South America and on. Their last stop was in a place that Miranda hadn't heard of, called Lae in Indonesia, and then they disappeared over the Pacific Ocean, with nothing but a dotted line marking the planned route to Honolulu and back to California.

Stepping away from the map, Miranda turned to the Snag beside it. She couldn't see it well and had to close her eyes, listening for any sounds. Voices drifted through, though she couldn't quite make out what they were saying, as if they were talking through a thick blanket. Then quite suddenly, she heard a familiar female voice ringing from the other side of the gallery, opposite of the Snag.

"Well, she can't stay out there forever. Sooner or later, she'll have to come back here and we'll be waiting for her."

Miranda ducked and slid behind the sign's large base, trying to see the speakers, but they stayed in the shadows.

"But we don't even know where she is!" another voice said. "She could've gotten on a plane—"

"She didn't," the woman snapped. "It doesn't matter anyway. She's not going to sit there and wait. She's a Woodward, remember? She'll want to keep resisting, she's too weak to handle the reality that— "

Miranda fumed inside. They were damn right she was a Woodward and she'd never stop fighting them. She thought about her father's instructions to sew up the holes, and steeled herself. Then she stood and pressed herself through the Snag and back to the other side. Hours had passed, but the museum looked closed. A single piece of spidery thread floated in the still air in front of her.

No one else followed her, and the voices sounded muffled again as she leaned around the sign. When she decided the others were still on the other side, she stepped out onto the gallery floor. As Miranda stood in front of the Earhart exhibit, her attention shifted to the Snag. She wondered why no one else came through it. They'd had no trouble following her through in the first place, so why stay on other side? Unless they didn't know she'd left already.

She stood in front of this very faint, very thin Snag and reached into her backpack for the little wooden box. She clicked the latch, and when the lid popped open, Miranda looked at the needle and the spool of thread, carried with her all this way, waiting. She set down everything else at her feet and, after two misses, threaded the needle. The golden thread shimmered, so fine she almost couldn't see a single strand of it, and she held her breath, feeling a little ridiculous standing with a needle in front of a piece of air.

The light in the windows grew lighter, and Miranda knew any minute someone would come to open the museum. With a final deep breath, Miranda took the threaded needle and, concentrating on the thickest spot in the air, pressed the sharp metal tip into the space beside it. The needle caught. Trying to keep her hand steady, Miranda looped the thread around and pressed the needle back into the spot, then pulled it through the loop to make a knot. The air felt a little lighter, but she could still see the thread, with its uneven knot, hanging in mid-air like a weird floating bug.

She made four more knots, looping her thread over the loose piece until it was blended with her own. Her anger shifted to elation as she pulled the fifth and final time, and secured a solid knot. She pulled out the tiny scissors from the bottom of the box and snipped the thread just above the knot. The stitches faded from view, and Miranda stood in front of the empty space, clutching the scissors in one hand and the needle in the other.

Chapter 17

Miranda gathered everything back into her bag and then stood, facing the Snag. She put her hand out where she knew the stitches were. At first, she didn't feel anything, but as she concentrated, she could just make out the slight resistance of uneven stitching. She listened for several minutes, but no voices came through. Miranda almost jumped up and down. She had fixed one of the Snags!

Sounds behind her made her stop, and she realized that the museum was opening. She headed around the end of the corridor and to the gift shop, ducking inside as a group of school kids poured into the gallery. She stood behind a rack of blue sweatshirts, trying not to laugh with relief and at the surreal quality of it all.

"Can I help you?" asked a familiar voice. The gray-haired docent was at the cash register, leaning so that she could just see Miranda behind the sweatshirts.

"No, I'm just looking," Miranda said, putting her face back into a neutral expression. As she came out from the rack, the woman winked at her.

"I'm glad you like the museum so much, but most people have already left by the second day."

"I missed my flight," Miranda said. "Just waiting to be picked up so I can go home."

The woman smiled. "You can wait in the lobby if you like."

"Thanks," Miranda said, and high-tailed it to a metal bench just inside the front door of the museum.

The feeling she needed to keep moving started to creep upon her. She thought about Bridget and the credit card and phone nestled in the side pocket of her bag, and of the long trip ahead of her and how much she wanted a shower. She couldn't linger much longer, and didn't know how much money was still on the prepaid card, but she also needed to choose her next move. After a few minutes of indecisiveness, Miranda picked up her phone and called the single saved number.

"Hey," she said as soon as she heard the line answered. "Sorry to bug you, but I need a plane ticket and I don't think they'll sell to a teenager."

"You're probably right," Bridget said. "Where are you, and where do you want to go?"

"I want to go home," Miranda insisted.

"You know you can't do that," Bridget replied.

"I know I can't go to my house and I can't be seen, but I need to come home."

"Let me check something," Bridget said, and put her on hold. After a few minutes she came back on the line. "That shouldn't be a problem, as long as you understand the risk you're taking."

"I do," Miranda said. "I can't see anyone, I need to lay low. And I have just the place to do it, if you can get me back in the area."

"There's a flight in three hours that will get you to Charlotte. Is that close enough?"

"Perfect," Miranda said.

"You'll be on your own for a bit from there," Bridget said.

"I understand," Miranda said. "This is my mission, and I've got to finish it."

"I'll text you the boarding information, go ahead and check in for the flight."

"Thanks again," Miranda said, then hung up. A moment later, a text message with flight and confirmation numbers dinged on the phone. She headed back to the airport.

Miranda walked up to the ticketing counter and got her boarding pass, a strange feeling since just yesterday or so, (time was a little difficult to follow sometimes) she'd done the same thing with her father. Once at the gate, she found a corner and sat on the floor with her back protected, scanning the crowd in case someone followed her. She didn't see anyone, and a few hours later, she boarded her flight back to Charlotte via the Atlanta airport.

It took nine hours, including a two-hour layover, to get back to North Carolina. When the plane landed, Miranda felt tired but antsy to get back on the ground in her home state. During the flight, she watched the landscape during the flight until it grew dark out. Even though she couldn't see anything, she knew the trees and rivers were waiting for her.

The next challenge was getting a ride north because to get in the general vicinity of home, she needed a car, or at least a bus. Somehow, she thought that if the Editors were tracking the museum, they were probably also waiting for her at her house, but she didn't intend to go there, tempting though it might be. She still wanted to see her mother, but knew the best way to do that was to stop them from changing her altogether. Instead, she needed to find out where they were Editing her life so she could put a stop to it.

Miranda decided on a bus, and followed signs to the shuttle area that could take her to the Greyhound station. The ticket wasn't as expensive she expected, and she was soon settled in the back of a long bus with tall-backed seats. She thumbed through the red journal as she rode, dozing with her head against the glass window pane, until it pulled into the station in her hometown at 3:15 in the morning. She yawned and gathered her things, then climbed down the steps.

No one else was at the tiny bus depot at that time of night, and the bus she'd taken pulled out about three minutes later, with no other passengers boarding. She walked to the edge of the parking lot where a few taxis waited to be called. She tapped on the window of the first one, but before she got inside, she heard someone calling her.

"Miranda?" Bridget stood beside her car.

"What are you doing here?" Miranda asked as she ran to the woman. She gave her a huge hug, which Bridget returned. "Oh, I guess we haven't met yet, have we?"

"It's okay. This sort of thing happens."

"Can we go—" Miranda began, but Bridget stopped her mid-sentence.

"I need to verify who you are. Can you tell me something only the real Miranda and I would both know?"

"Um. You've got a quilt from your grandmother on your bed?"

"Okay..." Bridget narrowed her eyes. "That's creepy, but not something hard to learn. Try again."

Miranda thought for a long moment, knowing they needed to get on the road. She tapped her fingers on the straps of her bag, and felt the loose threads, and her mind went to the Tailor.

"You told me the first time you Walked it was an accident. You were trying to get away from these girls at your school." She bit her lower lip and waited while Bridget appraised her. The woman nodded.

"All right. Now get in."

They climbed into the car and Miranda hugged her backpack to her chest, wondering where to start and if she should even tell her friend anything. After all, Bridget hadn't met her yet. Snags made life awfully confusing. They pulled away from the bus terminal and she swallowed hard.

"I need to get to Greenlawn Cemetery," she said.

"You sure?" Bridget asked she pulled out onto the dark road.

"I'm sure."

The ride to the cemetery took about twenty minutes without traffic, and Miranda stared out the window in the silence, unsure what to say as she watched so many familiar places glide past in the darkness. It was strange to see them for the first time in so long, and in the middle of the night, like she was living in a dream world version of her own memories. She realized how out-of-touch she felt with it all. The other Miranda was sleeping in her bed just a few miles from here, and it wouldn't be too long before weird things started happening to her. She hadn't gotten the box yet, though, and that weighed on Miranda's mind as they got closer to the cemetery. How much was she supposed to tell? How could she get this done without telling Bridget everything?

Bridget pulled up to the cemetery gates. "You sure you want to be here?" she asked.

"I'm sure," she said. "It's okay. I know what I'm doing." She tried to smile at Bridget, who gave her a small smile back.

"Well, just be careful," the young woman said. "There are some weird things in cemeteries, you know. Things that ought not be disturbed. So you watch your step. And Miranda? I can't stress this to you enough: *do not go home.*"

"Okay... I won't," she said. She wondered how much of her mind Bridget might guess.

"Anything else before I go?" Bridget asked.

"Yeah, there's one thing," Miranda said as she opened the car door. "My cat was named Perkins. I'll be upset about him, but that was his name, before. And it's how you'll know it's really me the next time you see me."

Bridget nodded and Miranda closed the car door. She waved goodbye, then shouldering her backpack, she strode up the driveway into the cemetery and toward her father's grave. She walked down the hill, in view of the mausoleum, and paused to look at it before continuing to the stone. Once there, Miranda knelt and plucked some of the overgrown grass around it and neatened the ground. She ran her hand over the little carving at the back, weighing her options. Before she did anything, she wanted to talk to her father one more time, but that was impossible. Sitting in front of the stone, she thought back to the airport and the way he'd looked at her, happy to see her and proud, but worried all the same. He assured her she wasn't alone, and yet he left anyway.

Maybe I'm not alone, she thought. There was another Threadwalker nearby, someone her father trusted. "He trusted Hestia, too," came the anxious thought, but there seemed little choice. Making her decision, Miranda stood up and patted the top of the stone, then headed toward the section of the cemetery with the Snag.

She crept forward, watching the stones until she recognized a couple of them, then turned to the left and picked her way between a few more, looking for the gossamer strands that marked the thin spot. It took a while, but then she found it, low to the ground behind the tall marker. She rubbed her forehead with the back of her shirt sleeve and knelt in front of the stone. Right along the side, where she expected it, she found the little threads, barely visible in the moonlight.

Miranda took another look around, but the cemetery appeared deserted. She knelt and leaned into the thin spot, falling through and landing on a pile of leaves on the other side. A light rain began falling on her. She was a little sweaty from the warm September night, and shivered in the sudden dampness. Miranda set off across the grounds toward the back gate, looking left and right as she went in case someone might be waiting. She didn't meet anyone and was soon outside the front door of the old farmhouse. Thinking it might be rude to barge in on someone else, she knocked. At first no one answered, so she knocked again. As she started to think he might not be there, the door opened a crack and figure peeked out at her.

"Yes?" the person whispered.

"I'm looking for Ja— "

"Don't say my name out there!" the person hissed. "Come inside, quickly."

The figure stepped out of the way and the door opened a little wider for Miranda to step through. As soon as she was inside, the door closed with a dull *thump*, leaving them in pitch darkness.

"Who are you?" the voice hissed.

"Miranda Woodward," she answered, turning on the spot, careful to keep her feet planted, lest she trip on anything in the darkness.

"Oh!" said a voice to her right. She turned quickly to see a figure pressed into the corner, a shocked expression on his face. "How can I trust you?" the man asked.

"You can't trust anyone," Miranda replied.

"Correct." Jake flipped on the lights, forcing Miranda to squint in the sudden brightness. "You know a few things. Jake Callahan, pleased to meet you."

"Hi," Miranda said. "I guess we haven't met yet, have we?"

"No, not yet, but I know who you are." He had one hand on his chest and was sucking in air like he'd just run a marathon.

"Sorry about that," she said. "I didn't mean to sneak up on you or anything."

"It's... it's all right," he said, recovering enough to pull the door closed. "I'm Jake."

"You said that," she said.

"You're late."

"What do you mean, I'm late?" she asked. "I thought I wasn't supposed to be here for at least a couple of weeks!"

"Yes and no," he said, turning and walking up the stairs, though glancing over his shoulder at her. She shook her head and followed him.

"Seriously, what's going on?" she asked as they reached the top and he went into the library. He had papers strewn across the desk and several piles of open books, laid on top of one another, at the corners and on the desk chair.

"I thought you'd be here sooner. Your father thought you'd come here early this year, and I expected he meant May or June. It's September, I was starting to think something had gone wrong..." He pulled open a desk drawer and rummaged inside, reappearing with a pen and some crinkled paper.

"He said I'd need to make sure everything was all right." Jake twisted his fingers and shifted his weight on his loafers. "What kept you?"

"I'm not sure I should say," she answered. "Things have gotten... complicated."

"Yeah, they always are with this stuff," Jake answered with a thin smile.

"I guess I was delayed a bit," she said. "And then I've been trying to pick up the pieces since then. How do *you* know it's September for me?"

"I keep track." He shifted again and glanced at the library door. "You shouldn't stay here long."

"I don't want to," she said. "I just need some help. I'm not sure where to go next and I was hoping you might be able to help me." She leaned against the large reading table and faced him. "Did my dad leave any messages for me? Not the envelope, I'm not supposed to get that yet, but something else?"

Jake started at the mention of the envelope but his voice remained steady. "He might have, but we aren't exactly being candid here."

"Do you have an idea then?"

"I'm not sure," Jake said.

"But, you said— "

"He told me there was something you needed to do, and gave me a message for you, but I need to make sure you're you." Jake's words came out rushed, all in one breath.

"Okay, so what do you want to know?"

"Just, prove to me that you're Sam Woodward's daughter somehow."

"I don't know how to do that," she said. "Usually people ask me questions about myself."

"Well, I need something a little more concrete. Anyone who does their research could find that information about you."

Miranda thought hard. She needed to think of something that would prove who she was that no one else would have found. Jake glanced out at the hallway again, and Miranda noticed how strained he looked. Suddenly she smiled.

"I have something my dad left for me."

Jake snapped around to face her. "Really."

"Really," she said. She shifted her bag where she could reach inside of it without taking it off one shoulder, and unzipped it. Reaching inside, she drew out the little wooden box and held it up. "I got this, or will get this, on my birthday. September ninth."

Jake smiled at her and seemed to relax. "Perfect! Yes, don't show it to anyone. Put it away."

"What's the message?" she asked, sliding the box back into its place and zipping the bag.

"He said three stitches should do it."

"Was that all?"

"That's it. Just 'three stitches should do it.' I don't know what it means, but he said that you would know."

"Oh," she said.

"I don't know that I've been much help," Jake said. "Now, you should go. I think someone else will be here soon, and I don't need paths crossing." He followed her back down the stairs. When they got to the front door, he pulled her into a hug. "Good luck, Miranda. I really hope you can fix everything."

"Thanks," she said, hugging back. "And you've been more help than you know yet."

"Your dad would be proud of you," he said.

"I'm just glad he picked a good Librarian." She pulled away and winked at him.

"Someone's got to do the job. We already had a Tailor."

"True enough." She reached for the door handle and took a deep breath. "See you in a few weeks! And be nice to me, I'll be scared."

Jake looked affronted. "I'm nice to everyone!"

Miranda laughed and slipped back through the door. She closed it behind her, then bowed her head and dashed off in the rain, back to the footpath. She had a hard time finding the right spot in the increasing downpour, but spotted the stone she needed and pressed herself through the Snag. She gasped in the warm air on the other side, and got to her feet. Miranda brushed herself off and headed toward the empty house, and the relative safety of being out of sight and with access to a bed.

Sometime late into the night, her phone buzzed. She sat up and hit the answer button, but the line was silent. Miranda set the phone back on the table and looked around. The lamp was off, though she didn't remember pulling the switch, and she felt cold. Her phone buzzed again and she snatched it from the table.

"Who is this?" she hissed into the phone. Still no-one answered.

"You know, you really ought to take better care, it's not like—"

A voice came from the other end of the hallway, near the bathroom. Miranda froze. She remembered this. She stood and hung up the phone, then made her way toward the library door to see if she could catch a glimpse of whoever was out there.

"It's the way things have to be, I'm afraid," murmured the second voice.

"But she's bound to find out..." replied the first, louder, just as she remembered. Miranda leaned into the hallway, looking toward the bathroom, and back toward the top of the stairs where her Other self should have stood. No-one was there. And yet, she could almost make out the outline of a familiar shape when she wasn't looking straight at the spot, like someone was standing just in her peripheral vision. Looking back to the bathroom, she saw a silhouette walk toward her down the hall.

"*Shit!*" She ducked across the hall and into the bedroom door to grab her backpack, ready to climb out the window if need be. Watching the hallway through the door, the figure vanished in front of her. She closed the bedroom door and propped the little wooden chair against it, though she knew it wouldn't stop anyone determined to come inside and find her.

Like an echo, she heard Abby's voice downstairs and faint footsteps. Miranda leaned against the tiny bedroom window, looking for headlights, and saw none. Something about the situation didn't feel right. If she counted the days, and realized it was the night before her birthday. She and her friends should be pulling away from the house. She balled her fist and pressed it against her forehead, frustrated and fighting against a rising pain in her gut. How could she have forgotten? She could almost sense them, though of course they weren't there. Something in the past was keeping them from knowing her, so why would they bring her to this house? Except, of course, they hadn't. It was like a shadow of her memory projected in front of her.

Miranda took several slow deep breaths, but her stomach twisted once more and then stopped, leaving a dull, cramped feeling behind. Wide awake, she lay in bed and watched as the sky slowly turned pale gray and the sun crested over the tops of the trees. As the day broke, Miranda made up her mind. Despite what she told Bridget, it was time to go home.

Threadwalkers

Chapter 18

Miranda pulled out her prepay phone and dialed Bridget's number. The phone rang seven times, and she was about to hang up when the line connected.

"Stitch in Time Tailoring," Bridget's cheerful voice said.

"It's Miranda," she said. "Is it safe to talk?"

"Of course," Bridget said. "He's with someone right now, but maybe I can help you?"

"I need the number for a cab company," Miranda said. "Local."

"Local to where?"

"Just in town." Miranda tried to sound casual, but her voice caught.

"All right, here it is," Bridget said after a moment. "But please trust me on this, *don't go home*. It won't be the same."

Miranda entered the number into the phone's keypad, thanked Bridget, and hung up. Then she called the cab company and asked them to come to the cemetery. She checked everything inside her backpack and made her way downstairs. She walked first to the tree line between the house and the cemetery, checking to make sure no one else was around. She peered up and down the road, afraid of unmarked SUVs pulling into the driveway before the cab could get there.

Miranda took a deep breath, checked the road one more time, and was about to run across the street for a better vantage point, when a car pulled around a bend in the road to the left. She froze, glad for her own hesitation. As the car got closer, she realized it was a black and white taxi, and she dashed out to the edge of the road, waving her arms for it. The driver slowed and rolled down the window.

"I'm on a call," he said.

"That was me!" she said, going around to the passenger door. "Can you get me into town?"

"Got an address?" the driver asked, eyeing her in the rearview mirror.

Swallowing hard, Miranda gave him her home address, then leaned back in the seat, sinking as low as possible to try and get below the windows. She set her backpack on her feet but kept a tight grip on it.

"Everything okay?" the driver asked.

"It's fine," she said, careful not to look at him.

They rode in silence for the next twenty minutes. She forgot how far out in the country the cemetery was. By the time they reached her neighborhood, Miranda's throat was dry and her stomach was doing somersaults. She asked him to stop at the entrance to the neighborhood, paid with her card, and waited for him to drive away.

She stood at the turn onto her street for a long time. She learned to ride a bicycle on that road, first drove a car on it, too, while her mother pressed one foot onto an imaginary brake from the passenger seat. The lessons felt far away now, like a different lifetime where some other girl called Miranda did normal stuff, and then somehow, those memories got implanted into her brain. She looked at the driveways opening on either side of the street and wondered if the neighbors would notice her. As she debated the best way to get home via a back route, the garage nearest her opened, and two boys on bikes raced out onto the street. Miranda froze, but they ignored her and took off down the block, laughing and calling to each other. She shrugged and walked in the same direction.

Three blocks down, she reached the turn into her own cul-de-sac. As she looked toward her own house, she expected to see her mother's car in the driveway, but the cement was empty. One of the neighbors pulled out of her garage then, and Miranda ducked behind a car parked on the street. She watched the woman turn left toward the neighborhood entrance, holding her cell phone.

As she stood to go around the neighbor's house and take the back way home, her stomach twisted and she doubled over in pain. Waves of nausea swept over her, making her face flush and her skin tingle as she clenched her arms against her stomach. Then, as quickly as it came, the feeling passed. She gasped in the chilly air and straightened. She cut behind the big house on the corner and ran through the yard, heading toward her own back door.

As she stood panting on the doorstep of her back porch, Miranda looked for the flowerpot where her mother kept the spare key, but couldn't find it. The back garden looked quite different, with paving stones marking a little footpath to a swing set she never owned. Puzzled, Miranda checked under a few decorative frog statues and found the spare. She turned the knob and prepared to step into her own kitchen for the first time in weeks. Thinking of the bald man, she pocketed the key. There was no sense in giving him an easy way in later.

It felt strange to be standing in the kitchen. Nothing looked as she remembered it, and a different table nestled in the breakfast nook. No mail littered its surface. The coffee maker still glowed in the corner, on a timer to turn itself off two hours after its last use. She inhaled to smell the fresh brewed grounds and tried to steady herself. Surely this was just another change that happened, like the cat. She strode out of the kitchen and ran up the stairs to the hall landing, outside her own bedroom. She looked into her room and felt her head swim.

Inside, the walls were painted a pastel blue, with leaping dolphins and bubble-shaped whales adorning them above a crib with a fuzzy green blanket draped over the side. A changing table with a little nightlight glowing beside it was in one corner. And a rocking chair sat in the opposite corner where her bookshelf should have been. Miranda began to tremble.

She ran from the room and slammed open her mother's bedroom door. It was filled with furniture she'd never seen, and portraits of a young couple with two small children, one of them just a few months old, covered the wall above the bed. Miranda leaned against the doorframe, fighting for air. She turned and stumbled back into the hallway. Everywhere she went, she saw unknown furniture, strange photographs, and children's toys that weren't hers. No trace of her mother or her own life remained. She longed for anything familiar, even for Polly the wrong cat to come trotting out of some corner. But then she heard them: voices downstairs.

"No, we.... wait...through..."

She crept back down the stairs, listening. The voices were faint, and familiar. As Miranda reached the foyer, she realized that these were the same voices she always heard in the living room. Leaning around the door, she peeked into that room, but no one was there. She tiptoed across the room, trying to make out the words, but they were still too quiet to discern. As she reached the pass-through to the kitchen, they got a little louder. She didn't know how much longer she might have before the current occupants came home, but she wanted to find the source of these voices, once and for all.

Miranda walked into the kitchen, past the table (behind which she now noticed a high chair), and to the back door. As she paused to look into the back yard, she heard the lock turn on the front door, and a much clearer female voice. She flung herself through the back door, pulled it closed behind her, and ducked beneath the kitchen window. She heard someone turn on the kitchen faucet. Her head spun, but she fought off the queasiness and went around the side of the house, crouching to stay below the windows. As she turned the corner, she saw it. Hanging in the air, just behind the living room window, was a Snag. The little tendrils of gold sparkled in the afternoon sunlight. The Snag was below the direct view of the window thanks to the slope of the yard, hidden in plain sight.

She walked up to it, keeping close to the house. The Snag was where she remembered having a shed years ago. Her dad tore it down one winter after an icy tree branch smashed its small roof. She wondered if the door to the shed was being used now as a convenient place to hide when moving back and forth. At any rate, as she leaned closer to it, she heard the voices again.

"...still on the other side," a man's voice said. "He should be in place tonight. Then we can take care of it."

"Good," a woman's voice replied. "We need to get this done soon before anyone notices the shift."

"Yes ma'am," the man said. "I think we've figured out where— "

The voices stopped. Miranda looked around and didn't see anything, but she could tell something wasn't right. If the Editors had a Snag right by her house, it explained why they were able to change so much of her life.

"Not anymore," she whispered. "It's time to find out what's really happening." Miranda got a firm grip on her backpack's straps and stepped into the Snag.

She arrived in her own side yard beside the little shed in the middle of a very warm afternoon. It felt like summer with the muggy humidity, and she turned on the spot to make sure she was alone. Ducking behind the shed, she listened for anything that might tell her when she might be.

Just then, she heard the front door of the house open and close, and noticed her mother's old station wagon, the one she used to ride in to elementary school. She watched as her mom backed out of the driveway and then disappeared down the street. As soon as the engine sounds faded, she stood up, her legs shaking. She took four steps toward the kitchen door, when someone grabbed her arm.

"Where are you going?" She was spun around and found herself face to face with the bald man. "How did you get through here?"

Miranda didn't answer. She tried to yank her arm free, but he tightened his grip.

"You're not going anywhere now that I've got you," he said, leaning in close. She could smell his breath and it was sour, like he hadn't brushed his teeth in several days. Miranda tried to twist herself free, but couldn't get loose from his grip. "I'm sick and tired of you, girl. All over the country I've followed you, and now, after everything, I've finally caught you. Now come with me and be quiet about it, or we'll have to go get your mother and have her convince you. I'm sure you don't want me to talk to your mother, now do you?"

"Leave her alone," Miranda said, trying to pry open his fingers with her free hand.

"Then shut up and move."

The man marched into the house and shoved her down on the couch. He was at least a foot taller than her with thick, muscular arms, and she didn't move from the spot where he'd shoved her. She glanced up at the photos on the mantle. In them, her family was whole. Her kindergarten school picture, the same one from her dad's wallet, was displayed in a frame right at the center. At least now she knew when she was. Her stomach twisted and she curled into a ball on the sofa, fighting nausea. Meanwhile, the man picked up the living room phone and dial someone.

"It's me." He listened to something on the other end, his face contorted. "Yeah, well, I had no choice, did I? No, you listen. *I've got her.* No, I'm serious, I've got her, and I'm bringing her to the office. She came through 117!" the bald man snapped. "I'm tired of chasing her across the country. Besides, she's not even supposed to be here. I don't care what *she* says, I had to do *something*. She screwed it up, and she's going to tell us how to fix it. Yeah. Okay."

The man hung up and became silent. Miranda watched him through half-closed eyes. His eyes kept darting toward the front door, and along the mantle at the photos of Miranda and her family. She fought against the feeling in her gut and was overcome by the familiar smell of the old couch, with the woven fabric that she always associated with home and the days when she was sick and her mother would have her sleep in the living room and watch cartoons.

The man unzipped his leather jacket and started pacing, muttering to himself, and running his hand across the top of his head. He went to the mantle and picked up the school photo, then one of just her parents, and then put them back down. As he turned and started to go up the stairs, she felt a deep anger well up inside of her, unlike anything she ever experienced. After everything, this man was inside her house, touching her family's things, and then had the nerve to go upstairs? What was he looking for? The anger cut through any pain she felt, and she jumped from the couch and plowed up the stairs after him.

As she got to the top, the bald man turned to face her from the doorway to her own bedroom. He held another framed picture in one hand, his other hand was balled in a fist, and his eyebrows shot up on his forehead as she came running at him, swinging wildly.

"Get out of my house!" she screamed, pummeling him and kicking him as hard as she could. "Get out get out get OUT!"

"YOU! You aren't even supposed to be here!"

"YOU AREN'T EITHER!"

The man pulled free and took off down the stairs with the photograph, Miranda right on his heels. He ran back through the kitchen and to the side yard, where he stopped right beside the Snag. Miranda lunged forward and grabbed the frame, holding on for all she was worth.

"What did you do in there?" she demanded.

The man didn't answer, but tried to twist the frame free from her grasp, inching toward the Snag. Miranda dug in her heels, pulling back even as she felt herself dragged forward. She could see the picture now: it was a portrait of her family, taken when she was just a few months old, in a professional frame with a paper backing. Though she didn't know why this man wanted a portrait, she wasn't about to let him have it. As they got to the edge of the Snag, she reached out in desperation and dug her fingernails into his hand as hard as she could. He yelled, and she was able to yank the frame away, tumbling back onto the grass.

The man slipped through the Snag, fading from view almost immediately. Miranda started to get up and charge after him, but paused, looking at the frame. The driveway was still clear, and none of the neighbors seemed to have heard anything, so she scooped up the picture and carried inside. Walking to the foot of the stairs, she saw the little hook where she remembered this portrait belonged. Miranda rehung the picture, and stood admiring it for a moment, before turning to the rest of the house. She wanted to make sure nothing else looked different before she left. After a quick glance at the mantle to see everything looked all right, she ran back upstairs to her bedroom.

Toys littered the floor and a pile of plastic dinosaurs dominated the center of the bed, ready to climb the mountain of plushies her six-year-old self had called the Volcano. She paced around the room, trying not to disturb anything, but flooded with memories. When she got to the bed, she reached for her brown teddy bear to give him a squeeze before leaving, but a tiny mew made her pause. She looked down in the plushie pile, and there, snuggled between a pink horse and a white rabbit, was a tiny black and white kitten.

"Perkins!" she whispered. She scooped him up and gave him a snuggle. The little kitten purred and licked her fingers. She laughed. Suddenly, she heard a car door slam outside, and then another. She set the kitten back on the bed and sped down the stairs and through the kitchen as she heard the front door's lock turn. Miranda dashed outside, leaving the back door ajar, and ducked under the kitchen window. She longed to stay and hear her parents' voices, but knew she needed to get back to the other side. She crept around the corner to the Snag and, with a last glance back toward the house, she pressed herself through the thick spot in the air and landed hard on the cold ground.

Miranda pulled out her needle and thread, and faced the Snag. Her father's message via Jake rang in her ears. *Three stitches ought to do it.* She reached down to the lowest place she could see and started to insert her needle into the thickest part of the air. Whatever this man wanted to do on the other side, she needed to stop, but this also meant cutting off the only place she knew for certain both of her parents were still alive, and together. She blinked back tears. Keeping her family safe was her priority, and if that meant blocking her only access to them, so be it.

Her hand shook as she pressed the needle into the base of the Snag and pulled it through. Her grip grew steadier as she looped three stitches through the air on either side of the floating golden bits, connecting them and pulling her own thread tight over them. With a last pass through the third stitch, she pulled her thread into a knot. As she raised the scissors to cut the final piece loose, she heard a shriek behind her.

"What have you DONE?" The blond woman from the campground was running toward her, the bald man right behind her, pointing.

"I live here!" Miranda said. "You don't!" She snipped the thread.

Her stomach twisted and she doubled over, dropping the scissors onto the brown grass in front of her. The woman screamed something else, but her vision swirled and the noises around her muddled into a cacophony of sound as she curled into a ball on the hard ground. Everything went dark for a moment and she nearly vomited. As Miranda's vision cleared, she sat up, ready to run, but the woman and the bald man were nowhere to be seen. Miranda scooped up her scissors and tucked them with the needle and thread back into their box. She stood up and glanced around once more, preparing to head back across to the neighbor's yard, but the place looked deserted. She pulled out her second phone, her Threadwalker phone. The battery was almost dead, but she was able to get a text through. It occurred to her that once again, Bridget might not know her, so she decided to use her whole name.

This is Miranda Woodward. At home, everything is okay. Can you pick me up?

Thirty seconds later she got a reply: *Be there in ten.*

Chapter 19

Bridget pulled into the driveway ten minutes later as promised, and Miranda hopped in the passenger seat. Bridget didn't say anything, so Miranda followed suit. They pulled into a narrow parking lot twenty minutes later behind a long building with a row of plain metal doors along the back of it. Bridget got out of the car and led the way to the back entrance to the Tailor shop. Miranda took a deep breath and followed her friend inside, pulling the door closed behind her.

"Be sure to lock it," Bridget whispered, and Miranda did. It clicked in a satisfying way that made Miranda feel safe, and they walked into the back of the shop.

"Sir?" Bridget called. "I'm here with... someone."

Miranda looked around the back room, where she hadn't been before. It looked more to her like the prop department in a theater than a tailor shop, with rows of clothing racks lining the walls and pressed against one another. The clothes looked like they spanned a huge range of styles and eras. As Bridget picked her way to the other side of the room, Miranda examined a rack with some bell-bottoms and flower print tops that looked more authentic than any she'd seen in the mall. As she ran her hands over some maroon crushed velvet, she wondered if the Tailor made these things, or if they were the accumulation of unclaimed clothing over decades in the business.

"Miranda!" Bridget whispered. She looked over her shoulder, and beckoned.

Miranda stepped over a heap of cloth that included bright rainbow colors and brown checkerboard patterns, and joined Bridget at the door to the main part of the shop. She leaned around the frame and peered into the semi-darkness beyond.

Though she'd only been to the shop a handful of times, she could tell right away something wasn't right. A tall floor lamp provided the only light, casting a pool of illumination on the area just in front of them. The rack of spools that usually hung on the wall was on the floor, the now-snarled threads rolling across the tile. Bridget's desk chair was close to the door where they stood. Loose pieces of fabric strayed across the floor in a trail leading to the workroom, the door of which stood halfway ajar. The small lobby was beyond the light so impossible to make out, but everything within view looked disheveled. Bridget reached out and gripped Miranda's arm.

"What's going on?" Miranda whispered, leaning close to Bridget's ear.

"I'm not sure. It looks like the place has been ransacked."

"It seems quiet now, at least," Miranda said. She took a step forward, stopping at the edge of the yellow-lit floor. "Tailor?" There was a faint sound that she thought might have come from inside the workroom, but she hesitated to walk into the light, or to get cornered in the small space. "Tailor? Are you here?"

A shuffling sound came more distinctively this time, then a groan, and a hand appeared on the doorframe of the workroom. Miranda choked back her own scream; the hand was covered in dark stains. Bridget's grip on Miranda's arm tightened, but they held their ground. The fingers contracted, and the Tailor pulled himself into view.

"Sir, you're hurt!" Bridget cried, rushing forward.

The Tailor slumped against the workroom door, holding onto Bridget with one arm while the other hung beside him. A dark gash across his temple seemed to be the source of the blood, and his breathing was unsteady. He nodded to Bridget and she helped him to her desk chair, where he sank onto the leather seat with a sigh.

"What happened?" Miranda asked. He looked up.

"I could ask you the same thing," he said, and his voice was stronger than she expected. "Who are you?"

"Miranda Woodward."

"Ahh, I thought you might be," he said, nodding. "That explains a lot. But you are here early! Is it done then?"

"I closed the Snag at my house," she said. Bridget looked at her, but the Tailor smiled. He studied her face, while Bridget looked back and forth between the two of them. He straightened himself in the chair and rolled his shoulders.

"How long?"

"I'm not sure."

"Days?"

"Weeks. Maybe months." She met his gaze and he smiled. "You remember me? I wasn't sure if you would."

"Walkers can remember things as they have been and as they should be. It is part of our gift, you see."

"She's been in California, sir," Bridget said. "I told you she called a few weeks ago?"

"Yes," he said. "Your father entrusted you with something, did he not?"

"Yes, he did," Miranda whispered, glancing around the shop, afraid of anyone else hearing this.

"I always knew he was my smartest student," the Tailor said, his face glowing with pride. "Much to the disappointment of the particular Editors who came here looking for that information today." He held up his hand to stop Bridget, who opened her mouth to interject. "No, I expected as much when you first made contact not long ago. Or months, as it would seem, for you." He paused and set both hands in his lap, pulling away from Bridget. "Please, get chairs. I will not be hovered over by the two of you."

"But your injuries--!" Bridget protested.

"I have a friend I will call to help me, but first Miranda must hear this. Her task is not finished yet."

Miranda and Bridget went into the workroom, both ignoring the torn and crumpled papers strewn around the desk, and the ripped fabric by the door. They each picked up a chair and carried them into the main room, sitting opposite the Tailor. Their faces were all half lit, half shadowed from the lamp, and Miranda leaned forward in the chair, her elbows on her knees and her hands outstretched toward the old man.

"How are you?" he asked.

"I'm okay," she answered, surprised to hear herself say it. "Tired of prepackaged food though, and I miss my own bed."

"You've learned a lot?"

"So much," she said. "And I even saw..."

The Tailor nodded. "I thought as much. Speak no more of it, as it was a dangerous thing, though it pertains to what I am about to tell you. Your task isn't finished."

"But you don't know— "

"I do know this. Just over a year ago, your father came into the shop. He couldn't stay long, because he needed to get back home for your birthday, but he was agitated and needed to discuss something. I was with a client. He waited. Once the client left, I found your father pacing back and forth in front of that rack of spools. I'd never seen him so excited, or so scared.

"I asked him to sit down, but he told me he didn't have long to stay. He then proceeded to tell me that he'd found a way to stop the Editors. Not just to detect their changes, though he'd been working on perfecting that for years. He found ways to discover the small Edits that had huge implications if you looked far enough down the line. No, he told me he'd found a way to stop them, to keep them from making the changes.

"I didn't believe him at first, but he needed my, ah, expertise. He needed something made that I could produce. We worked together over many weeks perfecting his plan, or at least the part of it I knew about, because he wouldn't tell me the whole thing.

"He told me it was too dangerous for me to know too much, that one day they'd come looking for me and he didn't want me to have to protect the information. But he also knew that it was

319

dangerous enough to need a backup plan. This is where you come in, Miss Woodward."

"I'm the contingency," she said. "He... I know about that."

"Yes," the Tailor replied. Bridget twitched beside him. "You are the backup plan. He said to expect you on or close to your sixteenth birthday, if he was unable to bring you in himself. He told me certain things would be set in motion that would change your life forever, and that I needed to teach you more and at a younger age than we ever train other Walkers. You needed to know.

"He also told me almost all of the information we needed to verify your identity. One of the hallmarks of a Walker is that she remembers the *correct* timeline, as it pertains to herself. It is how the Editors slipped in the past, revealing themselves by having knowledge of events that either never happened, or that should have happened differently. He told me things that would seem small to most, but important to you. You, of course, told us about your cat. He told us other things. Your mother's car. Your love of books."

"But why did he tell you all of that? I mean, who else would it be?"

"Miss Woodward, I had not met you before, and he did not intend to bring you here until necessary. Strictly speaking, Walkers begin training at nineteen years of age, and you were three years too young! I needed to be certain because it was possible that someone might research you, or get answers out of you, and then come here looking for information while posing as you."

"But you just said you didn't know everything!" Miranda said.

"Obviously *they* didn't know that. Even now, they may believe I am withholding information. And I did! Only you, and Bridget now, will know about your father's wishes."

"But I'm still not sure what I'm doing, I'm just kind of making it up as I go. What if I screw it up?"

"Somehow, I don't think you will," the Tailor said. "Your instincts are good, and your heart is in the right place. You want things to be Right, for your life to be whole again, and that, if nothing else, will keep you on the correct path."

"I don't know what to do, though," she said, looking down at her hands. "I can't think of what else to do, except that I want my mom back. I don't want anything else to happen..."

The Tailor didn't reply. His face now shadowed, he leaned back in Bridget's desk chair, and pulled a handkerchief from his pocket. He began wiping his hands clean, then folded it in half and half again, and pressed it to the cut on his head. Miranda watched him, her mind racing as she thought of everything she'd experienced, from meeting Jake and Hestia, to heading north to Virginia in the freezing cold and then getting taken across the country, only to lose her father all over again. Her father...

"All right. Well, I'm going to check my desk to see if they took anything." Bridget got up and walked back to the front of the office.

"What can you tell me about all those old clothes in the back of the shop?" Miranda asked, trying to give herself a little time as she worked through an idea forming. "They look like costumes."

"Oh, you saw those, did you?" the Tailor asked, chuckling. "They are not costumes, but the genuine article, every one.

Sometimes when you plan on going to a slightly more, ah, crowded area, even for a brief amount of time, the best way to not be seen is to hide in plain sight."

"Yeah, I guess that makes sense." She wondered if there were any outfits in the racks of clothes that might come in handy one day.

"Mostly the rule is to stay out of sight," he continued. "And, of course, if you are stranded..."

"The hermit protocol," Miranda finished.

"Correct."

They sat in silence for a few minutes while Miranda contemplated this. If you were stranded, you were, for all intents and purposes, dead. Hestia said she was supposed to be dead, but what if she was just stranded out of her own timeline? She'd been on the plane with Miranda's father. What could it mean? Her train of thought was interrupted as Bridget rejoined them, a piece of paper in one hand and an odd look on her face.

"What is it?" the Tailor asked.

"Sam's card is gone," Bridget replied. "I haven't noticed any others missing, though."

"What was on it?" The Tailor sat up straighter.

"Just his phone number, really. I don't think there was even an address or anything."

"You're certain?"

"Fairly certain. We don't keep notes on most people, just contact numbers," she said, glancing at Miranda. "Yours was all right, but I think someone checked it."

"What's on my card?" Miranda asked.

"Your birthday," Bridget said. "Nothing else. The Tailor keeps his notes somewhere else."

"So, why look at it?" Miranda looked from one to the other, but didn't understand what the point of this conversation was.

"They were trying to get any useful information they could find on you, Miss Woodward," the Tailor said.

"Like what?" Miranda felt her shoulders tightening at the thought of more people coming after her. She didn't know what the Editors could possibly do with her dad's old phone number, but it made her uncomfortable to think of them having any information at all.

"Anything that might tell them something about you," Bridget said. "Sir, you didn't say who came in here."

"No, I didn't," he said. "There were two, though, or I might have been able to handle them. But I think Miss Woodward has something to say." He turned and looked at her.

"I'm ready to go home." The words came out of her mouth before she even realized the thought existed in her mind, but as soon as she said it, she knew it was true. "I know there's a lot of other stuff going on, but I need to find my mom. And I need sleep. Sleep sounds really good."

Miranda looked at Tailor and he reached out to take her hand. "You are the best contingency plan Sam Woodward could have chosen. Another Woodward! They won't know what's coming! But you're right; for now, go home. Rest. Recuperate. We have time, thanks to you."

"Thanks," Miranda said, standing up. She turned to Bridget. "Can you take me?"

"Sure," the young woman said, going to get her purse. Miranda squeezed the Tailor's hand and then headed to the back door of the shop. As she reached it, he called to her.

"You've done well, Miss Woodward. Very well."

"Thank you," she said, and headed to the car.

When Bridget pulled into her driveway, Miranda got out and waved goodbye. She walked slowly up the sidewalk and stood in front of the door, unsure if she wanted to go inside or not. The turmoil of the last days, weeks, months, tore at her insides and though she felt some relief that she'd closed the Snag, she didn't feel prepared for whatever lay inside the house. Would it be empty? Would her mother's things be back? How would she know where to start looking for her mother? What if someone was still watching the house? She turned to look up and down the street to make sure she was truly alone, and didn't see anyone. While she hesitated on the doorstep, the front door opened behind her.

"Miranda?" said a familiar voice.

She froze. Her pulse quickened as she turned, her bag dangling in her hand.

"Miranda, honey, what are you doing out there?"

"Mom!" Miranda sprang forward, nearly tackling her mom in a giant hug. Her mom was wearing her purple scrubs and smelled faintly of the orange scented cleaner from the children's wing at the hospital, her brown hair was pulled into a bun at the base of her neck, just like always. Miranda felt a rush unlike anything she had felt since the night in the corn maze; here was her mom, and she was hugging her. She felt giddy and excited and relieved. Joy filled her up, swallowing the ache in her chest until she felt full and warm.

"Sweetie, what is it?" her mother asked, hugging her back. "You're acting like you haven't seen me in weeks!"

"It feels like I haven't, Mom," she said. Miranda followed her mom inside the house and then into the kitchen. The scent of something baking wafted across the room, and the coffee pot gurgled on the counter. There was the pile of mail on the kitchen table, her school schedule was stuck to the fridge, and Perkins' water dish was by the pantry. Everything was back where it should be.

"Well, I'm glad you're in a good mood. Your slumber party with Jae and Abby last night must have been fun!"

"What? Oh! Yeah, it was!" Miranda laughed and sat down at the kitchen table behind the pile of mail.

"You and Jae and Abby sure know how to have a good time," her mother said, leaning on the kitchen counter with a large coffee cup in her hands. "I'm so glad you've got friends like them."

"Me, too," Miranda said. She couldn't tell if she was about to cry or laugh and tried to take a deep breath. *Chill, Miranda,* she told herself. *She doesn't know you've been gone weeks and weeks.*

"Well, I'll want to hear all about it, but let's have breakfast first, all right?"

"Sure, Mom. Whatever you want." Miranda felt so glad to have her mother right there with her, and kept having to look away when her mom caught her watching everything she did.

The oven timer beeped. As her mom reached for her oven mitts to pull a pan of cinnamon rolls from the oven, Miranda rummaged in her backpack to find her cell phone, tucked away for so long she wasn't sure it would even turn on. She found the charging cable her mother always left by the kitchen phone and plugged in her cell before she pressed the power button. As soon as she did, the phone started buzzing as message after message appeared, from Jae and from Abby and other people from school, texting to wish her a happy birthday.

Miranda texted her friends back, the warm feeling from seeing her mom swelling like a balloon inside of her as she replied to each one. Abby had sent photos from the slumber party and Jae wanted to know what she was doing later, and it was as if nothing had ever changed. And, Miranda thought, for them, nothing had. She looked up to find her mom looking at her, an odd expression on her mother's face. She quickly put her phone down, thinking her mom was about to scold her for being on it at the table, but realized that her mother wasn't looking at the phone.

"You okay, Mom?" she asked.

"Yes, but..." Her mother nodded toward her wrist. "Where'd you find my watch? I could've sworn I'd hidden it better."

Miranda looked down at the gold watch she'd been wearing since, well, her birthday and felt a slight panicky feeling. Her mother hadn't given it to her yet!

"Oh, well, I found it and I thought I was supposed to have it," she said. "I really love it, Mom. Thank you!"

"You are too good a snoop, Miranda Jane Woodward," her mother said, shaking her head and sitting down beside Miranda at the table. "Happy birthday, sweetheart."

"Thanks, Mom," Miranda said, leaning her head on her mom's shoulder. She made a mental note to check the pantry for the gift box as soon as she could and to ask the Tailor what to do with the duplicate watch, hoping that was the most complicated thing she'd face after everything. Her mother smiled at her and she relaxed.

"Tell you what, Sweet Pea," her mother said. "These cinnamon rolls need to cool a little bit. Why don't you take your overnight bag upstairs and change into some clean clothes? You look like you slept in what you wore to the corn maze."

Miranda looked down at her outfit. She was wearing the jeans and t-shirt she'd been pretty much living in for the last couple of weeks. The thought of clean clothes and being in her own room suddenly sounded like the best idea in the world. She stood up, hugged her mom again, and headed upstairs.

The door to her bedroom was cracked open and the lights were off, but the screensaver on her computer scrolled past with all the photos she recognized. Her dad was back in the old family pictures, and the photos of Jae and Abby were back, too. Miranda stood for a moment transfixed, watching them all go past. She dropped her backpack onto the floor, and realized she was truly letting it go for the first time in days. The thought thrilled her.

But then all thoughts of her backpack evaporated: there, on the bed, lay Perkins, snuggled into her pillows with his tail tucked around his paws. He picked up his square head and trilled at her in his usual greeting. She tumbled onto the bed, gathering him into her arms, tears of happiness streaming down her cheeks.

Miranda was home.

About the Author

Joanna Volavka is the author of the young adult science fiction novel *Threadwalkers*. She currently lives in Chicago with her husband, two cats, and extensive book collection.

A writer for Geek Girl Pen Pals, Joanna spends her time alternately between creative artistic pursuits and has a passion for conservation and wildlife while working on whatever story she's got brewing in her overly active imagination. She still hasn't decided what she's going to be when she grows up, though she suspects it will probably be herself.

Read more about Joanna and her adventures on her website www.joannavolavka.com

You can connect with Joanna on Twitter: @joannavolavka and on Instagram: @joannavolavka and @geekyjo

Acknowledgements

Per usual, there are too many people who have helped along the way to acknowledge individually, but I will attempt it just the same.

Thank you to Mrs. Bush, my 7th grade English Lit teacher, who first planted the idea that this whole writing thing was even possible. You gave me an outlet, and I have never forgotten you.

Thank you to Ruth Moose, for your mantra of persistence over perfection and also the constant reminders that I needed a writing group. You were right. I hope that you enjoy this story, even if it is sci-fi.

Thank you to my writing group partners, Debbie and Kat. I'm so glad I found you at just the right time. Timing is everything, isn't it? Thanks always for your honesty and insight.

Thank you to all of my beta readers, Arielle, Brandon, Danae, Elise, (other) Joanna, Rosa, and anyone else who read a portion. You each met Miranda at a different part along this journey and I appreciate all of your feedback and encouragement (and honest suggestions). I hope you like the final version. Now please burn all copies of the mess some of you may have squirreled away. ;)

Thank you to the staff of the International Geek Girl Pen Pals Club, past and present: Emma, Farq, Jen, Kara, Kim, Rosa, Stewie, Summer, Toasty, Val. You've helped in so many ways, have been there for me when I needed it, and have listened to me ramble about this story for long enough. You ladies rock. <3

Thank you to Cosmo. I hope folks enjoy your cameo.

Thank you to my family, for always supporting me, and also for letting me occasionally hole myself up in the dining room with my laptop during holidays.

Most importantly, thank you to Jared, who has put up with this whole escapade for over a decade and deserves an award for patience many times over. I love you.

And lastly, thank you to YOU, dear reader! I put this tale into the world for you to read, and I hope it was fun. If you've read all the way to the end of this, come say hi on Twitter and tell me your favorite dinosaur.

Freedom for Me
Coming Soon from 50/50 Press!

As the Civil War rages, Thomas longs to fight for his country. When he is assumed to be a slave because of his appearance, he's determined to find a way to fight for the Union cause. Thomas battles against the Rebels with his regiment, but when he befriends a runaway slave, he begins to understand the true meaning of freedom in America. *Freedom for Me* is a historical novel based on the life of one of the only Chinese soldiers who served in the American Civil War.

Killerjoy
Now Available from 50/50 Press!

This epic novel is set in a dangerous world of mysterious monsters, ruined kingdoms, vast cities, and superheroes for hire. A young outcast with the ability to walk through walls leaves her mercenary life behind to join a team of royal guards. At the same time, a young man gets recruited by masked vigilantes to take on the caped heroes who abuse their power. This unique science fiction novel is the first in a trilogy and celebrates diverse voices not often shared in epic fantasy adventures.

Undercover Chefs
Coming Soon from 50/50 Press!

Three unlikely friends join forces to win a baking competition and save their school's culinary classroom. Isaac, a nationally-ranked runner; Jane, a shy artist; and J.C., a rebellious scooter rider—all have a secret passion for cooking. The promise of a cupcake contest lures them to an unusual classroom on the outskirts of campus. As they share friendship and a love for cooking, the pressures of the contest start to boil over—a recipe for disaster that could destroy their chances at winning! The heat is on, and Isaac, Jane and J.C. must figure out a way to salvage their cupcakes, save the classroom, and protect their secrets before the judges cast their final votes.

Made in the USA
San Bernardino, CA
03 June 2019